ROMANCE

OF THE

PERILOUS LAND

SCOTT MALTHOUSE

OSPREY GAMES
Bloomsbury Publishing Plc
PO Box 883, Oxford, OX1 9PL, UK
1385 Broadway, 5th Floor, New York, NY 10018, USA
E-mail: info@ospreygames.co.uk
www.ospreygames.co.uk

OSPREY GAMES is a trademark of Osprey Publishing Ltd

First published in Great Britain in 2019

A catalogue record for this book is available from the British Library.

ISBN: HB 9781472834775; eBook 9781472834782; ePDF 9781472834751; XML 9781472834768

19 20 21 22 23   10 9 8 7 6 5 4 3 2 1

Originated by PDQ Digital Media Solutions, Bungay, UK
Printed and bound by Bell & Bain Ltd., Glasgow G46 7UQ

Osprey Games supports the Woodland Trust, the UK's leading woodland conservation charity.

To find out more about our authors and books visit **www.ospreypublishing.com**. Here you will find extracts, author interviews, details of forthcoming events and the option to sign up for our newsletter.

Artwork: John McCambridge, Alan Lathwell, and David Needham

ACKNOWLEDGEMENTS
I'd like to thank Natalie for putting up with me while I wrote this. I'd also like to thank Steve, Pete, Dave, McB, and Neil for helping me bring this to life. Finally I want to thank Ken St. Andre for putting me on the path.

CONTENTS

INTRODUCTION

It is the Age of Valour.

A cloaked thief thrusts a glittering dagger into the throat of a cockatrice, taking care not to meet its gaze, which could instantly turn her to stone. A broad-shouldered knight gallops over the Plains of Perrin, spear in hand, on the hunt for the giants terrorizing a nearby village. A wise cunning woman conjures black tentacles from the ground as malevolent spirits try to breach a chapel. A stalking ranger looses arrows at lightning speed, sending a trio of brigands into the underworld. A raging barbarian faces down a huge water-dwelling knucker, cleaving the serpent in two with his axe. A worldly bard chants a battle song as the Knights of the Round Table charge the fearsome Questing Beast.

The Perilous Land is a place of magic, valour, and darkness. It is a realm similar to the British Isles of older times, viewed through a hazy lens of its rich history of folklore and oral tradition. This is land where creatures of British mythology lurk, whether under stone bridges, hidden in shady woodland, or secreted in some forgotten corner of an old ruin. It's a world where the celebrated heroes of legend are found, where Robin Hood stalks the night and King Arthur is ruler of Camelot, his ever-loyal Knights of the Round Table at his side.

The Age of Valour has dawned on the Perilous Land and a new hope has emerged as King Arthur brings together the greatest heroes from all four corners of the land to fight the tide of evil led by the sinister knight Mordred and dark enchantress Morgan Le Fay. While some kings and queens have been seduced by these powers with promises of land and riches, others have allied themselves with Camelot to battle the monsters that darken their doorsteps and bring peace back to the land. The fight won't be an easy one and only the most valiant will prevail in this new age.

Romance of the Perilous Land is a game very much inspired by the oldest fantasy roleplaying game created in the 1970s, but it is also its own creation. Players will take on the role of courageous knights, sneaky thieves, mystical cunning folk, and other characters as they try to stop the forces of evil from dominating the Perilous Land. Together they will forge epic stories inspired by the folklore of Britain, creating tales they will remember for years to come.

In this book you will find all the rules and inspiration you need to start playing *Romance of the Perilous Land*.

WHO ARE THE PLAYERS?

In *Romance of the Perilous Land*, the players take on the role of heroes who are roaming the land hunting evil creatures and righting wrongs. Together they will form a party as allies of Camelot, battling the hordes of Mordred and the sinister Sisters of Le Fay. As with many good folk tales, morality in this game is black and white – there are forces of good and forces of evil. The players are righteous and true, but don't take that to mean that they can't be flawed too.

The players are building their own legends. By the time their characters reach level 10 they will have songs sung about them and books written about them for centuries to come. The beauty of the game is that the players get to watch their own legends flourish – both their trials and also their triumphs.

WHAT IS A ROLEPLAYING GAME?

A roleplaying game is a type of group storytelling game. It blends improvised acting with game rules, producing a structured narrative where players take on the role of different characters in a fantasy world. However, one player does not play a character, but rather the referee, or the 'Game Master' (GM for short). It's this player's job to run adventures, create towns, cities, underground lairs, monsters, non-playing characters (NPCs), and more. They facilitate the game and uphold the rules, keeping the action flowing so that everyone has an excellent time.

Games of *Romance of the Perilous Land* are played with an array of unusual dice: four-sided (d4), six-sided (d6), eight-sided (d8), ten-sided (d10), twelve-sided (d12) and twenty-sided (d20). Sometimes the rules will ask for a flip of a coin, which is represented as d2. Usually dice are denoted with a number at the beginning, like 2d6, meaning you roll an amount of dice equal to the first number. For instance, if you were told to roll 4d8, you would roll four eight-sided dice. Each player also gets a character sheet that explains their character's statistics, what they are good and not so good at. Games can be optionally played with grid-paper and miniatures to represent the location of the characters at a given time, but some people prefer the 'theatre of the mind' approach where actions are described in abstract terms – either way works just fine.

Players will also require pencils, erasers, a notebook and some healthy snacks for the session (carrot sticks are always a winner). Sessions tend to last for a few hours, so it's a good idea to keep fed and hydrated as you play.

THE GOLDEN RULE OF ROLEPLAYING

Roleplaying games are collaborative games where friends come together to tell exciting stories. The golden rule to remember when playing is that fun outweighs the rules as written. If a certain rule makes something less fun in a given situation and everyone agrees, change the rule. Like most roleplaying games, you should feel free to create your own house rules for *Romance of the Perilous Land* if it enhances the fun of the game.

EXAMPLE OF PLAY

In this example, Larry is taking on the role of GM. Chris is playing Sir Rod the knight, April is Harna the barbarian, and Ben is Eld the Wise, one of the cunning folk. The players have arrived at an ancient ruin dedicated to Cerridwen, Keeper of the Cauldron and demi-goddess of prophecy, but they have managed to disturb some of the spirits that lurk there.

Larry (GM): After several hours you arrive at the site of an old ruin where shattered masonry lies on the grass. You can make out a statue of a female who seems to be standing over a large pot.

Ben: Eld is wise in the ways of ancient things. Can he try to figure out who this woman is with his religion skill?

Larry (GM): Of course. Make a Religion check with edge.

Ben: [Rolls a 10 and an 8 – taking the lowest number of the two.] My Mind is 14, so 8 is a success.

Larry (GM): You recognise the statue as Cerridwen, keeper of the cauldron of the underworld and demi-goddess of prophecy. It's likely that this was once a small temple built in her honour. April, what do you do?

April: Harna isn't exactly the inquisitive type, but she's aware of her surroundings. I want to see if there are any nasty surprises lurking around the area.

Larry (GM): Cool, no problem. Make a Perception check.

April: [Rolls a 5]. Ok, that's a pretty good roll!

Larry (GM): As you inspect your surroundings further you hear whispering coming from behind one of the ruined walls.

April: Guys, I don't think we're alone here. Harna draws her club.

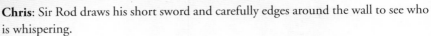

Chris: Sir Rod draws his short sword and carefully edges around the wall to see who is whispering.

Larry (GM): Rod notices three squat creatures wearing conical red hats. Their eyes are like glittering emeralds and their teeth like razors. You recognise them as vicious redcaps.

Chris: Rod bellows at the beasts and points his sword at them: "Lo, who conspires against us?"

Ben: Be careful Rod, redcaps may be small but they can tear a man limb from limb.

Larry (GM): The redcaps growl at you and bare their fangs. Time to make a combat order roll.

[All players roll a d20 to discover the order of combat.]

Larry (GM): Rod's up first. Take an edge on this attack since you bellowed so loudly.

Chris: Hah, great. I swing my sword at the one closest to me. [He rolls a 19 and a 6 as his attack rolls – taking the lowest.]

Larry (GM): Your sword slices a gash into the redcap's chest. Roll your damage.

Chris: [Rolls a 4.] Take that!

Larry (GM): The creature cries out in agony, slightly knocked back by the blow. Ben, you're up.

Ben: Eld rushes around the corner and casts Dazzle with Glittering Lights on one of the redcaps to try to blind it. [He rolls a Mind check to cast his spell and gets a 16 – unsuccessful.] Ah! That sucks.

Larry (GM): Your spell fizzles out before you can even cast it. Unlucky, Eld. Harna?

April: Harna is going to go into a full barbarian rage and charge at the closest redcap, swinging her club.

Larry (GM): Great, the fire of rage fills your eyes as you attempt to club the redcap. Roll your attack.

April: [Rolls a 6.] I've hit. [Rolls her club damage plus rage damage.] Ok, so that's 10 damage to the redcap.

Larry (GM): You crack it square in the face, causing it to fly back into the wall. Its body sinks to the ground and the light leaves its eyes. Through the trees you see a hulking figure emerge, standing nine feet tall and wearing nothing but a sheepskin loincloth. The giant roars, picks up one of the redcaps and devours it in a single bite before noticing you. What do you do?

The World of the Perilous Land

The Age of Doom

Darkness once held its malevolent grip over the Perilous Land. A multitude of beasts, phantoms, and magical beings rose from the forgotten places of the world to assert their dominance over mankind in what came to be known to scholars as the Age of Doom. The ordinary people of the land feared for their lives on a daily basis, not knowing whether they would be waylaid by a giant when hunting for food, or if their children would be snatched from their cribs by the green hags of the marshlands. Gargantuan red dragons scorched towns and witches placed curses on the halls of kings. Death and pestilence were a daily occurence and only a brave few chose to stand against the darkness with blade, arrow and spellcraft. It would take a young man in a kingdom called Camelot to become the catalyst for the true battle against the forces of evil.

Before Uther Pendragon died of a sickness brought on by black magic, his ally Merlin, a powerful cunning man, was entrusted with a great secret. Uther's illegitimate son, Arthur, was given to Merlin to raise in a hidden location. Neither the people of Camelot nor Arthur himself knew that he existed as the rightful heir to the throne, disgraced as Uther was. After Uther's death, bitter battles were fought over the throne with much blood shed. Merlin, seeing the valiant young man Arthur had become, decided to reveal the new king in a test of might. He placed an enchanted sword deep within a large stone and declared that the one who could pull the blade out would become the true king of Camelot. Knights and nobles from Camelot and beyond heard of the wizard's challenge, but none were able to retrieve the sword after weeks of trying. Arthur, seeing an opportunity to make a difference in this Age of Doom, decided to attempt the feat, not knowing that Merlin had placed a spell to enable only Arthur himself to remove the sword. When he did so, all in the kingdom bowed to him and his fight against the evil that pervaded the land began.

THE DARK POWERS

King Arthur brought together the greatest warriors in the land under the banner of the Knights of the Round Table, named after the circular table they would meet around, shaped so that every member was seen as an equal. With his knights he would do battle against the most ferocious beasts in the kingdom and tackle the growing threat of black magic. But as Arthur was building a foundation for good in the world, there were those who sought to stop him and his ilk at all costs. The sorceress Morgan Le Fay arose from the shadows of the Wytchwood Forest to defend the creatures who she saw as victims of Arthur's tyrannical rule. She gathered followers all over the Perilous Land who sympathised with her plight to fight against the Knights of the Round Table, many of whom used deception, enchantment and murder to make their stand, believing that the end justified the means. Their kind became known as the Sisters of Le Fay, with members of the group located around the land.

Le Fay wasn't the only one to rise against the king. Mordred, Arthur's nephew, believed that he was the legitimate heir to the throne of Camelot and would stop at nothing to usurp his uncle. He trained as a knight in Arthur's court for years before disappearing – seemingly killed on a quest where no other knight returned. In reality, Mordred led his fellow knights purposefully to their doom before fleeing to the kingdom of Norhaut to build his forces. There he consorted with a variety of cunning folk, evil warriors, and monsters, who swore fealty to him under the banner of The Black Lance. Now, like the Sisters of Le Fay, members of The Black Lance can be found all around the Perilous Land, causing chaos wherever they go.

THE GREAT SEARCH

With enemies rising around him, Arthur knew that he had to gain his own allies beyond his realm. The battle had grown larger than just Camelot, so he would need to find valiant heroes across the Perilous Land to fight against evil wherever it reared its head. In a journey known as The Great Search, he sent knights out to scour the Perilous Land for those who could lend their blade, arrow, or magic to Arthur's cause. In the forest of Sherwood they met Robin Hood and his Merry Men, who swore to protect the wild places of the world from doom. Those knights who rode out to the Kingdom of Corbenic were greeted by the Order of the Fisher King who allied with Camelot in an effort to gain help from Arthur to cure their ailing king, mortally wounded by Mordred in battle. In the northern lands the knights met the Iron Hawks, a group of monster hunters led by grizzled veteran Bors the Younger. Seeing his prowess in battle, Camelot promised to furnish the hunters with arms and armour should they serve Arthur. Bors reluctantly agreed, not one to swear oaths to anyone but himself. Finally, Merlin himself traversed the land to find like-minded cunning folk to use their magic for the good of the Perilous Land, forming the Fellowship of Enchanters.

For the first time in over a century, the darkness has something to fear. With his allies, Arthur has brought about the Age of Valour, where good finally has a chance of triumphing over evil. But the fight will be long and arduous and death will be waiting around every corner.

PLAYING IN THE AGE OF VALOUR

Games of *Romance of the Perilous Land* take place in the Age of Valour after Arthur has undertaken The Great Search. His effort to unite the various kingdoms against the powers of darkness have not been without problems. Many rulers refuse to join him, some believing that he wishes to unite the Perilous Land so he can be its sole ruler, while others sympathise with Morgan Le Fay or Mordred. Others just want to keep to their own affairs.

The Age of Valour is a time of great heroism and is an exciting era for play. Players will be doing their best to keep monsters and evil-doers at bay, trying to win over new allies for Arthur's cause, rubbing shoulders with legendary characters such as Merlin and Robin Hood, battling the hordes of Mordred and perhaps even coming face to face with the enchantress Morgan Le Fay herself.

Players also have the option to become a member of a faction, either from character creation or through the course of a campaign. These factions add further depth to how players roleplay their characters, whether it's becoming a hunter of magical treasure with the Order of the Fisher King, bringing the corrupt to justice with the Merry Men of Sherwood or even joining the Knights of the Round Table.

In this world where dragons dwell, where dark wizards battle brave knights, and where the fate of the Perilous Land is in the hands of the players, the possibility for adventure is truly endless.

TIMELINE OF THE PERILOUS LAND

The history of the Perilous Land is deep and full of world-shaking events that have shaped the land for centuries to come. The following timeline shows the various eras of the Perilous Land, seperated into 'ages'. An age occurs once a large event has happened, often changing the status quo of the Perilous Land. These are further separated into Before Camelot (BC) and Camelot Era (CE).

THE AGE OF GIANTS (1000–560BC)

The first age of the Perilous Land saw the arrival of the giants, led by their emperor Gogmagog. The Perilous Land was known to the giants as Ashta, meaning 'Place of Peace' as all giants lived harmoniously for a time.

THE GALESH UPRISING (850–828BC)

After more than two centuries of Gogmagog rule, a faction of giants led by Galesh grew unhappy with their emperor, who they agreed was holding them back from exploring the wider world. Galesh, therefore, wanted to become emperor and lead his people, so he gathered 300 giants against Gogmagog. After more than 20 years of fighting, Gogmagog made a pact with the dragon Xeran to destroy Galesh in return for rule over the many mountains of Ashta. Xeran agreed and ambushed Galesh, killing him and many of his forces.

THE FOUNDATION OF SPELLS (560BC)

Gogmagog did not desire another uprising and so set out to harness the magic that flowed through the veins of the world. He gathered worldspeakers, giants who were most in tune with nature, to attempt to use magic. After three years of meditation one worldspeaker, Rado, was imbued with magic and cast the first ever spell – light. Soon all of the worldspeakers were able to cast spells and Gogmagog was pleased. This would set into motion the first new age in the world – the Age of Magic.

THE AGE OF MAGIC (560–420BC)

The worldspeakers would become the most powerful enchanters to ever live and much to Gogmagog's dismay they were treated as gods by many of the giants. They would create fantastic monoliths dedicated to the worldspeakers and sing songs about their magic. Gogmagog grew furious at this treachery and sought Xeran for advice on the matter. Xeran, who knew much about magic, told of another world of powerful creatures who could match the powers of the worldspeakers.

THE ARRIVAL OF THE OTHERWORLD (540BC)

Gogmagog convinced one of the worldspeakers to open a door to the Otherworld where the fairies dwelt. The worldspeaker did as he was asked and soon the fairies began to enter the world. They were creatures formed of pure magic unlike anything the giants had ever seen. In the night, Gogmagog met with Queen Mab of the Unseelie Court, a dark fairy (although Gogmagog was not to know this). She agreed to bring her forces against the worldspeakers so long as they would be able to come and go as they pleased from the Otherworld to Ashta. Gogmagog agreed and soon the beasts and spirits of the Otherworld were pouring forth and forming a great army.

THE BATTLE OF THE EMERALD PLAIN (539BC)

Gogmagog and Mab led their army of giants, beasts and fairies against the worldspeakers and their followers. Thousands died that day and the race of giants dwindled. Ultimately the worldspeakers fell and Gogmagog was victorious. But Mab was devious and sought to topple all of giant kind, and so during the great victory feast she had Gogmagog drink an enchanted wine that would put him to sleep for centuries. Once he was unconscious Mab proceeded to destroy most of the giants. Those who survived fled underground.

THE ARRIVAL OF HUMANKIND (420BC)

The gods sensed an imbalance in the world as a result of Mab's treachery and created humans to right the balance. Humans turned out to be tenacious and industrious creatures, building the first cities and forming borders around the land for the first time, with each of the four kingdoms named after its founder: King Escose, Queen Norhaut, King Hutton and Queen Ascalon.

THE AGE OF HUMANITY (420–0BC)

With humans came engineering, crafting and building. Soon towns, cities and villages were cropping up across the Perilous Land, so named by the humans for the magical beings that stalked the land with evil in their hearts. The first kings and queens had been crowned and the Age of Humanity had dawned.

THE DAWN OF CUNNING (418BC)

It did not take long for humans to master the art of magic, though many still looked on it with distrust. The cunning folk became magical conduits and after some initial trepidation were viewed as integral members of society, having gifts of healing as well as destruction. King Escose was the first to employ cunning folk in his court, a practice that was mirrored around the Perilous Land.

THE GREAT EXPANSION (400–1BC)

With just four kingdoms, there was still a vast area of fertile land for the taking. Humans created new kingdoms, usually to the chagrin of neighbouring monarchs who saw this as treachery of the highest order, resulting in many a battle over four centuries. At the end of that time six more kingdoms had arisen and humans truly ruled over the Perilous Land.

THE AGE OF CAMELOT (0BC–50CE)

At the end of the great expansion a kingdom was founded that would become the home of legends. King Constantine founded Camelot and set about building the city over a period of thirty years with the aid of his advisor, a young cunning man called Merlin.

THE DEATH OF CONSTANTINE (30CE)

Constantine fell gravely ill towards the end of his life and when he passed there was a great mourning across Camelot. His son Uther Pendragon would take up the throne, an inexperienced and somewhat reckless young leader who would have to learn the art of governance quickly.

THE COMING OF XERAN, LORD OF DRAGONS (42CE)

Over centuries, the dragons had taken over the mountains of the world and had become numerous. The pact Xeran had made with Gogmagog had been beneficial to dragonkind, and now Xeran wanted to take advantage of humanity's desire for riches. He demanded from Uther a tax, where at the end of each month Camelot's most prized treasures would be sent to him in his lair. At first Uther refused and cursed the dragon, but days later Xeran destroyed several villages in revenge and returned to Uther asking again for the tax. This time Uther saw no other option than to oblige. Over the years, Camelot grew poorer as its treasures dwindled and Uther's favour fell rapidly.

THE DRAGONWAR (50CE)

Uther met with Merlin and his most trusted knights to devise a plan to bring down Xeran. Merlin spoke of the enchanted sword White Hilt and the magical shield Pridwen, both of which would aid in the dragon's destruction. Uther led his men on a quest to find both of these magical items in the Wretched Caves, where they were said to lay. The great cockatrice that guarded these treasures killed many a knight, but Uther managed to cut off its head. Retrieving the sword and shield, Uther led his knights to Xeran's lair and fought him for four hours. Finally Uther bested the creature and reclaimed Camelot's treasures. The city rejoiced and Uther became a hero.

THE AGE OF DOOM (51–62CE)

In 51CE all the kingdoms of the Perilous Land fell under a great shadow. The malevolent creatures and spirits that had waited in dormancy since the Age of Magic became active. People became afraid to leave their homes, believing that they would be snatched away by a foul bugbear or their children drowned by hags.

THE DEATH OF UTHER
AND THE CROWNING OF ARTHUR (53CE)

Treachery found its way into the halls of Camelot in the winter of 53CE when Uther was found dead in his chamber, leaving a withered, dry corpse. Witnesses say they saw a woman cloaked in black fleeing from the castle and those who could identify her recognised the woman as Morgan Le Fay, the dark enchantress. Uther's illegitimate son Arthur, who had been taken into foster care, was the next in line to the throne, though Arthur did not know it. Merlin placed an enchanted sword in a large stone and proclaimed that anyone who should remove the sword would become the next king of Camelot. Arthur swiftly removed the blade to the disbelief of all in the city and was crowned king.

THE KNIGHTS OF THE ROUND TABLE (54CE)

Arthur had inherited a poisoned chalice of a kingdom when he took the throne. Morgan Le Fay was a threat that loomed over him like a black cloud, and every day there were reports of evil beasts attacking villages and wicked sorcerers spreading their darkness across all the kingdoms of the Perilous Land. Times were desperate, so Arthur decided to form an elite group of knights to help battle against the onslaught of evil in the world. He named them The Knights of the Round Table, for he saw them as equal in value and valour as he. The Knights of the Round Table undertook many quests to rid Camelot and wider regions of the terror at their doorsteps, winning the praise and admiration of all who lived in Camelot.

THE BETRAYAL OF MORDRED (56CE)

Camelot once again became a shining beacon of hope in the world and its knights were hailed as among the strongest and most chivalrous in history. But there was great treachery afoot in the halls of Camelot. Mordred, Arthur's nephew, grew tired of his uncle's rule and believed that it was he who should have inherited the throne. Mordred betrayed Arthur by leading a retinue of knights to their doom before fleeing to Norhaut where he would plot against his former king and raise an army under the banner of The Black Lance.

THE WOUNDING OF THE FISHER KING (57CE)

Mordred sought to gain a tactical advantage against Camelot by invading its neighbour Corbenic in the humid summer of 57CE. He led his army onto the Plains of Perrin where the Fisher King and his gleaming knights met Mordred in battle. It was a bloody skirmish and ultimately Mordred's force was routed, but not before he had struck the Fisher King in the leg with an enchanted lance. The king was poisoned and helpless, but his faithful knights would undertake a quest to find a cure for this malady. As the Fisher King's health deteriorated, so did his kingdom as it fell into the hands of foul creatures and deadly brigands.

THE GREAT SEARCH BEGINS (58CE)

Mordred saw that Camelot would not easily be won – it would take time and patience to raise an army that could take on Arthur. Therefore The Black Lance spread like a spider's web throughout the Perilous Land, growing stronger with each passing year. At the same time Morgan Le Fay had mustered a following in kingdoms further from Camelot, and the Sisters of Le Fay had begun to take shape. Seeing this expanding threat to not just his own kingdom, but all good kingdoms in the land, Arthur began The Great Search in order to unite the Perilous Land against a common enemy.

THE AGE OF VALOUR
(63CE TO THE PRESENT)

After a year of The Great Search, Arthur had found his champions from all over the Perilous Land. From dukes and enchanters to warriors and thieves, Camelot drew together like-minded people from most kingdoms to fight the growing darkness.

Now the tide of battle is turning and evil is on guard, for the greatest heroes in over a hundred years have joined the battle and will stop at nothing until light is returned to the Perilous Land.

The is the beginning of your story. Let your legend unfold.

CHARACTER CREATION

A character is the player's avatar in the world of the Perilous Land. Each player (apart from the GM) will create their own character to control in the game, whether they choose to be a crafty thief, one of the magical cunning folk, a noble knight, or something else. These character types are known as 'classes' – a type of template used to define the roles and abilities of a character. It is recommended that a player create and control only one character, but they may have more if the GM allows it. Ultimately the class a player chooses depends on what kind of character they want to play. Would you prefer to be a battle-hardened melee fighter who wades into battle with a sword in hand? Or maybe you like the thought of keeping to the shadows with a dagger in hand? Do you like the idea of being a charismatic bard who can persuade and uplift others? Maybe you would love to be able to cast spells as a cunning folk? Whatever you want to play, think first about what would be the most fun for you.

Players should discuss the ideas they have for their characters during creation to ensure they have a party that has all bases covered. An adventuring party consisting only of rangers, for example, would suffer greatly in melee combat, so try to assign a different class to each player. After all, to survive in the Perilous Land requires teamwork.

Characters gain new abilities as they become more experienced, giving further play options for the player as their campaign progresses. Characters begin at level 1 and continue to level 10, where they are considered at the pinnacle of their abilities.

To start creating a character, you will need a character sheet. Every player apart from the GM will have a character sheet to record details about their character, in

addition to equipment, treasure and magic items they may find on their adventures. You can find the character sheet at the back of this book or on our website, **www.ospreypublishing.com/gaming-resources**.

The character creation process is as follows:

1. Roll attributes
2. Select a class
3. Select a background
4. Select a starting talent
5. Note down starting money and equipment
6. Create a name, age, and backstory

CHARACTER ATTRIBUTES

There are five main attributes that sum up a character's strengths and weaknesses. It's unlikely that any one character will be great at everything, which is why having a well-balanced party of adventurers is important. The five attributes are as follows:

Might: How physically strong a character is and how well they perform in melee combat. Might also affects bonuses to damage after a successful melee attack as per the below table.

Reflex: How nimble and dexterous a character is and how well they perform in ranged combat. Reflex also affects bonuses to damage after a successful ranged attack as per the below table.

Constitution: How hardy a character is. This attribute is used for testing resistance against poison and other harmful effects.

Mind: How intelligent and wise a character is. This attribute is used for casting spells and understanding specific knowledge. For every point of Mind over 13, a character may learn an additional language at character creation. All characters start understanding common and their own language from the languages section.

Charisma: How diplomatic, attractive, and well-spoken a character is. This attribute is used for social interactions and resisting enchantments.

The damage bonus to a successful melee or ranged attack, based on their Might or Reflex score:

MIGHT/REFLEX SCORE	Less than 12	12–14	15–17	18–20	21–23	24+
DAMAGE BONUS	+0	+1	+2	+3	+4	+5

These attributes will change as the character gains experience, reflecting characters becoming more agile, crafty, and knowledgeable about their environment.

For each attribute, roll 4d6 and remove the lowest roll, noting the total next to each attribute. It is up to the player and the GM to determine what order they assign these scores. Some like to roll in order of each attribute and keep the results as they are (this is a particularly 'old school' method), while others prefer to write down all the totals before assigning to their desired attributes. The latter is the best way if the player already has an idea of the kind of character they want to play.

EXAMPLE

Jenny decides to roll her five totals first before assigning them to attributes. After considering it with the other players, she wants to play a thief who can talk her way out of any situation. She rolls a 10, 9, 10, 12 and 16. Jenny assigns the 16 to Reflex, an important attribute for a thief, the 12 to Charisma, one 10 to Might, the other 10 to Mind and the 9 to Constitution.

OPTIONAL RULE: THE ARRAY

Some gaming groups aren't fond of the random nature of rolling for attributes, so instead of rolling players may instead choose an array of scores to assign. This prevents some characters from being more powerful than others. This array is 9, 10, 12, 14 and 16.

HIT POINTS

Characters have hit points, or HP, to denote their state of health and fatigue. The higher the number of hit points, the more damage a character can take. Hit points are by their very nature abstract and don't necessarily always represent physical wounds, but weariness, being caught off-balance, and narrow misses. At character creation the player will use their Constitution score as their starting HP. For example, if your character's Constitution score was 16, your starting HP would also be 16.

CHARACTER SKILLS

Each class and background has its own set of skills that represent what the character excels at. Skills are tied directly to a specific attribute and allow the character to roll with an edge on the attribute when using that skill in the game. Skills are as follows:

MIGHT

Athletics: A character skilled in Athletics will be better at physical tasks such as swimming through rough currents and sprinting.

Riding: A character skilled in Riding is better able to saddle and ride mounts such as horses and ponies.

REFLEX

Acrobatics: A character skilled in Acrobatics is better able to leap over chasms, move out of the way of danger, and land without being harmed.

Climb: A character skilled in Climb can better ascend walls, cliff faces, or other surfaces suited for climbing without aid.

Stealth: A character skilled in Stealth can better skulk in the shadows to remain unseen, and has light footsteps and good spatial awareness.

Thievery: A character skilled in Thievery is better able to pick pockets without being noticed, pick locks, and forge counterfeit documents.

CHARISMA

Animal Husbandry: A character skilled in Animal Husbandry can better calm an animal in the wild.

Bluff: A character skilled in Bluff is better at tricking others into believing a lie and causing distractions.

Intimidate: A character skilled in Intimidation is better at threatening others into doing what they want, whether through violent tactics or an imposing demeanour.

Perform: A character skilled in Performance is better able to entertain others through song, dance, or poetry.

Persuasion: A character skilled in Persuasion is better suited to diplomacy, able to use their silk tongue to make others more likely to do their bidding.

MIND

Healing: A character skilled in Healing understands physiology and how to care for those who have been injured or fallen ill.

History: A character skilled in History is able to better recall the past events of a region, the succession of monarchs, or understand the political workings of a specific court.

Languages: A character skilled in Languages is able to read and speak certain tongues and understand the written word better than most.

Magic Knowledge: A character skilled in Magic Knowledge has a better understanding of the esoteric rites and rituals of cunning folk, in addition to being able to surmise the enchantments placed on items and deduce the nature of magical creatures.

Nature: A character skilled in Nature better understands the lay of the land, having knowledge of the geography of a kingdom, and is more proficient in identifying the nature of beasts and monsters.

Perception: A character skilled in Perception has better senses than most, being able to spot hidden doorways, hear quiet murmurings from behind a wall, or sense when someone might be lying through physical or verbal indicators.

Religion: A character skilled in Religion has a better grasp on the various deities and religions of the Perilous Land.

Survival: A character skilled in Survival is able to live longer in the wild through knowledge of foraging, tracking, and hunting.

CLASS FEATURES

Each class has a set of features that are unlocked when the character reaches a certain number of levels, representing gaining experience and self-improvement. These are special abilities unique to that class, giving them the ability to pull off impressive feats in a range of situations, although most prominently in combat. Further information about class features can be found in the classes section.

TALENTS

Talents give a character special abilities, whether in battle or while adventuring. They are abilities distinct from class features, some of which are universal while others are tied to a specific class. At certain levels, a character will be able to select a new talent, allowing for further class customisation.

STARTING MONEY AND EQUIPMENT

Each level 1 character begins the game with 3d6 x 10 gold pieces (gp), the currency of the Perilous Land. These can be spent on travelling equipment, weapons, and armour during character creation. Each class also has its own starting equipment, as do the optional character backgrounds, so be sure to note these down on your character sheet.

CHARACTER CLASSES

There are six classes to choose from in the game, each with their own part to play in your shared stories. Players should try to use a variety of classes to form a rounded and interesting team of adventurers. The classes are as follows:

- Knight
- Ranger
- Cunning folk
- Thief
- Barbarian
- Bard

CLASS TERMINOLOGY

Hit Dice (HD): These dice are rolled when a character levels to determine their new HP.

Hit Points (HP): A number that represents the amount of damage a character can take before falling unconscious or dying.

Weapon Proficiency: The weapon types the class is able to use without having to roll a setback in combat. These are divided into melee and ranged categories.

Armour Proficiency: The armour types the class is able to use without penalty in combat, in addition to a setback on Might and Reflex saving throws.

Save Proficiency: The class gains an edge on saving throws in which they are proficient.

Skills: A list of skills that the class is able to use.

Class Features: Special class abilities that are unlocked by increasing your character's level.

KNIGHT

HD: 1d10
Weapon Proficiency: Light, medium, and heavy melee. Light and medium ranged.
Armour Proficiency: Light, medium, and heavy armour.
Save Proficiency: Might and Reflex.
Skills: Choose three from: Athletics (Might), History (Mind), Perception (Mind), Riding (Might), Survival (Mind).
Starting Equipment: Flail, leather armour, and small shield; or shortbow, leather armour, and 20 arrows.

Knights are the hardiest of fighters and are experts in warfare, trained to identify the enemy's weaknesses and strike at an opportune moment. In the Perilous Land, the Knights of the Round Table are the most famous of these chivalrous warriors, standing for justice, honour, and righteousness. Knights abide by a code of honour and would rather die than break that code. While knights have historically come from noble bloodlines, the Age of Valour has brought with it a need for knights outside of nobility, meaning anyone who will swear the knight's oath, and has the right physical and mental capabilities, can become one of these brave warriors.

Knights are versatile warriors who can easily adapt to using several types of melee and ranged weapons. While some choose to walk into the fray with a short sword and shield, others prefer to hold their enemies at a distance with their short bow before pulling out their blade if the enemy comes too close. If they see an ally being attacked, they will quickly jump to their aid, preferring to take the brunt of the damage themselves rather than see their friends injured. More experienced knights can rally their comrades in battle to help them win the day.

Most civilised places in the Perilous Land venerate knights and will offer them a warm welcome. It is much easier for knights to be granted audiences with royalty than others, and news of a knight in town will travel rapidly, often resulting in a new quest.

KNIGHT CLASS FEATURES

Aid the Defenceless: A knight must act by a code of honour to put their life before others, for this is the truest act of heroism. They will constantly be assessing the battlefield for threats to their allies, throwing themself in the way of an enemy's blade. At level 1, if someone within 5ft of the knight takes damage from a non-magical source, the knight may choose to take some or all of that damage instead.

Weapon Expert: After spending time with various weapons, a knight begins to favour one over the others. At level 3, the knight chooses a favoured weapon type, such as a longsword. The knight rolls with edge on attacks with this weapon.

Never Surrender: Knights are sworn to protect others and to defend their kingdom at all costs. At level 5 they can summon the strength of will to stay standing even when badly wounded. The knight can still perform a single action until they reach negative HP equal their level, after which they are knocked unconscious.

Valiant Effort: Even in the midst of battle, a knight can get their allies back on their feet to help them fight another day. At level 7, once per combat as an action the knight can replenish all armour points for themselves and all allies within 30ft.

Double Strike: The knight is able to manoeuvre through the battlefield, cutting through their enemy's front line. At level 9, the knight may attack twice on their turn. The second attack may target another enemy they are able to reach.

Level	Knight Class Advancement
1	Class Feature: Aid the Defenceless, Talent
2	Talent
3	Class Feature: Weapon Expert, +2 to all attributes
4	Talent
5	Class Feature: Never Surrender, +2 to all attributes
6	Talent
7	Class Feature: Valiant Effort, +2 to all attributes
8	Talent
9	Class Feature: Double Strike, +2 to all attributes
10	Talent

RANGER

HD: 1d8

Weapon Proficiency: Light, medium, and heavy ranged. Light and medium melee.

Armour Proficiency: Light and medium armour.

Save Proficiency: Reflex and Constitution.

Skills: Choose three from: Acrobatics (Reflex), Healing (Mind), Nature (Mind), Stealth (Reflex), Survival (Mind).

Starting Equipment: Shortbow, 20 arrows and a dagger; or a short sword, sling and 20 stones.

Rangers are born hunters, expertly able to track their quarry through the wilderness, often for days on end, to corner their target. The forest is the place they feel most at home, hiding in the treetops and foraging for berries to keep themselves alive even in the harshest weather conditions. Due to this, rangers are excellent travelling companions, especially if the party isn't going to see civilisation for days at a time. They are able to concoct herbal remedies using plants and berries to revitalise themselves and their allies.

The most famous ranger in the Perilous Land is Robin Hood, a figure of both celebration and dread, depending on your point of view. Robin and his Merry Men stalk the forest of Sherwood, raiding bandit camps and making life miserable for corrupt nobles and priests.

Rangers prefer the wilds to large cities and are often uncomfortable around large groups of people. The reek of nature on their bodies does tend to aid them with this, especially considering their faces are usually covered in mucky camouflage.

In battle, rangers often stay out of the fray, picking off enemies with the deadly aim of their bow, but can handle themselves in close combat when required.

RANGER CLASS FEATURES

Herbalism: Rangers are masters at picking out beneficial plants to concoct a revitalising remedy. From level 1, twice per day the ranger may spend five minutes to make a remedy with the herbs they have foraged. The remedy heals 1d6 HP, and at level 6 heals 1d10 HP. The remedy is a one-use item and lasts for two days before becoming unusable.

Mortal Enemy: At level 3, at the start of the day select a creature to be the ranger's mortal enemy . This must be a specific creature (i.e. bugbear). The ranger rolls with edge when making attacks against this creature. Choose another mortal enemy at level 6 and a further one at level 9.

Deadly Shot: Rangers have a keen eye and after many hours of practise, they are able to hit their enemy's vital spots. At level 5 the ranger does an extra 1d4 damage on ranged attacks.

Split Shot: Rangers are able to quickly reload and shoot off arrows at lightning speed. At level 7, the ranger makes two ranged attacks as an action. The second attack may target a different enemy.

Snap Reflexes: Rangers must be on their toes at all times, able to move quickly at a moment's notice. At level 9 enemies have a setback on ranged attacks made against the ranger.

Level	Ranger Class Advancement
1	Class Feature: Herbalism, Talent
2	Talent
3	Class Feature: Mortal Enemy, +2 to all attributes
4	Talent
5	Class Feature: Deadly Shot, +2 to all attributes
6	Talent
7	Class Feature: Split Shot, +2 to all attributes
8	Talent
9	Class Feature: Snap Reflexes, +2 to all attributes
10	Talent

THIEF

HD: 1d8

Weapon Proficiency: Light and medium ranged. Light and medium melee.

Armour Proficiency: Light and medium armour.

Save Proficiency: Reflex and Mind.

Skills: Choose three from: Acrobatics (Reflex), Bluff (Charisma), Perception (Mind), Stealth (Reflex), Thievery (Reflex).

Starting Equipment: A dagger, leather armour and lockpicks; or a sling, leather armour, and lockpicks.

Despite being vilified by general society, the skills possessed by thieves are more useful than one thinks when it comes to adventuring. They silently skulk in the shadows, jumping out at their target at the opportune moment with a flash of the blade. Locks are no match for the thief's nimble hands as they break into homes and chests storing away family heirlooms and forgotten treasures, and as expert trap finders, they can sniff out a suspect wire or pressure plate more easily than most, disarming it before it's tripped.

Thieves come in all flavours, from the lowly pickpocket trying to survive day by day, to the romantic gentleman thief who not only steals treasure, but hearts too. While only a few manage to live a life of luxury, some are more selfless in their thievery – stealing only to give to the poor.

In battle the thief likes to stick to the shadows, using cover to sneak around their enemies and strike without warning, moving in a swift, precise manner to down their foes before they know what's hit them.

THIEF CLASS FEATURES

Sneak Attack: Thieves are masters of waiting in the shadows for the right moment to strike. From level 1, when a thief has an edge on attacks against an enemy they roll an extra 1d4 damage.

Trapfinder: The thief has a nose for traps. At level 3, the thief gains an edge when attempting to check for and disarm traps.

Critical Strike: At level 5, when the thief hits with sneak attack, they do 1d6 extra damage (instead of 1d4).

Disguise: At level 7, the thief is able to craft cunning disguises using only the materials at their disposal. They may make a Charisma check to disguise themself. Enemies must make a successful Mind check with a setback to recognise the thief.

Deadly Strike: At level 9, when the thief misses an attack, they may treat it as a hit twice per combat.

Level	Thief Class Advancement
1	Class Feature: Sneak Attack, Talent
2	Talent
3	Class Feature: Trapfinder, +2 to all attributes
4	Talent
5	Class Feature: Critical Strike, +2 to all attributes
6	Talent
7	Class Feature: Disguise, +2 to all attributes
8	Talent
9	Class Feature: Deadly Strike, +2 to all attributes
10	Talent

CUNNING FOLK

HD: 1d6
Weapon Proficiency: Light ranged. Light melee.
Armour Proficiency: Light armour.
Save Proficiency: Mind and Charisma.
Skills: Choose three from: Healing (Mind), History (Mind), Languages (Mind), Magic Knowledge (Mind), Religion (Mind).
Starting Equipment: A staff and cloth armour; or a sling and cloth armour.

Cunning folk, also known as wizards, enchanters, and sorcerers, are masters of the magical arts, performing wonders and even astonishing miracles. They are often hired as witch hunters, using good magic against those who practice dark arts. Most dedicate themselves to the gods, choosing to heal the sick and cast away the devils that infect the world.

Cunning folk are usually seen as solitary, keeping to themselves, prizing knowledge over human companionship. However, some choose to use their powers to serve their monarch, joining bands of adventurers looking to hunt down evil in the Perilous Land. Some of the most powerful people in the land are cunning folk, including the legendary Merlin and Morgan Le Fay.

Every day, cunning folk prepare a variety of spells using poultices of animals bones, runes, scrying mirrors, and other magical ingredients that allow them to cast powerful incantations when they're required. Because of their ability to craft curses and conjure beings from other worlds, some people find them unsettling and some in power have gone so far as to outlaw certain forms of magic. Others see wizards as a boon to society, hiring them to find witches and defeat monsters lurking on the fringes of society.

CUNNING FOLK CLASS FEATURES

Spellcasting: From level 1, cunning folk are able to cast spells from the spell list. They begin with the same number of spell points as their Mind attribute.

Magic Discipline: At level 3, cunning folk can choose to specialise in a certain magic discipline: charms, conjuring, curses, healing, or scrying. The spell costs for spells in the chosen discipline are halved (rounded up).

LEVEL	CUNNING FOLK CLASS ADVANCEMENT
1	Class Feature: Spellcasting, Talent
2	Talent
3	Class Feature: Magic Discipline, +2 to all attributes
4	Talent
5	+2 to all attributes
6	Talent
7	+2 to all attributes
8	Talent
9	+2 to all attributes
10	Talent

BARBARIAN

HD: 1d12

Weapon Proficiency: Light, medium and heavy melee. Light ranged.

Armour Proficiency: Light and medium armour.

Save Proficiency: Constitution and Might.

Skills: Choose three from: Animal Husbandry (Charisma), Athletics (Might), Intimidate (Charisma), Riding (Might), Survival (Mind).

Starting Equipment: A longsword and cloth armour; or a club and shield.

Barbarians exist on the edge of society in the Perilous Land, living in tribal communities on the grassy plains, foothills, and even in the harsh cold of the mountains themselves. They paint their faces with plant dye in order to look more intimidating to their enemies and are fiercely loyal to their kin. Barbarians are able to throw themselves into a blood rage, pummeling their enemies with no remorse.

Most of the barbaric tribes believe that armour is a weakness, with many eschewing full suits in favour of lighter materials. Similarly, they hold the belief that weapons are sacred objects forged by the hands of their gods. The larger and more deadly the weapon the better, with some tribes even blessing their blades and axes before any battle. You would be hard pressed to find a ranged weapon in a barbarian encampment. Bows are taboo in their societies as they believe that a true warrior meets their foe face-to-face. As a result, barbarians and rangers often don't see eye-to-eye.

Barbarian societies venerate animals, which can be seen in the names of their tribes, such as The Blue Adder, Savage Wolf, and Blind Boar. They wear animal skins that are blessed by their tribal shamans so the animal spirit will follow them wherever they go. Barbarians do not do well in civilised society, but to know one is to have a loyal friend for life.

BARBARIAN CLASS FEATURES

Barbarian Rage: Barbarians can throw themselves into a blind rage. From level 1, once per combat the barbarian may go into a rage. For 3 rounds, their attacks do an extra 1d6 damage. Barbarian rage is not counted as an action.

Quick Step: Barbarians are able to move quickly overland. At level 3 the barbarian increases their speed by 5ft.

Natural Armour: At level 5, barbarians gain 3 points of natural armour. This is in addition to any armour they are wearing.

Burning Rage: At level 7, when the barbarian rages they do an extra 1d8 damage instead of 1d6. On a critical hit, the enemy is also knocked prone.

Epic Rage: At level 9, when the barbarian rages they do an extra 1d10 damage instead of 1d8. On a critical hit, the enemy is also knocked prone and is paralysed for one round.

Level	Barbarian Class Advancement
1	Class Feature: Barbarian Rage, Talent
2	Talent
3	Class Feature: Quick Step, +2 to all attributes
4	Talent
5	Class Feature: Natural Armour, +2 to all attributes
6	Talent
7	Class Feature: Burning Rage, +2 to all attributes
8	Talent
9	Class Feature: Epic Rage, +2 to all attributes
10	Talent

BARD

HD: 1d8
Weapon Proficiency: Light and medium melee. Light ranged.
Armour Proficiency: Light and medium armour.
Save Proficiency: Charisma and Reflex.
Skills: Choose three from: Bluff (Charisma), History (Mind), Nature (Mind), Perform (Charisma), Persuasion (Charisma).
Starting Equipment: A sling and leather armour; or short sword and cloth armour.

Bards are gifted storytellers, musicians, and entertainers who travel the land gaining inspiration from their experiences, whether plundering the depths of ancient caves said to hold untold treasures, or sailing the freezing oceans to lost islands. Bards are orators, able to persuade others that their way is the right way, but they can also inspire others to go above and beyond their normal capabilities. With a hymn of battle, they can inspire warriors to continue the fight when all hope seems lost.

While some classes are fierce with weapons, or can cast mystical spells, bards are designed to uplift the whole adventuring party to help them achieve their goals. Even Robin Hood has a bard as a member of his Merry Men to ensure victory in their raids on the crooked nobility of Sherwood.

However, don't mistake a bard for someone who doesn't get their hands dirty when they have to. With their training in a variety of melee weapons, they can hold their own in a fight. Most often they will hang back behind their more heavily-armoured allies, boosting their attacks, healing their wounds, or even intimidating the enemy.

There are several bardic institutions set up across a number of cities in the Perilous Land, including the prestigious Taliesin's College of Bards. These colleges have produced some of the most famous bards in the eleven kingdoms.

BARD CLASS FEATURES

Battle Song: From level 1, as two actions a bard may sing a battle song (max two times per combat). One target within 10ft gains an edge on attacks and spells until the start of the bard's next turn.

Replenishing Verse: At level 3, once per combat (or once per hour outside of combat) as an action the bard may heal a target 1d8 plus half the bard's level in HP (rounded down).

Tale of Doom: At level 5, as two actions, a bard may tell a tale of doom (max two times per combat). One target within 30ft a setback on attacks until the start of the bard's next turn.

Inspirational Song: At level 7, as two actions a bard may sing an inspirational song (max two times per combat). One target within 40ft gains an additional 1d8 to damage rolls until the beginning of the bard's next turn.

Greater Replenishing Verse: At level 9, once per combat (or once per hour outside of combat) as an action a bard may heal all targets within 40ft by 2d8 plus half the bard's level in HP.

Level	Bard Class Advancement
1	Class Feature: Battle Song, Talent
2	Talent
3	Class Feature: Replenishing Verse +2 to all attributes
4	Talent
5	Class Feature: Tale of Doom +2 to all attributes
6	Talent
7	Class Feature: Inspirational Song, +2 to all attributes
8	Talent
9	Class Feature: Greater Replenishing Verse, +2 to all attributes
10	Talent

CHARACTER BACKGROUNDS

Backgrounds are designed to flesh out your character's history while offering them additional skills, money, and equipment to reflect their background. A player should select a background for their character as a way of enhancing roleplay and offering further depth to the game. Backgrounds also differentiate characters who share the same class.

ARISTOCRAT

You come from a wealthy family and have wanted for nothing. You are who the peasantry aspires to be, but those lacking noble blood could never reach your status. But perhaps this life became too comfortable for you and you have found a calling elsewhere.

Background Skills: Languages (Mind) and Riding (Might).

Starting Gear: A feathered hat, quality cloak, quarterstaff, and a leather purse containing 10gp.

ARTISAN

You have skilled hands adept in crafting objects with materials such as leather, wood, or steel. Artisans have a keen eye, able to pick out fine imperfections and spot things that maybe others couldn't. You may have even owned a shop or smithy to sell your wares.

Background Skills: Perception (Mind) and Nature (Mind).

Starting Gear: A bolt of leather, workman's tools, commoner's clothes, and a leather purse with 4gp.

COURTIER

You have worked in the halls of kings and queens as an advisor or attendant. As a result you know the right (and wrong) ways to address royalty, sometimes having to bend the truth in order to keep your head firmly on your shoulders.

Background Skills: Bluff (Charisma) and History (Mind).

Starting Gear: Lavender perfume, quill, parchment, signet ring, and 8gp.

FALCONER

Over the years, you have trained and developed a close bond with a bird of prey companion in order to hunt game in the wilderness. You are comfortable around animals, almost having a sixth sense when it comes to understanding their needs.

Background Skills: Animal Husbandry (Charisma) and Nature (Mind).

Starting Gear: Falconry glove, a bird of prey (see Hawk in the bestiary), and a bag of rabbit meat.

FARMER

In the past you were a salt-of-the-earth farmer, undertaking back-breaking labour mucking the pigs, tilling the fields, and working night and day to put bread on the table. Spending most of your life in the outdoors, you're attuned to nature more than most.

Background Skills: Nature (Charisma) and Riding (Might).

Starting Gear: Weather almanac, chicken feed, whistle, and 3gp.

GUARD

You were a town or city guard, hired by a local landowner, or monarch to deal out justice in the streets. Wearing battered armour and carrying a blade that had seen better days, you spent your time patrolling the streets looking for hooligans and thieves, sometimes being put on gate duty. Through this experience, you know how criminals operate and think.

Background Skills: Intimidate (Charisma) and Perception (Mind).

Starting Gear: A small bludgeon, a list of wanted criminals from your hometown, and a pair of leather gloves.

INNKEEPER

You have spent your days and nights behind a bar counter, serving beer and wine to locals and travellers alike. Through your job you've heard the tall tales, town gossip, and even the odd conspiratorial rumour. Because of this you learned how to talk to people, even if it was just to persuade them to buy another round of drinks.

Background Skills: Persuasion (Charisma) and History (Mind).

Starting Gear: A corkscrew, a list of ingredients to make a potent ale, and 5gp.

Jester

You once had a position as a court jester, bringing amusement to the aristocracy through tricks of dexterity and slapstick humour. You are able to tease a smile out even the most serious of people through a mix of wit and comic performance.

Background Skills: Perform (Charisma) and Acrobatics (Reflex).

Starting Gear: Four juggling balls, jester's make-up, a yellowed joke book, and 5gp.

Militia

You were once a sword for hire, a freelancer looking to scrape a wage, covering everything from guard duties for a local aristocrat to a baron's private army. You work best with a weapon in your hand and an order from a superior.

Background Skills: Athletics (Might) and Intimidation (Charisma).

Starting Gear: Knife, cloth cap, leather purse, waterskin, and 4gp.

Outlaw

You were a no-good street rat, a petty thief living from hand to mouth. The streets are your home – you know them like the back of your hand and you likely have several underground connections to help you out in a fix.

Background Skills: Stealth (Reflex) and Thievery (Reflex).

Starting Gear: A makeshift dagger, a black cloak, a set of lockpicks, and 3gp.

Priest

You were, or perhaps still are, a member of an order of priests, devout to the core and never veering from your faith. Everywhere you go you waste no time spreading the word of your patron deity, giving blessings to the meek and smiting the evil that lurks in the hearts of sinners.

Background Skills: Religion (Mind) and Healing (Mind).

Starting Gear: A holy symbol, priest's vestments, and a vial of holy water.

Scholar

You are a member of the intelligentsia with a thirst for knowledge. For most of your life the library has been your home, never feeling more comfortable than when your nose is stuck in the pages of a scholarly tome – whether it's about the histories of kings or the developing work on alchemy.

Background Skills: History (Mind) and Languages (Mind).

Starting Gear: The Book of Histories, a quill and ink, and 4gp.

Seafarer

You are happiest when the salt air is filling your lungs and the wind is in your sails. You have travelled far and have a great knowledge of the oceans and stars.

Background Skills: Perception (Mind) and Survival (Mind).

Starting Gear: A sextant, a map of local seas, a small telescope, sailor's garb, and 4gp.

Travelling Merchant

With a cart and wagon you have set off across the Perilous Land selling your wares, whether it's fine silk, spices, weapons, or magical ingredients. As a merchant you're a people person with a silver tongue that persuades customers to part with their gold.

Background Skills: Persuasion (Charisma) and Riding (Might).

Starting Gear: Merchant's clothing, lucky four-leaf clover, wineskin, and 5gp.

TALENTS

Talents are designed to add further customisation to your character, giving them enhanced abilities based on experience to aid them on their many quests. All classes begin with a talent from level 1 and gain new talents as they increase in level. Some talents have prerequisites that a character must meet in order to be able to take them. This could be: a class prerequisite, meaning only a specific class can use the talent; an attribute prerequisite, allowing only characters with a certain attribute score to use it; or a talent prerequisite, where only a character who has previously taken a specific talent is able to use it. Talents sometimes offer multiple benefits, or just a single benefit. Be sure to note new talents on your character sheet.

When selecting talents, think about how you want to play your character and choose the talent that suits this play style. For example, if you're a barbarian who wants to focus on combat, you would select talents that are going to help you in the midst of a battle.

GAINING TALENTS

All classes gain a new talent at levels 2, 4, 6, 8, and 10.

RETRAINING TALENTS

Sometimes you might choose a talent that feels right at the moment, but in a few levels' time you want to change your strategy or you simply don't feel the talent is useful for your character. You have the option of retraining a talent if you wish when you increase a level that would ordinarily allow you to gain a new talent. You may only retrain one talent at a time. To retrain, select a new talent from the list. This now replaces a previous talent. When you retrain a talent, you also gain the new additional talent. However, you may want to consult your GM before doing so, especially if you've retrained a talent multiple times.

For example, Sir Kristoph the knight hits level 6 and is able to gain a new talent. In addition to choosing a new talent, he chooses to retrain his current Agility talent, replacing it with the Armour Recovery talent.

TALENT LIST

AGILITY

You have honed your reflexes and athletic prowess, able to dodge near misses and leap further than most.
- Increase your Reflex score by 1, to a maximum of 20.
- When jumping over a distance, the difficulty is lowered by 10ft.
- You cannot fall prone as a result of an attack.

ARMOUR EXPERT

Prerequisite: Armour Recovery
You can make your armour last longer.
- All armour you are wearing, including shields, increases by 2 armour points.

ARMOUR RECOVERY

Prerequisite: Knight
You have trained in your armour for many hours, growing used to its weight and how it handles.
- When you take a regroup action you gain 3 armour points instead of 2.

BARDIC RESONANCE

Prerequisite: Bard
You can hold a note when performing amazing feats, making your bardic effects last longer.
- Your bard class features last an extra round.

BLACKSMITH

You are able to forge weapons and armour with the right materials.
- So long as you have relevant materials worth half the value of a piece of armour, you can spend time to craft the item as long as you have access to a forge. The type of item being crafted determines the length of time it will take to craft. Light weapons and armour take 1d3 days, medium weapons and armour take 1d4+1 days, and heavy weapons and armour take 1d6+3 days.

BRAWLER

You have trained in hand-to-hand combat, using only your fists and legs to take your opponent down.
- Your unarmed attacks do 1d6 damage instead of 1d4.

CHARMING

You have a way with words and an agreeable nature making it easier for you to persuade others.
- Increase your Charisma score by 1, to a maximum of 20.

CONNECTED

Prerequisite: Charisma 12
You have eyes and ears around the Perilous Land to aid you in your hour of need.
- When you are in a city, there is a 3 in 6 chance you have at least one contact from whom you can gather information. In a town this becomes a 2 in 6 chance and in a village it's a 1 in 6 chance.

CRITICAL BLOW

Prerequisite: Might 12 or Reflex 12
You are able to take advantage of your enemy's weaknesses in combat and strike a lethal blow.
- You score a critical strike on a 1 or 2.

CRITICAL KNOCK DOWN

Prerequisite: Critical Blow
When you strike true, you force your opponent to the ground.
- When you make a critical hit, the target is knocked prone.

DARKSIGHT

Your eyes have adapted to the dark.
- You treat darkness as if it were shadows when in combat.

DETERMINED

You can keep fighting even with wounds that would cause others to fall.
- Increase your Constitution score by 1, to a maximum of 20.
- You only fall unconscious when you reach -1 HP.

DODGE

Your fast reflexes allow you to quickly move out of the way of an oncoming attack of opportunity.
- You gain proficiency with Reflex saving throws.

FLEETFOOT

Prerequisite: Reflex 12
You are light on your feet, able to move over natural obstacles with ease.
- You are unaffected by difficult terrain in the wilderness.

IMPROVED LEADERSHIP

Prerequisite: Leadership
You are an experienced leader, able to easily take command of others in battle.
- All allies within 40ft, including yourself, gain an edge on Combat Order Rolls.
- All allies within 20ft, including yourself, gain an edge on Mind saving throws.

INSTRUMENT OF VALOUR

Prerequisite: Bard
Your inspirational songs are heightened by a valorous tune played on your instrument.
- Once per combat you may choose a bard class feature. You may use that feature one extra time during this combat.

HARDY

You have an increased constitution, allowing you to take more physical punishment than others.
- Increase your Constitution score by 1, to a maximum of 20.
- Increase your HP by 4.
- You gain proficiency with Constitution saving throws.

JACK-OF-ALL-TRADES

Prerequisite: Mind 12
You have dabbled in many skills.
- Gain two additional skills. These do not have to be your class skills.

LEADERSHIP

Prerequisite: Charisma 12
You are confident and charismatic, a born leader.
- All allies within 20ft, including yourself, gain an edge on combat order rolls.

MAGIC INITIATE

Prerequisite: Mind 12, non-cunning folk
You are attuned to the magic in the world and have studied enough to cast simple spells.
- You gain spell points equal to your Mind attribute.
- You are able to cast spells up to level 1. You cannot attempt to cast spells above level 1.

MAGIC SENSITIVITY

Prerequisite: Cunning folk
You can feel the vibrations of magic running through your body when you are near a magical source.

- You roll with edge when attempting cast the Sense the Presence of Magic spell.

MASTER HEALER

You can aid those on death's door and increase the potency of healing potions.

- When you use a healing potion on either yourself or another, it provides an extra 1d4 HP healing.
- You roll with edge to stabilise a dying creature.

MIGHTY

You are able to attempt impressive feats of strength.
- Increase your Might score by 1, to a maximum of 20.
- You gain proficiency with Might saving throws.

MONSTER HUNTER

You have studied many types of foes that walk the Perilous Land and understand their nature.
- You roll with edge when making a Mind check to identify a non-human creature, including its name, HD, and any special abilities.
- You roll with edge when attempting to track a non-human creature.

MYSTICAL INTUITION

Prerequisite: Cunning folk
You are able to more effectively draw magic from your surroundings.
- Increase your total number of spell points by 3.

POTENT REMEDY

Prerequisite: Ranger
You are an expert in crafting potent healing tinctures and salves.
- Remedies you create using your Herbalist class feature heal an extra d4.

QUICK SHIFT

You are able to move swiftly in order to gain a tactical advantage on the battlefield.
- After making a melee or ranged attack, you may make a 5ft move without using an action.

RAZOR BOW

Prerequisite: Reflex 12
You are able to use your bow in combat as if it were a melee weapon.
- You do not have a setback when attacking with a bow in close combat.

SHADOW FLOURISH

Prerequisite: Thief or ranger
You have have gained a deadly expertise with the use of a certain light melee weapon.
- You make attacks with light or medium melee weapons using Reflex instead of Might, gaining a Reflex damage bonus.

SHARP-WITTED

You are cunning and clever, able to outsmart your enemies.
- Increase your Mind score by 1, to a maximum of 20.
- You gain proficiency with Mind saving throws.

SHIELD EXPERT

You have trained in the art of shield defence.
- Gain a +2 armour bonus when using a shield.

SPELLSWORD

Prerequisite: Cunning folk
Despite being a magic-user, you have trained in the use of some melee weapons.
- Increase your Might score by 1, up to a maximum of 20.
- You gain a proficiency with medium melee weapons and medium armour.

SPRINTER

Prerequisite: Reflex 12
You are able to cover ground quicker than most.
- Increase your movement speed by 5ft.

SWIFT RECOVERY

Prerequisite: Constitution 10

After a short rest you are able to heal faster.

- You gain bonus HP equal to half your level (rounded up) after a short rest.

TRAINED CASTER

Prerequisite: Cunning folk

You do not need to summon as much energy to cast spells.

- Increase your Mind score by 1, up to a maximum of 20.
- Your spell casting costs are reduced by 1 point per three spell levels.

TRAPPER

Prerequisite: Ranger or barbarian

You are able to create traps from your environment to harm or impede your enemies.

- You can spend 10 minutes to create a simple trap. This trap takes up 5ft in space. If someone occupies this space they set off the trap. The victim must make a Reflex saving throw. If they fail, they take 1d6 damage and fall prone. If they succeed, they just fall prone.

TREASURE HUNTER

You can expertly appraise items and spot the most valuable treasure.

- When selling treasure, you receive an extra 20% of its value.
- After ten minutes inspecting a treasure, you are able to identify its use and value.

TWO-WEAPON EXPERTISE

Prerequisite: Two-Weapon Fighting

You have mastered the art of battling with an off-hand weapon.

- You do not gain a setback for using two weapons in combat.

TWO-WEAPON FIGHTING

You are proficient in using two weapons at once in battle.
- You may use two single-handed weapons in combat.

WILD SWING

Prerequisite: Barbarian
You can cleave your foes in a huge arc, injuring multiple opponents.
- After dealing damage to a target with a melee weapon, you may make a second attack against one other target within 5ft of you. You may only use Wild Swing once per round.

WILDERNESS EXPERT

You are able to survive in the wild for weeks at a time, foraging and finding the most defensible camp spots.
- When in the wilderness, you may spend one hour foraging for food and water, returning with enough for the party.
- You can automatically tell whether food found in the wild is suitable to eat or poisonous.
- When making camp, anyone attempting to find the encampment has a setback on Perception checks.

WITCHFINDER

You are able to sense the presence of witches and have spent years studying how to kill them.
- You can tell if a witch has been in a location in the past 24 hours.
- When a witch is within 100ft your witch sense alerts you.
- You have an edge on melee or ranged attacks against witches.

FLESHING OUT
YOUR CHARACTER

Once you have chosen your class and background, it's time to flesh out your character further with a name, age, deity, description, and backstory.

AGE

A character's age can determine how they are roleplayed. Choose an age before you start a game with a character. This won't affect any of the character's attributes, but the age could help explain why they have certain scores. For instance, an older character may have a higher Mind score but lower Reflex, while a character in her twenties may not be as worldly but might have a higher Constitution or Might.

DEITY

The vast majority of people in the Perilous Land worship some kind of deity, who helps guide them in their daily endeavours by providing a philosophical framework from which to live their lives. There are deities dedicated to the forest, like Cernunnos, poetry like Fachea, and hunting, like Nodens. This book contains a list of deities, along with their domains and class affinities to help you decide who you character should worship. Deities offer great roleplaying potential, offering an insight into what a character might find important and how they might react to certain situations.

OPTIONAL RULE: STARTING FACTION

You may decide that you want your character to start having joined one of the factions of the Perilous Land. If you would like your character to start as a Knight of the Round Table or a member of the Fellowship of Enchanters (or another faction), you can note that down on your character sheet. To read moew about the factions of the Perilous Land, see page 170.

CHARACTER DESCRIPTION

What does your character look like? Note down a few key aesthetic traits and don't be afraid to make them unusual. Is his beard in plaits? Is her face covered in swirling tattoos? Does she have a voice like thunder? Thinking about what your character looks like and their mannerisms will help you when it comes to roleplaying. Perhaps he has a nervous tic, or bellows every sentence.

CHARACTER BACKSTORY

Creating a backstory for your character is a great way to aid roleplay and give the GM material to work into the campaign. This is where you can work your background and faction (if you choose to join one) into your story: How did you become an outlaw? What drove you to joining the Iron Hawks? Think about what your character most desires from their life and what their greatest fear is. This could be a need to impress Sir Lancelot of the Round Table and you might fear rejection from the knights. Perhaps you ran away from home at an early age and became a sailor before realising you had an innate magical gift, so sought out others like you. GMs can use these details to make games of *Romance of the Perilous Land* more personal to the players.

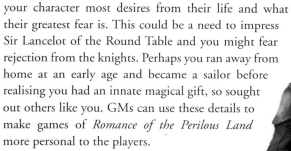

CHARACTER EXAMPLE

Overleaf you can see an example of a finished character, Thania of Corbenic, Knight of the Fisher King.

ROMANCE
—◆ OF THE ◆—
PERILOUS LAND

CHARACTER SHEET

Name Thania of Corbenic

Player Scott

Level 1

Experience

Attribute	Score	Save
Might	16	X
Reflex	13	X
Charisma	12	
Constitution	14	
Mind	10	

Class
Knight

Background
Falconer

Faction
Order of the Fisher King

Deity
Epona

Skills	
Athletics (Might)	X
Riding (Might)	X
Acrobatics (Reflex)	
Stealth (Reflex)	
Thievery (Reflex)	
Animal Husbandry (Charisma)	X
Bluff (Charisma)	
Intimidate (Charisma)	X
Perform (Charisma)	
Persuasion (Charisma)	
Healing (Mind)	
History (Mind)	
Languages (Mind)	
Magic Knowledge (Mind)	
Nature (Mind)	X
Perception (Mind)	
Religion (Mind)	
Survival (Mind)	

Total HP 14

Current HP 14

Total Armour 10

Current Armour 10

Valour Points 3

Weapon	Range	Type	Damage
Flail	Melee	Medium	D8+2

Class Features

Aid the Defenceless

Talents

Critical Blow

Description

Long raven hair, emerald eyes, a look that could stop a person dead in their tracks. She is not the most personable woman in the world, but get past her defences and you will find a compassionate soul and a loyal friend.

Backstory

Thania grew up in the tiltyard of Castle Corbenic and under the guidance of her mother learned the ways of falconry. After her king was struck down with his malady, Thania made it her goal to help find a cure for him by joining the Order of the Fisher King.

Languages

Common, Corlish

Equipment

Flail, leather armour, small shield, falconry glove, bag of rabbit meat, 30gp

Notes

Aid the Defenceless: Take some/all damage of characters within 5ft.

Critical Blow: Critical strike on a 1 or a 2.

EQUIPMENT

To survive the Perilous Land, a hero must be equipped with the right items, be that a sword on her back, mountain clothing and provisions for three days, or a riding horse, bow, and tent for the night ahead.

Equipment can be bought in many places, from large, bustling marketplaces where merchants offer their wares, to small esoteric shops that sell magical tinctures to offer healing in the darkest of hours.

ENCUMBRANCE

Characters can carry a number of items equal to double their Might score. If they carry more than this, their movement is halved and they take a setback to Reflex checks. Heavy weapons and armour count as two items. When it comes to ammunition, 10 of one type of ammunition counts as one item.

ARMOUR AND SHIELDS

Armour is worn to help keep a hero alive in combat, whether being pelted with arrows or receiving a blow to the chest from a flail. Armour comes in three types: light, medium and heavy. Certain classes will receive penalties for wearing armour they are not proficient in.

Armour Name: This denotes what kind of armour it is. For example, chain armour.

Armour Points: When a character wearing armour receives damage, they first reduce their armour points before their hit points. Generally speaking, the heavier the armour, the more armour points it has.

Type: The type of armour will be either light, medium, or heavy.

Cost: How many gold pieces the armour costs.

ARMOUR PROFICIENCY

Different classes are able to move and fight better in certain types of armour. Stronger classes that focus on melee combat are more likely to be trained in heavy armour, while others who skulk in the shadows or try to keep out of the fray wear light or medium armour. This is reflected in the armour proficiencies listed for each class. Classes who wear armour types they are not proficient with add their armour points to attack rolls and have a setback on Might and Reflex saving throws. Furthermore, if they are not proficient with heavy armour and they choose to wear it, they also must halve their speed.

LIGHT ARMOUR

Characters who need to be nimble or who aren't trained in combat are more likely to wear light armour.

Cloth: Cloth armour is little more than a padded shirt that offers a small amount of protection.

Leather: Made from tanned hide, leather armour is expertly crafted to provide protection from cuts and gouges.

Small shield: A round buckler held with a leather strap.

MEDIUM ARMOUR

Medium armour is a step up from light in terms of protection. It strikes a balance between allowing for freedom of movement and defence.

Chain: Crafted from linked rings that are draped over the body, chainmail covers the arms and head. This type of armour is most common among soldiers.

Wooden shield: This shield is wide enough to cover most of the torso and crafted from fine hardwood.

HEAVY ARMOUR

Heavy armour offers the most protection, but wearing it is likely to take its toll on anyone who isn't trained in its use.

Plate: This full suit of armour offers covers the majority of the body, making it highly protective.

Tower shield: This is a tall shield used by elite soldiers, covering the entirety of the body.

Armour Name	Armour Points	Type	Cost
Small shield	2	Light armour	30gp
Wooden shield	3	Medium armour	60gp
Tower shield	4	Heavy armour	100gp
Cloth armour	6	Light armour	15gp
Leather armour	8	Light armour	50gp
Chain armour	10	Medium armour	100gp
Plate armour	12	Heavy armour	350gp

Weapons

Each class has one or more weapon proficiencies listed, based on their training and experience. Like armour, weapons come in three types: lights, medium, and heavy.

Weapon Name: This denotes what kind of weapon it is. For example, dagger.

Damage Die: This is the die that is rolled in combat when an attack with this weapon is successful. The total roll is deducted from the target's hit points after taking armour into account. The minimum amount of damage that can be done on a successful attack is 1, even if the rules would make it 0.

Type: The type of weapon will be either light, medium, or heavy.

Cost: How many gold pieces the weapon costs.

Range: How far a ranged or thrown weapon can shoot/be thrown.

Weapon proficiency

Different classes are trained in the use of certain weapon types. Knights are able to wield all types of melee weapon, having trained heavily in hand-to-hand combat, while rangers are experts in light to heavy bows. Some, such as the cunning folk, can only use light weapons because they have spent their time focusing on spells rather than combat. Classes who use weapon types they are not proficient with have a setback to attacks.

Light weapons

Characters who are perhaps not as strong, or who need to fight with speed, will find light weapons to be easier to wield. The maximum damage for light weapons is the lowest of all weapon types.

Dagger: Daggers are perfect for concealing on a character's person. They are swift but do not inflict as much damage as a heavier weapon such as a sword. However, daggers can be thrown.

Staff: Staves are crafted from wood and the top ends are often carved into an animal head. They can be used one- or two-handed and are favoured by cunning folk.

Sling: This light strip of leather can be loaded with a stone and spun above the head before releasing the stone at the enemy at great speed. Slings only have a shorter range, but ammunition is inexpensive.

Medium weapons

Medium weapons are slightly heavier than light weapons and require more skill to use. Those trained in some ranged or melee combat will be able to use this weapon type.

Short sword: This double-edged blade is longer than a dagger but remains light enough to wield with a single hand. Short swords are the most common swords used in the Perilous Land.

Club: A smooth piece of hardwood with a wider top and narrow handle. Clubs are particularly favoured by wild people.

Flail: A flail is a spiked iron ball attached to a wooden handle by a chain. Knights often use flails during melee tournaments.

Spear: A sharp metal point on the end of a long wooden pole. Spears are effective for fighting at range, with wielders able to attack from behind an ally, effectively shielding themselves from oncoming blows.

Shortbow: The smallest of the bow family, the shortbow is most effective at close range.

HEAVY WEAPONS

Heavy weapons require extensive training and often great strength to use effectively. This weapon type is capable of causing great damage.

Longsword: Longswords have a straight, double-edged blade and a crossed hilt. They are favoured particularly by knights in battle.

Claymore: This two-handed war sword is a creation of Escose warriors, who needed a large sword to battle the giants of the mountains.

Lance: A lance is a type of pole weapon, similar to a spear, that is used on horseback in battle and during a joust. Lances are excellent when riding against infantry, but soldiers always have a lighter weapon to spare when they eventually come into close combat with the enemy.

Longbow: This tall bow is the size of the wielder and is capable of shooting arrows at great distances.

Heavy crossbow: A large, two-handed crossbow that must be loaded with both hands. This weapon shoots bolts at much quicker speeds than bows, and is able to tear through armour.

Weapon Name	Damage Die	Type	Cost	Range
Dagger	1d6	Light melee	3gp	20ft
Staff	1d6	Light melee	2gp	-
Sling	1d6	Light ranged	1gp	50ft
Short sword	1d8	Medium melee	30gp	-
Club/Flail	1d8	Medium melee	30gp	-
Spear*	1d8	Medium melee (one- or two-handed)	60gp	-
Shortbow	1d8	Medium ranged (two-handed)	30gp	80ft
10 x Arrows/Bolts	-	Ammo	10gp	-
Longsword	1d10	Heavy melee (two-handed)	90gp	-
Claymore	1d12	Heavy melee (two-handed)	350gp	-
Lance**	1d12	Heavy melee (one- or two-handed)	400gp	-
Longbow	1d10	Heavy ranged (two-handed)	90gp	150ft
Heavy Crossbow	1d12	Heavy ranged (two-handed)	350gp	100ft

*A spear can be used both one- or two-handed. If it is used two-handed, gain a +1 to damage.
**When mounted, a lance may be used with one hand, but when unmounted it must be used with two hands. The lance does +2 damage when the wielder is mounted. The wielder gains a setback when fighting unmounted.

64

ADVENTURING EQUIPMENT

The following section details the types of adventuring equipment characters can buy in the game. The list of items is not exhaustive, but offers some of the more common pieces of equipment they may use on their adventures.

Backpack: This pack is made from leather and slung over the shoulders. It is quite spacious, allowing the adventurer to fit in the equipment they require for a long journey. Pockets sewn onto the sides allow for quick access to smaller objects.

Bedroll: A bedroll folds out onto the ground, offering a soft surface on which to sleep in the wilderness.

Bell: This small brass bell creates a noticeable chime when rung.

Book: A book can be entirely blank, allowing it to be used like a journal, or it may contain information, stories, poetry, or art. Cunning folk write their spells in a large tome, often bound in leather.

Candle: A small white candle with a wick. When lit it casts light in a 10ft x 10ft area.

Chalk: A small stick of chalk used to draw on rough surfaces. The markings will fade after a while when exposed to the elements.

Chest: A 1ft wooden box with a hinged lid and a lock. Often used to store precious objects.

Fishing tackle: This includes a wooden fishing rod, line, several hooks, and enough bait for a single fishing trip.

Flask of oil: A small leather container filled with oil used to light lanterns.

Flint and steel: When the flint and steel are struck together they create a spark used to ignite a campfire or torch.

Hammer: A short wooden-handled hammer with a heavy iron head used for woodworking.

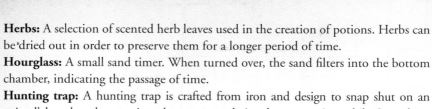

Herbs: A selection of scented herb leaves used in the creation of potions. Herbs can be dried out in order to preserve them for a longer period of time.

Hourglass: A small sand timer. When turned over, the sand filters into the bottom chamber, indicating the passage of time.

Hunting trap: A hunting trap is crafted from iron and design to snap shut on an animal's leg when they step into the centre, rendering the creature immobile. Something stepping into a hunting trap takes 1d4 damage and 1 damage for every round thereafter. The hunting trap can be removed with a simple Athletics or Might check.

Instrument: A selection consisting of a lyre, a stringed U-shaped instrument from the harp family; a flute, a woodwind pipe; and a drum crafted from wood with animal skin stretched over the top.

Lantern: A metal lantern with a glass case housing a candle. Oil is poured in to fuel the light. The lantern lights an area 30ft x 30ft.

Lock: A small iron padlock.

Lockpicks: A set of tools used to pick locks, including a torque wrench. Using a lockpick offers a -2 bonus to Thievery or Reflex rolls when attempting to pick a lock. If a natural 20 is rolled, the lockpick breaks.

Manacles: A set of thick iron cuffs that lock shut around wrists or ankles, tethered by a chain.

Mirror, small: A small mirror that can be used to look around blind corners.

Parchment: Fragile paper used to write letters.

Pole (10ft): A long steel pole used for checking the immediate areas for hazards and traps.

Quill and ink: A feather that can be dipped into ink in order to write on paper.

Quiver: Hung around the shoulder, a quiver has enough space to fit 20 arrows or bolts.

Rope (50ft): A 50ft length of silk rope that can be used to tie around objects, people, or creatures. It is strong enough to withstand the weight of multiple human-sized climbers.

Sealing wax: A red stick of wax that can be melted to seal a message.

Shovel: A small wooden shovel that can be used to dig in soil.

Tent: A two-person tent made from brown linen. A series of metal poles allows the tent to stand upright.

Trail rations: Trail rations contain dried food, including salted meats and nuts that are used to sustain travellers on the road.

Torch: When lit, a torch provides a 20ft x 20ft area of light. A torch will burn out over time.

Whetstone: A smooth stone used to sharpen a blade.

Wineskin: A leather bladder that can be filled with liquid, most often water or wine.

Wooden stake: A sharpened piece of wood. If used as a weapon, it does 1d4 damage.

Work tools: A selection of craft tools including nails, a hammer and a bolt of leather.

Item Name	Notes	Cost
Backpack	Carry 4 extra items	40gp
Bedroll		3gp
Bell		2gp
Book		2gp
Candle	10 uses	1gp
Chalk		1gp
Chest		4gp
Fishing tackle		1gp
Flask of oil	10 uses	1gp
Flint and steel	10 uses	3gp
Hammer		1gp
Herbs	10 uses	10gp
Hunting trap		4gp
Hourglass		1gp
Instrument	Lyre, flute, or drum	4gp
Lantern		10gp
Lock		1gp
Lockpicks		20gp
Manacles		3gp
Mirror, small		2gp
Parchment (10)	10 uses	1gp
Pole (10ft)		3gp
Quill and ink	10 uses	1gp
Quiver		2gp
Rope (50ft)		1gp
Sealing wax	5 uses	1gp
Shovel		2gp
Tent	Holds 2 people	6gp
Torches (3)	5 uses per torch	1gp
Trail rations	5 uses	4gp
Whetstone		1gp
Wineskin		1gp
Work tools		6gp
Wooden stake	10 uses	10gp

HOSPITALITY

The following section lists purchasable items related to hospitality, including inn rooms and meals.

Small meal: A single meal usually containing a piece of fruit, some cold meat, bread, and cheese.

Hearty meal: A large meal with cooked meat, a loaf, pastries, vegetables, and fruits.

Jug of ale: A jug full of ale containing enough for three pints.

Common room: A modest quarters with one or two beds and a stool.

Aristocrat room: A large room with a soft bed, an armchair, mirror, and changing screen.

Stables: Used to keep horses. Horses will be fed if kept overnight in the stables.

Hospitality Name	Notes	Cost
Jug of ale or wine		1gp
Small meal	Sustain 1 person for 1 day	2gp
Hearty meal	Sustain 1 person for 2 days	4gp
Common room	Per night	5gp
Aristocrat room	Per night (includes hearty meal, bath, and ale)	20gp
Stables	Per day per mount	1gp

TRANSPORTATION

The following section lists transportation available for purchase. All riding beasts come equipped with saddles and harnesses.

Carriage: A laquered wooden carriage with a plush interior that can fit four inside in addition to a rider on top.

Mule: A cross between a donkey and a horse, mules are bred to carry heavy loads cross country.

Pony: A small horse bred for pulling small wagons.

Riding horse: A strong horse used for riding long distances.

Wagon: A wooden cart pulled by horses. Wagons are often used by traders for storing their goods.

Transport Name	Notes	Cost
Pony		20gp
Mule	Can carry up to 20 items	10gp
Riding horse		50gp
Wagon		40gp
Carriage		150gp

PLAYING
THE GAME

CHARACTER ATTRIBUTES

very player character in a game of *Romance of the Perilous Land* has five main attributes that denote how they perform physically, mentally and socially. This section goes into further detail around what these attributes mean and what they are useful for during play.

MAKING ATTRIBUTE CHECKS

One of the most frequent rolls that a player will make is an attribute check, or simple 'check'. This is done when a character is attempting something that would pose some kind of challenge to one of the five main attributes. The GM will ask a player to roll an attribute check when the situation demands it, noting the attribute that is involved in the check. The challenge posed should be something that has consequences if the check is failed. For example, jumping over a 2ft wall wouldn't necessarily require an attribute check because there is little risk and consequence. However, scaling a 20ft wall could result in the character plummeting to the ground and getting injured.

When attempting something requires a check, the GM will select the most appropriate attribute or skill for the check and set a difficulty rating, which is a number deducted from the attribute in question. The player must then roll equal to or under that final number with a d20 to succeed. This is called the target number (TN).

**Attribute check = Roll equal to or under a
relevant attribute score – difficulty rating**

For example, if Sir Kristoph was attempting to scale a 20ft wall, the GM would ask him to roll a check to be able to pull himself up. The GM sets a difficulty rating of 4, as it's fairly tough for a level 1 character. In this example, Sir Kristoph has 15 Might, so must roll 11 or less to succeed the check. He takes the d20 and rolls an 11, which means he successfully scales the wall. If he had failed the check by rolling 12 or over, he would have faced the consequences as determined by the rules as written or what that GM decides should happen. In this case, it could mean Sir Kristoph takes some damage from the fall and lands prone.

DIFFICULTY RATINGS

Difficulty ratings are set by the GM to determine how challenging a check is. This is a number that is deducted from an attribute to determine the target number for a given check. There are four types of check:

Simple: Jumping a low wall, recalling common bird species, swimming in calm waters.

Regular: Riding a horse, picking a common lock, smashing a wooden box.

Tough: Taming a hawk, bashing down a metal door, understanding another language.

Severe: Lifting a horse, holding your breath for 10 minutes, decrypting a long dead language.

DIFFICULTY RATING TABLE

As characters gain levels and their attributes increase, difficulty ratings for checks also increase. Consult the table below to find out the correct difficulty rating for a given task.

Difficulty	Level 1	Level 3	Level 5	Level 7	Level 9
Simple	0	0	0	0	0
Regular	2	3	4	5	6
Tough	4	5	6	7	8
Severe	6	7	8	9	10

EDGES AND SETBACKS

Even after setting a difficulty rating, a challenge may be more difficult or easier to accomplish depending on its context. Taking the example of Sir Kristoph attempting to scale a wall, let's suppose that the wall is rain-slicked and mossy. The GM determines that the character would have a harder time climbing the wall than if it were dry and full of footholes. In this case, the player would make their Might attribute check with a setback. This means the player rolls 2d20 and takes the highest number, using this as the result of their check. However, if Sir Kristoph had a rope and the wall was dry the GM would determine that the check would be easier, so would be rolled with an edge. This time, the player would roll 2d20 and use the lowest number as the result of the check.

It should be noted that if the GM determined that the character had both an edge and a setback in the same challenge, they would cancel each other out and the player would roll the check as normal. For example, Sir Kristoph might have an edge by scaling the wall with a rope, but the GM also determines that since the wall is slippery he should also have a setback. Because of this, the player rolls 1d20 on his Might attribute, as normal.

CONTESTED ATTRIBUTE CHECKS

Sometimes a challenge will be a direct contest between two people, such as an arm wrestle. This is called a contested attribute check because the challenge involves another active participant trying to prevent a character from succeeding.

Most creatures and NPCs in *Romance of the Perilous Land* have an HD (hit dice) score that determines how strong or experienced they are, acting just like player character levels.

When a player character is making a contested attribute check against an opponent with an HD score, the character attempts to roll equal to or under a relevant attribute as normal. However, because there is an opponent, the character reduces this attribute score by a number equal to the opponent's HD to get the target number the player must roll.

Creatures with an HD also have a TN (target number) score rather than any attributes. The creature must roll equal to or under their TN to succeed, but they must reduce this TN by the player character's level. The participant who succeeds their check is the victor. If both succeed, the lowest roll is the victor. If neither succeed, they may be able to continue making checks until one succeeds.

In summary, when making a contested check against a creature with an HD score:

- The player character reduces their relevant attribute by the HD of the creature to determine their target number.
- The creature reduces their TN attribute by the player character's level to determine their target number.
- Both attempt to roll equal to or under their target numbers.
- One succeeds by either passing the check where the opponent does not, or rolling the lowest score if both are successful.
- Any ties are rerolled.

For example, Sir Kristoph is attempting to hide from a giant after trespassing in its lair. Sir Kristoph is level 2 and the giant has HD6 and TN16. The GM tells Kristoph's player that he needs to roll a contested Reflex check to stay out of sight. Kristoph has a 14 Reflex attribute score, which he reduces by 6 because this is the HD of the giant, giving a target number of 8 to roll. The giant, who is trying to sniff Kristoph out, reduces its TN by 2, equal to Kristoph's level, giving it a final target number of 14 to roll. Kristoph's player rolls a 10 and the GM rolls a 12 for the giant. In this case, the giant has succeeded and Kristoph has failed, meaning the giant manages to find him in his hiding place.

IF A PLAYER CHARACTER IS MAKING A CONTESTED CHECK AGAINST ANOTHER PLAYER OR NPC WITH A LEVEL

While it is less common, sometimes a player character will have to make a contested attribute check against another player character or an NPC who has a level (these are usually 'named' NPCs that have all the same stats that a character would have).

The method is nearly the same as making a check against a creature with an HD, but instead both participants reduce their relevant attribute scores by the opponent's level. Both then must attempt to roll equal to or under this new target number to succeed.

For example, Sir Kristoph (level 2) is arm wrestling Sir Galahad (level 8) as part of a wager. The GM determines that both will be making the check with their Might attributes. Sir Kristoph reduces his Might of 15 by Sir Galahad's level, giving him a final target number of 7. Sir Galahad has a Might score of 18, reducing this by Kristoph's level, giving him a final target number of 16. Kristoph rolls a 2 and Galahad a 17. Against all odds, Kristoph manages to best Galahad in the arm wrestle and win the wager.

USING SKILLS WITH ATTRIBUTE CHECKS

Characters have a list of skills that allow them to roll with an edge on attributes when using a skill relevant to the challenge at hand. If an attribute check can be tied to a skill a character possesses, they roll with an edge on the attribute that is connected with that skill. For example, a character who is trying to convince a merchant to lower their price on a sword would ordinarily make a Charisma check. However, if the character has the Persuade skill, which is connected with Charisma, they would roll with an edge.

SAVING THROWS

Saving throws occur when a character needs to actively resist something that could cause them harm or an adverse effect. Saving throws act just like attribute checks, but a player cannot choose to roll one. Instead, the GM decides that the player must roll a saving throw (also called a 'save'). Most commonly, saves are used to resist magical damage, poisons, physical harm, and mind-altering effects. Saving throws are tied to each attribute, so you may be required to make a Mind save or a Reflex save. Just like attribute checks, saving throws can be modified to be easier or more difficult, granting an edge or a setback. Each class has its own save proficiency, which gives it an edge on certain saves.

If a creature has caused the saving throw, whether through an attack or otherwise, the creature's HD must be deducted from the attribute the player is using to determine the target number.

For example, Sir Kristoph is battling an incubus, a foul spirit that is attempting to control his mind with a charm attack . The GM tells the player that he must make a Charisma save. Because the incubus is HD5, Kristoph reduces his Charisma of 12 by 5, giving him a target number of 7 to roll in order to succeed.

If it was not another creature that caused a saving throw (for example, an environmental hazard), the GM assigns a difficulty rating as though it were a check.

The following attributes are tested for avoiding specific harms:

Might: Used to avoid physical harm that can't be dodged.

Reflex: Used to avoid physical harm that can be dodged.

Mind: Used to avoid spell effects, illusions, or enchantments.

Constitution: Used to avoid poisons, disease, or death.

Charisma: Used to avoid charms.

SAVING THROW PROFICIENCIES

Every class has its own set of saving throw proficiencies, indicating an aptitude towards avoiding a particular kind of effect. A class proficient in a certain kind of save gets to roll with an edge on that save.

MIGHT

The Might attribute is tied to how powerful the character is physically. A high score means they are more adept at athletic tasks such as climbing, vaulting, lifting and swimming. Might also determines how well a character uses melee weapons. Might can be used for the following checks:

- Trying to pry open a stuck door
- Climbing a tree
- Lifting a boulder
- Jumping a ravine
- Digging a ditch
- Riding a horse

SKILLS CONNECTED TO MIGHT

- Athletics
- Riding

REFLEX

Reflex determines quickness, agility, the ability to move quietly, and how well you can use a ranged weapon. A high score means that the character is light on their feet, able to dodge blows more easily, and stick to the shadows without being noticed. Reflex can be used for the following checks:

- Moving silently through a room
- Shooting an arrow at a distant target
- Leaping out of the way of an oncoming hazard
- Picking a pocket
- Unlocking a door with a pick

SKILLS CONNECTED TO REFLEX

- Acrobatics
- Stealth
- Thievery

MIND

Mind determines how intelligent and wise a character is. This includes being able to deduce, understand complex subjects, read magical languages, and identify objects or creatures. A high score means that the character is deeply learned in one or more subjects, is highly perceptive and has a great amount of common sense. Mind can be used for the following checks:

- Determining the type of creature that left a certain track
- Stabilising a dying ally
- Understanding their location geographically without a map
- Realising if there is a trap up ahead
- Spotting an enemy in the undergrowth
- Understanding a dead language
- Recalling a certain piece of history about an area

SKILLS CONNECTED TO MIND

- Healing
- History
- Languages
- Magic Knowledge
- Nature
- Perception
- Religion
- Survival

CONSTITUTION

Constitution determines how well a character can take punishment, survive in harsh conditions, or survive at length without food. A high score means a character is hardy, able to shrug off wounds better than most, and withstand the effects of poisons. Constitution can be used for the following checks:

- Protecting against the cold when travelling over a mountain pass
- Negating or slow the effects of a poison
- Surviving for longer without sustenance
- Holding your breath
- Staying awake for a long period of time

CHARISMA

Charisma determines how persuasive, entertaining, or intimidating a character is. A high score means a character is good at getting people to do their bidding and have effective leadership skills. Charisma can be used for the following checks:

- Singing a beloved shanty to entertain guests
- Playing the lute
- Bartering with a merchant
- Persuading a guard to set them free
- Calming an agitated horse
- Interrogating an enemy

SKILLS CONNECTED TO CHARISMA

- Bluff
- Persuasion
- Intimidate
- Animal Husbandry
- Perform

COMBAT

There is no doubt that your adventures will pit you against foes who wish you dead, so combat is a necessary factor in the game. Whether you're throwing punches in a tavern brawl or trying to plunge your sword into the belly of a heaving sea monster, the following section deals with rules for conducting battle in a game of *Romance of the Perilous Land*.

How combat works is similar to how attribute checks operate, but with a slightly different structure that allows the players to simulate a dramatic encounter on the tabletop with miniatures.

COMBAT ORDER ROLLS (COR)

Combat works in a series of turns, with each player and opponent acting in a certain order. To determine the order of combat, player characters taking part in the fight must make a combat order roll (COR). This is simply a Reflex attribute check with no difficulty modifications. If the roll is successful, the player character acts before the enemies. If not, then that player character acts after the enemies. The players may decide among themselves in what order they act in after the CORs are made, but the order is fixed once a decision is made.

The GM does not have to make a COR for creatures. Once the players have made their rolls to determine whether they will act before or after their opponents, the GM is free to determine the order the creatures act in, and as with players, the order is fixed after this has been decided.

For example, Bryan, Anna, and Ben are about to go into combat with three grotesque redcaps. Bryan's Reflex is 15, so makes a Reflex check, rolling a 10. Bryan will be acting before the redcaps. Anna's character has a Reflex of 10 and rolls a 14, so will be acting after the enemy. Ben's Reflex is 12 and rolls a 18, meaning he will also act after the Redcaps. Anna decides it's best for Ben to go first, as she wants to get a good flanking position and Ben agrees. The GM then decides the order the redcaps will act in.

TIME

Combat is split into turns and rounds. A turn is the time it takes for a single participant to act, while a round is the time taken for all participants to act. A combat round is the equivalent of 10 seconds of time, representing the fight moving swiftly, with swords clashing and spells being uttered almost simultaneously. In some cases, you won't need to record how long a combat is taking; however, in certain situations you will need to note down how many seconds have passed, for instance if a spell effect is time sensitive.

SURPRISE

At the beginning of a combat, the GM determines whether the players or NPCs gain a surprise round. This could be due to an ambush or simply that one side is unaware of the other's presence. The side with the surprise round acts before any opponents for a single round. Any attacks made by the side with surprise gain an edge.

ACTIONS IN COMBAT

Combatants are able to take two actions per turn from the following list:

- Perform a melee or ranged attack (once per turn)
- Move their movement speed or less
- Use a class feature (if an action is required)
- Use an item from their pack
- Pick a lock
- Perform a non-combat physical action (i.e. jumping over a table)
- Perform a social action (i.e. intimidating an enemy)
- Make a combat manoeuvre (i.e. ferocious attack)
- Cast a spell

CASTING SPELLS

Spells may cost one or more actions in combat. This will be noted on the spell's stats.

MOVEMENT

A combatant may move up to 20ft on their turn. If you are using miniatures, count a single square as 5ft. If you are playing without miniatures then you can use the close, near, far method. Here the GM establishes how far away you are from your enemy using either close (0–5ft), near (5–25 ft) or far (25ft or more). Using their movement, the combatant can move one 'step', so from near to close, or far to near.

It is assumed that the combatant has the time to draw and sheath weapons as part of their movement, so these are not counted as separate actions.

MELEE ATTACKS

A melee attack is made using a melee weapon in close quarters with an enemy. To make a melee attack, you must be adjacent to the opponent. Declare to the GM that you are making a melee attack and roll a Might attribute check, reducing the target number by the HD or level of the target to get your 'to hit' number. For instance, if a character with 14 Might was attacking a HD2 foe, the hit number to roll would be 12 (14–2=12). If you succeed the check, you have scored a hit and have damaged your target. Roll the damage die of the weapon you are using, plus your Might damage bonus, and deduct this first from any armour points the target has, then from the target's HP. A successful attack will always do a minimum of 1 damage, even if the damage would ordinarily be reduced to zero. For example, you score a hit against an enemy with 2 armour points and 12 HP. You roll a 4 for damage using your short sword, with a +2 damage bonus from your Might, for a total of 6 damage. The GM deducts the first 2 points from the creature's armour and the remaining 4 points from its HP, leaving it with 8 HP at the end of the turn.

When an NPC attacks a player character, the GM will refer to the target number, or TN, of the NPC. The GM will then reduce this TN by the level of the opponent it is attacking to get its 'to hit' number. Damage is then rolled on a successful hit.

For example, Sir Kristoph is attacking a boggart, a HD1 creature, with his longsword. Sir Kristoph has 15 Might and so reduces this by the enemy's HD, which in this case is 1. This gives Sir Kristoph the 'to hit' number of 14. He rolls an 11, which is a hit. He then rolls his longsword damage die, d10, plus his damage bonus of +2, and gets a 3, which is deducted first from the boggart's armour of 1, then from its HP. The boggart then attacks Sir Kristoph with its gnarled claws. The boggart has a TN of 11, but because Sir Kristoph is level 2, the final 'to hit' number is 9. The GM rolls a 17 for the boggart's claw attack, missing entirely.

RANGED ATTACKS

When attacking with a ranged weapon such as a bow or sling, a combatant is able to deal damage from a distance. This works in much the same way as a melee attack, except that a Reflex check is rolled when attacking, with the target's HD deducted from your Reflex attribute. Successful ranged attacks gain a damage bonus based on the character's Reflex attribute. Ranged weapons have a distance they are effective up to. Every 5ft beyond this range reduces the 'to hit' number by 1. For example, a shortbow has a range of 80ft, but if you were to attempt a shot at 100ft you would reduce the 'to hit' number from your Reflex by 4.

CRITICAL HITS AND FUMBLES

When attacking, a natural 1 rolled on the d20 means a critical hit has been made. Roll the damage die twice when this occurs, totalling the numbers and doubling any damage bonuses you receive. Rolling a natural 20 means the player has fumbled and the attack is an automatic miss, even if it would have ordinarily hit.

CLOSE RANGED COMBAT

If a ranged attack is made in close combat, the attacker takes a setback.

UNARMED AND IMPROVISED COMBAT

When fighting unarmed or with an improvised weapon, the damage die rolled is 1d4.

MOUNTED COMBAT

Mounts, such as horses, can be used during combat. Anyone attacking a mounted combatant may choose to attack either the mount or the rider. If the attacker is unmounted, they take a setback to melee attacks against the rider. If the mount is unwilling to be ridden, the rider must make a successful tough Charisma or Animal Husbandry check to ride it. On a fail, the mount will do one of four things. Roll 1d4:

1. The mount does not move and remains in its position for the turn.
2. The mount bucks and the rider is thrown off, falling prone.
3. The mount runs in a random direction.
4. The mount bucks, the rider is thrown off and falls prone, and the mount flees at full speed away from the combat.

ARMOUR IN COMBAT

Armour points are reduced when damage is taken. Once all armour points have been reduced to 0, damage is taken from HP as normal due to weariness and fatigue. For example, a knight with 10 armour points can take 10 damage before damage starts to affect her HP. Armour fully regenerates after 10 minutes of rest as the player character patches it up and carries out general maintenance. A regroup action can also be taken in combat to replenish a small amount of armour points

Note that shields cannot be used with two-handed weapons.

COMBAT MANOEUVRES

The following is a list of manoeuvres that can be taken in combat that go beyond just attacking an opponent. Some of these combat manoeuvres require the use of an action, while others do not.

FLANKING

A combatant is flanked when they have two melee attackers within 5ft of them on opposite sides. Any combatant who is flanking gains an edge to attacks against the flanked target.

TOTAL DEFENCE

As two actions, a combatant can make a total defence manoeuvre to lower the chances of them getting hit on their opponent's turn. Attacks against someone using total defence take a setback. Total defence lasts until the start of the combatant's next turn.

FEROCIOUS ATTACK

As an action, a combatant in melee can make a ferocious attack manoeuvre to try to do more damage to the opponent. A ferocious attack is made with a setback, but deals +2 damage if it hits.

KILL SHOT

As an action, a combatant using a ranged weapon can make a kill shot manoeuvre to gain a bonus to their attack. When performing a kill shot, the attacker gains an edge on their next ranged attack.

RESTRAIN

As an action, a combatant may make a Might or Athletics atribute check to try and restrain an opponent. If successful, the opponent has the restrained condition. On its turn, a combatant may try to break the restraint with an opposed Might or Athletics check. This counts as an action. A combatant who is restraining a creature may attack with a single-handed weapon only. If the combatant who is restraining the creature moves away at their full speed, the restraint is broken. The combatant may choose to move the creature they are restraining by moving at half speed.

REGROUP

As two actions, a combatant can rest a moment to regain two armour points.

FIGHTING WITH TWO WEAPONS

A character with the Two-Weapon Fighting talent is able to fight with two one-handed weapons, gaining a second attack which can be made against a different enemy than the original target. Fighting with two weapons gives a character a setback when attacking.

COVER

During combat, cover can offer a defensive position from which to fight or recuperate, whether crouching behind a fence or ducking behind a statue. There are two types of cover: obscuring cover and blocking cover. Obscuring cover means that the character is partially hidden behind cover, but can still be seen and potentially hit by the enemy. This could be behind a waist-high wall, around a corner or behind a cart. They are still partially exposed, so ranged attacks against them take a setback. Blocking cover means they are totally concealed and cannot be seen by the enemy and cannot be hit by attacks. A regular Stealth check can be made to become hidden when behind obscuring or blocking cover. While hidden, a combatant has an edge on attacks. If they attack an opponent while hidden, they are no longer considered hidden at the end of their current turn.

CONDITIONS

Combat is usually frantic and fast-paced, with creatures being thrown around, poisoned daggers sinking into flesh, cunning folk paralysing their foes, and tricky spirits turning invisible. Conditions can be triggered by an effect such as a spell, special ability, or a combat manoeuvre.

INVISIBLE

An invisible creature is much more difficult to hit. If an attack against an invisible creature is successful, before rolling damage roll 1d6. On a 4–6 the attack misses and no damage is done. On a 1–3 the attack does damage as normal. Invisible creatures receive a –10 bonus to Stealth checks. Invisible creatures still make noise.

PARALYSED

A paralysed creature is unable to take any actions. At the end of each of their turns, they may attempt a Constitution save, with the difficulty of the save equal to the HD or level of the source of the paralysis.

PRONE

When a creature falls prone it is lying on the ground. Melee attacks against a prone creature have an edge, while ranged attacks have a setback. A prone creature must use a movement action to stand. Prone creatures may move in a prone position by crawling, moving at half their initial speed. A prone creature gets a setback on attacks.

RESTRAINED

A restrained creature is unable to move. Attacks against a restrained creature get an edge.

SLEEPING

A sleeping creature is treated as unconscious until awoken. A sleeping creature awakens if it takes damage, is subject to loud noise, or interfered with physically. Sleeping creatures take a +10 penalty to Mind checks to spot or perceive something.

SLOWED

A slowed creature moves at half its normal speed. Creatures cannot be slowed again if they are already slowed.

UNCONSCIOUS

An unconscious creature cannot take any actions until they are conscious again.

HEALING AND DYING

It's inevitable that characters will get innumerable scrapes and wounds on their adventures.

Player characters heal naturally when they rest, allowing them to regain all of their lost HP after an eight-hour rest. Resting must be uninterrupted non-strenuous activity, such as sleeping, sitting, or meditating. Characters can also recuperate lost HP after a 10-minute short rest. After a short rest, roll your class HD, the result being the amount of HP your character regains. You can heal from a short rest a number of times per day equal to your class level.

FALLING UNCONSCIOUS

When a player character reaches 0 HP, they are considered unconscious and cannot take any actions.

DYING

Player characters are considered dead when they reach negative half their HP (rounded down). For example, a character with 15 HP will die when they reach –7 HP. It is possible to be resurrected by magical means (such as with the Resurrect the Recently Deceased spell). While in negative HP, they are considered bleeding out and take 1d4 HP damage every hour. However, ordinarily when a character is dead, they are gone for good and that player should roll up another character.

AID THE DYING

Anyone can try to stabilise a dying character with an aid the dying check. Make a Mind or Healing check and reduce the target number by the amount of negative HP the dying character currently has. For instance, if a dying character has –3 HP and a character attempting to aid the dying has 13 Mind, their target number to roll is 10. If the check is successful, the character's HP returns to 0 and they are considered just unconscious. If the check is unsuccessful, the dying character takes 1 HP of additional damage. A character can only make an aid the dying check once per hour.

VALOUR POINTS

In any traditional tale of good versus evil, good will always win out in the end, even if it's a struggle to prevail. Knights manage to land the final killing blow just as their opponent is about to fatally wound them, an enchanter heals an ally just as they are about to fall unconscious, and fate intervenes before a thief springs a deadly trap. Heroes need that extra edge to keep them alive, which is why every player character has a pool of valour points.

Valour points can be spent to help a hero prevail in the face of adversity, when all seems to be going to the way of darkness, a valour point can ignite the small spark of light needed for good to triumph. At the beginning of every session, each player gets three valour points.

Players can gain and spend valour points throughout the game for bonuses and effects.

SPENDING VALOUR POINTS

Valour points can be spent on a number of boons. Each boon has a set cost associated with it, which is the number of valour points a player needs to spend to activate the boon. A boon is activated immediately and not saved for future use. Only one boon may be used in a turn. Boons are as follows:

- **Boon of Luck:** Re-roll a die and keep the second roll (1 valour point).
- **Boon of Restoration:** Gain 3 HP (1 valour point).
- **Boon of Instinct:** Gain an edge on your next attack (2 valour points).
- **Boon of Resolve:** Reduce damage taken by 5 (2 valour points).
- **Boon of Second Chances:** If you were to fall unconscious, you instead return to 1 HP (3 valour points).

ADVENTURING IN THE PERILOUS LAND

Romance of the Perilous Land is a game first and foremost about heroic adventure. The legends of King Arthur and the Knights of the Round Table are known for their dangerous quests and deadly foes, where brave heroes travel across the land to right wrongs and seek glory in the name of Camelot. *Romance of the Perilous Land* allows players to carve out their own legend in this Arthurian realm, going toe to toe with sinister knights, strange spirits, and grotesque monstrosities conjured from the folklore of the British Isles. Adventures are a dangerous business and there is no guarantee of returning alive from the journey. This section contains rules on adventuring, including travelling overground, hazards, traps, and dungeons.

TRAVELLING

The quests players undertake will likely take them through multiple kingdoms, over rugged terrain, mountain passes, and deep forests. As in real life, travelling in the game takes a certain amount of time depending on the means of getting from point A to point B. Characters travelling at walking speed over regular terrain, such as a dirt road or over a field, will move at three miles per hour. If mounted on a riding horse travel becomes significantly faster at 15 miles per hour, while a pony moves at eight miles per hour. A horse pulling a wagon or cart moves at 10 miles per hour.

MOVING AT SPEED

Characters walking or with mounts may choose to move at speed. On foot they move at four miles per hour, while riding horses move at 20 miles per hour, ponies at 10 miles per hour and horse-drawn carts/wagons at 14 miles per hour. While moving at speed a character on foot or on a mount is in danger of becoming exhausted after five hours of continuous travel (see: Exhaustion).

MOVING OVER DIFFICULT TERRAIN

Not all traversable land will be simple to cross. Sometimes moving through foothills or across snow can hinder travel. When moving across difficult terrain, characters and mounts move at half their usual speed.

EXHAUSTION

Too much continuous travel can be a strain and at some point, characters and mounts will become exhausted. If travelling on foot, characters may walk for eight hours continuously. After eight hours, they are in danger of becoming exhausted. For every hour over eight travelled, a player must make a regular Constitution save. If they are unsuccessful, the character is exhausted and takes a setback to attribute checks and attacks. If they continue to travel while exhausted, they must make a tough Constitution save and if they don't succeed, they fall unconscious. Riding horses and ponies may also travel for eight hours per day, but will refuse to travel any more after this. A character may attempt to push the horse with a regular Charisma attribute check. If successful, the horse will continue for another hour until another regular Charisma check needs to be rolled, this time with a setback. If successful for the second time it will travel for another hour before automatically stopping and resting. If a Charisma check is unsuccessful, the horse or pony refuses to move until it has had at least a six-hour rest.

CLIMBING

Characters are able to scale rock faces, walls, or cliffs. When climbing they move at half speed and must make an Athletics or Might check before they attempt to move, with the difficulty of the check determined by the GM. If they fail this check, they fall and take 1d4 falling damage for every 10ft they had climbed. When using a rope that is tightly secured, they roll with an edge. If the climbing surface is slippery or dangerous in any way, the check is rolled with a setback.

SWIMMING

Sometimes characters will have to cross lakes, rivers, or even swim in the ocean. Similar to climbing, a character attempting to swim must make an Athletics or Might check before their movement and move at half speed if successful, with the difficulty of the check determined by the GM. If unsuccessful, they drop below the surface and are in danger of drowning. For every round they are underwater they take 1d4 damage. At the end of each round they must make an Athletics or Might check to return to the surface. If someone tries to help them return to the surface, the drowning player rolls with an edge. If a character is wearing heavy armour, they roll with a setback on their Athletics or Might check when attempting to swim.

MOVING STEALTHILY

Characters can attempt to move while remaining unseen by making a Stealth or Reflex check after movement. The check is opposed against opponents' Perception or Mind checks. When moving stealthily, they must move at half speed. If they choose to move stealthily at full speed, any Stealth or Reflex check is rolled with a setback. While they are unseen, they gain an edge to attacks. If they attack an opponent while hidden, they are no longer considered hidden at the end of their turn.

NATURAL HAZARDS

Nature can be dangerous and depending on the terrain, one wrong move could be a hero's last. Natural hazards include extreme temperatures and unstable environments that prove harmful on an adventure.

FALLING ROCKS

Those climbing mountains or walking under cliff faces are at risk of falling boulders that could easily dash open the skulls of the unwary. A falling rock does 1d4 damage for every 20ft it has fallen. Characters can make an Acrobatics or Reflex save in order to dodge out of the way and prevent damage, with the difficulty determined by the GM. Larger rocks may do 1d6 damage.

POISON GAS

The vapours that arise from some swamps can be poisonous when inhaled. Poison gas hangs in the air and is often invisible, though sometimes has an odour like the stench of death. For every round spent in an area of poison gas, a character must make a Constitution save, with a difficulty determined by the GM. If unsuccessful, they take 1d4 damage from the gas. More potent gases could do up to 1d10 damage.

EXTREME TEMPERATURES

While much of the Perilous Land is temperate, the northern regions can get incredibly cold, especially in the mountains. For every hour a character is exposed to extreme temperatures they must make a Constitution save with a difficulty determined by the GM. If unsuccessful they are exhausted, taking a setback to attribute checks and attacks. The second time they are unsuccessful, they fall unconscious. If they remain for another hour in extreme temperatures after falling unconscious they die.

STRONG WINDS

Gale force winds can pick up seemingly from nowhere and hinder travel. Movement in strong wind is halved and any Acrobatics checks are rolled with a setback.

FOG

Fog is an obscuring weather condition that makes seeing things around you difficult. Heavy fog should be treated as darkness and light fog as shadows.

BLIZZARDS

When strong winds and heavy snow mix, blizzards are born. Blizzards obscure vision and make movement difficult. If a character is caught in a blizzard, use the same rules as extreme temperatures. Vision is treated as if in shadows and movement speed is halved.

SINKING MUD

Adventurers travelling across marshland run the risk of being caught in sinking mud. This area of soft mud drags down anyone who steps in it, usually to waist height. Every round a character is in sinking mud they must make a Might save with regular difficulty to pull themselves to safety. If unsuccessful they sink below the surface but are still able to breath due to air pockets in the mud. Once in the mud they are unable to escape without aid. Another person may attempt to pull a character out of the mud with an Athletics or Might check.

TANGLEWEED

Beneath the surface of some ponds and lakes grows tangleweed – long tentacle-like plants that wrap around legs, dragging their victims into the murky waters. Characters caught in tangleweed must make a Reflex save, with the difficulty determined by the GM. If unsuccessful, they are unable to move. They may make a Reflex save with regular difficulty at the end of each round they are caught in the tangleweed. After a second failure they are dragged into the water and are considered to be drowning, taking 1d4 damage for every subsequent round they are unsuccessful in their Reflex save.

MUSHROOM SPORES

All manner of mushrooms grow across the Perilous Land, some beneficial, but most poisonous. Mushrooms release spores that occupy a 20ft x 20ft area for 1d6 rounds. Different types of mushrooms have different spore effects:

Gassy webcap: Spores are poisonous. Anyone who breathes the spores takes 1d6 damage. Constitution save with regular difficulty negates.

Devil's fingers: Spores cause temporary paralysis for 1d4 rounds. Constitution save with tough difficulty negates.

Dark crazed cap: Spores cause madness in the individual. For 1d4 rounds anyone breathing the spores must attack their closest ally. Mind save with regular difficulty negates.

Vampire's bane: Spores cast daylight around the area.

Fingered candlesnuff: Spores heal wounds. Anyone who breathes the spores heals 1d4 HP.

Witches' butter: Spores cause fear. Anyone who breathes the spores must move away from the mushroom for 1d4 rounds and may take no other actions. Mind save with regular difficulty negates.

LIGHT AND DARKNESS

There will be plenty of times when characters will be travelling by the light of the moon, or delving into an underground ruin with only a torch to light the way. Light sources are important when adventuring as they can mean the difference between seeing the edge of a ravine and stepping over it.

DAYLIGHT

Daylight is when everything is illuminated as if it were in broad daylight. Everything in the area can be seen clearly. Torches, candles and lanterns create an area of 'daylight' around them.

SHADOWS

Shadows are areas that have little light, but shapes may still be made out within them. Some natural light may be filtering in, but the area is obscured. Characters attempting to spot something in shadows take a setback. If combat is taking place in shadows, attacks take a setback. Stealth checks made in shadows get an edge.

DARKNESS

Darkness is total concealment. One can't see their hands in front of their faces – all is black. Characters attempting to spot something in shadows must add +10 to their check. If combat is taking place in darkness, attacks take a setback and must roll a d6 after they have hit but before they do damage. On a 1–2 their attack misses because of the darkness. Stealth checks rolled in darkness automatically succeed.

ILLUMINATION

Certain items or organic materials can light dark paths, allowing characters to see. Light sources cast an area of daylight in a certain radius:
Candle: Lights a 10ft x 10ft radius.
Torch: Lights a 20ft x 20ft radius.
Lantern: Lights a 30ft x 30ft radius.
Glowing fungus: Lights a 10ft x 10ft radius.

EATING AND DRINKING

When travelling out in the wilds or wandering around a city, it's important that characters are sustained by adequate food and water. When in civilisation this can be found in taverns, inns and from merchants, but out in the wilds it must be foraged, caught, or found.

Characters must eat at least a small meal with water once per day to prevent themselves from suffering the effects of exhaustion. This could consist of bread and honey, or an apple and a wineskin of water. For every day they go without a meal, they must make a Constitution check. If unsuccessful they are exhausted and take a setback to attribute checks and attack rolls. If they are unsuccessful a second time they fall unconscious. If they go two weeks without eating or two days without drinking water they take 1d4 damage for every subsequent day without nourishment.

HUNTING AND FORAGING

In the wilds characters may have to find their food in order to survive. This not only involves being able to kill an animal, but setting traps, following tracks, and understanding which berries are suitable for eating. For every hour spent hunting and foraging, a character may make a Survival or Mind check, with the difficulty determined by the GM. If it is successful, the character has found enough food for four people for a day. If a character or multiple characters decide to hunt while they are travelling, their movement speed is reduced by half. If the terrain in which they are hunting and foraging is snowy or rocky, they take a setback on Mind-related checks.

CHARACTER ADVANCEMENT

Throughout a campaign characters will face many foes, embark on dangerous quests, and ultimately test themselves to the limit. The more adventures a character survives, the more experience they gain and the more skillful they will become. In the game, this is represented by levels – milestones where characters gain increased attributes, new class features, and an increase in hit points. Every class has its own character advancement table that shows what that class gets per level. However, at every level all classes roll their HD and increase their maximum HP value by the result.

At levels 3, 5, 7, and 9 characters increase all attributes by 2. This is to represent characters becoming more competent, even with their weaker attributes.

There are two ways in which a character can gain a new level and it is up to the GM and players to discuss which method they prefer.

Quest levelling

This is where characters advance to the next level after completing a certain quest. The length of a quest is determined by the GM – they could be short and simple or longer and more complex. Once the players have achieved the main objective of the quest, they are allowed to gain a new level.

Experience point levelling

Levelling through experience points (xp) is the most traditional method of character advancement. Experience points are gained through adventuring for deeds such as slaying creatures, completing quests and excellent roleplaying. After gaining enough experience points, characters may advance to the next level. This method of advancement usually takes longer than quest levelling. The following experience points should be shared between all participating characters.

Completing a short quest: 100 xp
Completing a regular quest: 200 xp
Completing a long quest: 400xp
Good roleplaying (per session): 20xp
Killing a creature: Creature HD x 10xp

Level	Experience points required
1	0
2	500
3	1,000
4	2,000
5	4,000
6	8,000
7	16,000
8	32,000
9	64,000
10	128,000

SPELLCASTING

agic plays a key role in the Perilous Land and though its practitioners are few and far between their powers can be extremely potent. Cunning folk and some other magical creatures are able to harness the thread of magic that runs through the ancient veins of the land. Practitioners call this magical wellspring the Wyrd and only those with the innate gift to tap into the Wyrd are able to cast spells. But magic can be fickle and difficult to control in the hands of less experienced enchanters. Many who attempt to manipulate stronger magics end up dead, meaning coming across a powerful magic-user is a rare occasion indeed. It is thought that Merlin and Morgan Le Fay are the greatest cunning folk in the Perilous Land, but there are other members of the Fellowship of Enchanters that show promise.

Spells range from small, subtle conjurings such as creating a light in the dark or making a noise from thin air, to grander, less stable deadly magic that creates disease or casts a hex. As casters grow in experience, so does their ability to manipulate the Wyrd and cast more powerful spells without fear of harming themselves.

Cunning folk and certain creatures are able to harness the energies of nature to cast magic spells. Spells can cause all kinds of effects, including those that are harmful and beneficial, but most importantly spells are wondrous – magic is rare and those that wield it are looked upon with awe and fear.

MAGIC DISCIPLINES

Magic is separated into five disciplines denoting the kind of magic that is being employed. Practitioners can spend years perfecting a specific discipline, while others prefer to cast from a variety of disciplines. At level 3, a cunning folk will decide on which discipline to take. The five disciplines are as follows:

HEALING

Healing magic focuses on crafting tinctures and salves to bring allies back from the brink of death, cure debilitating diseases, and remove poisons from the bloodstream. Healing magic relies on the use of different kinds of herbs to concoct life-giving potions.

CURSES

Curses are harmful to their intended targets, bringing immediate or future doom on them. Whether it's a relatively minor misfortune, such as losing money, to becoming infected with a plague, curses are a particularly potent magic and a discipline not to be trifled with. Witches and dark enchanters often specialise in curses, crafting small poultices filled with animal bones and human hair.

SCRYING

Scrying is the most common service a community cunning man or woman will provide, the act of divining the future and seeing what is hidden from mortal eyes. Practitioners usually use a scrying mirror or a crystal ball in order to predict what is to come, whether that's determining whether the current path will lead to danger, or to reveal hidden doors and objects.

CHARMS

Charms are designed to protect and offer boons of wit and strength to those who need it. Charms take the form of magical symbols called runes that are etched onto a natural surface such as stone or wood, or casting salt circles on the ground, offering a one-off boost to an ally's abilities. Of course, charms can also be negative, placed on an enemy to drain their skills, slow them down, and ultimately make them weaker. These are often the quickest for a cunning folk to prepare and are usually the least volatile magic.

CONJURING

Conjuring is the act of using magic to create things, from a spark of fire to summoning Otherworldly beings to fight on the behalf of the caster. Conjurers are adept at inflicting damage on the battlefield, casting bones on the ground and writing spell runes on their skin with charcoal to create various effects.

CASTING SPELLS

Cunning folk are able to cast spells to help them on their adventures or change the tide of battle. They prepare spells ahead of time, crafting healing salves from herbs they find in the nearby forest, wrapping poultices imbued with curses, etching runes with a knife, and covering their skin with strange and beautiful symbols that glow in the moonlight. Spell preparation is a key part of a cunning folk's day, with each spell requiring a certain length of time to prepare, which typically occurs in the morning but can happen throughout the day if there are spell points available.

SPELL LEVEL

Every spell has a level, ranging from 0 to 10. Levels represent how powerful and difficult to cast a spell is. Cunning folk are able to cast spells of any level, but there could be dire consequences for trying to wield magic that is too powerful for them.

PREPARATION TIME

It takes time to prepare spells, with some of the more potent magics taking longer than others. Each spell lists the time needed to prepare it ahead of casting. This time represents the caster finding herbs and mixing into salves, discovering the right stones to create charm runes, create poultices from animal bones, and any other requirements a spell has. If a cunning folk is interrupted during this time they must start over from the beginning. A preparation time of 'instant' means that the spell can be prepared and cast in the same round, with preparation costing one action. The same spell can only be prepared a maximum of three times per day unless its preparation time is listed as instant, in which case there is no limit.

Spell form

When a spell is prepared it takes on a certain form, such as a poultice, bag of salt, or rune stone. The spell form lists what is physically prepared during the spell's preparation time. It is assumed that spell users carry all ingredients and materials required to carry out these spells and always have enough when they are preparing a spell.

Spell cost

Each spell has a spell cost. This is the amount to reduce your spell points by when preparing the spell, symbolising you imbuing your ingredients or runes with magical energy. Once you have reached 0 spell points you are unable to prepare any more spells. Characters who are able to cast spells have a total number of spell points equal to their Mind attribute. Any time a caster has unused spell points, they may prepare a spell if they are able to pay for it.

For example, Willa, a caster, has prepared several spells in the morning, using up most of her spell points. Later in the day she uses the handful she has left over to prepare another spell.

Spell targets

Some spells require the caster to target a creature. This means that the caster can choose a PC or NPC for the spell to affect.

Replenishing spell points

After an eight hour rest a caster regains all of their lost spell points.

SPELL TESTS

In order to cast a spell, the caster must be able to speak the spell's activation words and move their arms, whether they are throwing a poultice or using a salve. If a caster's mouth is gagged or they are unable to move their arms, then they are unable to cast a spell. To cast a spell, the caster must select a spell from their list of prepared spells, or a spell with an instant preparation time, and make a Mind check. The spell level is subtracted from the caster's Mind attribute to get the target number required to cast the spell. For example, a character with Mind 14 casting a level 2 spell will need to roll a 12 or lower to succeed in casting. If the roll is successful, the spell has the effect as intended. If the spell fails, the spell fizzles out, but the caster does not 'lose' the spell and may try to cast it again in another round.

USE TIME

Each spell has a use time, which shows how long it takes to cast a spell in actions or minutes. Some quick spells may only take one action, which some more complex spells could take up to an hour to cast.

CASTING HIGHER LEVEL SPELLS

Casting spells of higher levels than the caster can be risky. If the caster fails their roll to cast the spell and the spell is of a higher level than the caster, there is a chance that the spell could backfire. For every level the prepared spell is above the caster level, roll that many d6s. Take the highest number rolled on a single d6 and consult the table below.

SPELL BACKFIRE TABLE	
D6 Roll	**Effect**
1	No effect
2	No effect
3	No effect
4	The caster has a setback on all checks and saves for 1d4+2 hours
5	The caster takes 1d10+2 damage
6	The caster is paralysed for 1d4 hours

For example, Feldor is a level 3 cunning folk who is attempting to cast a level 4 spell, which he prepared earlier in the day. With a Mind attribute of 17 he must roll 13 or less to cast the spell. He rolls his Mind check and fails with a 15, with the spell fizzling out. Because the spell is one level higher than his own, he rolls 1d6 on the spell backfire table, getting a 4, meaning he has to take a setback on all checks and saves for 1d4+2 hours.

Spell list

Level 0 spells

A heavenly light

Discipline: Conjuring
Preparation Time: Instant
Spell Form: Charcoal rune etched onto the palm
Spell Cost: 1
Use Time: 1 action
Effect: The rune drawn onto the palm of your hand glows a brilliant white light in a 40ft radius of daylight. The light can be dimmed at will by using an action and extinguished completely with action. If it is not extinguished beforehand, the light lasts an hour. Closing the palm does not affect the light, glowing as brightly as if it were open.

Good luck charm

Discipline: Charms
Preparation Time: 5 minutes
Spell Form: A small piece of wood etched with a rune
Spell Cost: 2
Use Time: 1 action
Effect: You touch a creature with your glowing green charm and it imbues them with a sense of luck. The charmed creature rolls with edge on their next check.

SENSE THE PRESENCE OF MAGIC

Discipline: Scrying
Preparation Time: 1 minute
Spell Form: A glowing light in the scrying mirror
Spell Cost: 1
Use Time: 1 action
Effect: After peering into the scrying mirror, you can identify the source(s) of magic within 100ft. This includes being able to tell whether an item is imbued with an enchantment or whether a creature has innate magical abilities. You cannot identify the enchantment of specific magical effects, unless you spend an extra spell point when preparing.

THE VOICE OF A HOUND

Discipline: Conjuring
Preparation Time: Instant
Spell Form: A sprinkle of magic salt on the tongue
Spell Cost: 1
Use Time: 1 action
Effect: You sprinkle the prepared salt on your tongue and feel your voice grow deep and hoarse. For the next minute you are able to perfectly mimic the bark, whine, or howl of a common dog or wolf. Anyone hearing the sound may attempt to succeed a Mind check to determine that the hound voice is of human origin.

LEVEL 1 SPELLS

CHANGE THE MUNDANE INTO TREASURE

Discipline: Charms
Preparation Time: 5 minutes
Spell Form: A rune etched onto wood or stone
Spell Cost: 1
Use Time: 1 action
Effect: Using the power imbued in a charmed rune, you make one creature believe that a mundane item, natural or crafted, is worth much more than in reality. The enchantment gradually wears off over 10 minutes once you are 100ft away from the

target. Anyone inspecting the treasure can attempt to succeed a Mind check, reduced by the caster's level, to identify the actual value of the treasure after 15 minutes of inspection.

CONJURE WATER FROM THE AIR

Discipline: Conjuring
Preparation Time: Instant
Spell Form: A sprinkle of magic salt
Spell Cost: 2
Use Time: 1 action
Effect: After sprinkling a pinch of magic imbued salt into a container, the container instantly fills with cool drinkable water to its brim. This spell can fill up to two gallons in one container, or split across multiple containers.

DAZZLE WITH GLITTERING LIGHTS

Discipline: Conjuring
Preparation Time: 5 minutes
Spell Form: A small bag of salt
Spell Cost: 2
Use Time: 1 action
Effect: You take a pinch of salt from the bag and blow it into one creature's eyes within 20ft. The affected creature sees a blinding array of dazzling lights dancing around his vision. The creature has a setback on attacks for the next 1d3 rounds.

REPLENISHED THE BATTERED AND BRUISED

Discipline: Healing
Preparation Time: 5 minutes
Spell Form: A herbal tincture
Spell Cost: 2
Use Time: 1 action
Effect: You craft a diluted healing tincture from local herbs and plants. When applied to a creature within 5ft of you, the tincture heals 1d6 HP. A creature who is unconscious is unable to drink the tincture.

WITCH DOLL

Discipline: Curses
Preparation Time: 10 minutes
Spell Form: A crude doll and several pins
Spell Cost: 2
Use Time: 1 action
Effect: You have three pins. When you insert a pin into the witch doll, a target that you can see within 50ft takes 1d4 damage, ignoring armour. You may insert multiple pins as one action.

LEVEL 2 SPELLS

BREAK THE SKIN OUT IN BOILS

Discipline: Curses
Preparation Time: 10 minutes
Spell Form: A poultice full of bones and hair
Spell Cost: 3
Use Time: 1 action
Effect: You throw the poultice up to 20ft at your intended target, or place it under their bed while they sleep. The target creature's skin becomes red and breaks out into hideous boils. The affected creature takes a setback to Charisma checks and is unable to wear armour without suffering 1d4 damage per hour. The curse lasts 24 hours, after which time the boils fade away. The creature may attempt to succeed a Constitution save to only take the setback to Charisma checks.

CAUSE THE ALERT TO SLUMBER

Discipline: Charms
Preparation Time: 10 minutes
Spell Form: A stone etched with an eye rune
Spell Cost: 3
Use Time: 2 actions
Effect: You hold aloft your glowing purple sleep charm. The intended target must be able to see the charm for the spell to have an effect. The target creature with HD equal to the caster's or lower falls asleep for 1d4 rounds. The target creature may make a Charisma check. If it succeeds, it falls asleep for only one round.

FIND SAFE SUSTENANCE IN THE WILD

Discipline: Scrying
Preparation Time: Instant
Spell Form: A scrying mirror
Spell Cost: 2
Use Time: 1 action
Effect: You gaze into the swirling colours of the scrying mirror where it presents you with a vision of where to find enough safe food and water to feed four people within a one mile radius.

HAVE VISION IN DARK PLACES

Discipline: Charms
Preparation Time: 10 minutes
Spell Form: A small wood charm etched with a rune
Spell Cost: 2
Use Time: 1 action
Effect: You or another creature can wear the charm to be able to see in total darkness as if it were daylight for up to an hour per caster level. Those wearing the charm are unable to make out colour in total darkness, but otherwise they can see their surroundings clearly.

REPLENISH THE FRACTURED AND WOUNDED

Discipline: Healing
Preparation Time: 10 minutes
Spell Form: A herbal salve
Spell Cost: 3
Use Time: 2 actions
Effect: You create a soothing herbal salve that quickly repairs open wounds and broken bones. The salve heals a creature within 5ft with 1d8 HP. The salve may be applied to an unconscious creature.

LEVEL 3 SPELLS

BEFRIEND THE WILDEST OF BEASTS

Discipline: Charms
Preparation Time: 5 minutes
Spell Form: A small stone etched with a rune
Spell Cost: 3
Use Time: 1 action
Effect: Showing a wild animal (not a monster or other supernatural being) the charm causes it to calm down. The animal will not attack you or anyone you do not want it to. The charm wears off after one minute.

CAUSE LIMBS TO STOP MOVING

Discipline: Curses
Preparation Time: 10 minutes
Spell Form: A poultice of bones and hair
Spell Cost: 4
Use Time: 1 action
Effect: You throw the poultice at a creature within 20ft, where it opens up on impact. The creature's limbs seize up and it becomes paralysed until the start of your next turn. The creature may attempt to succeed a Constitution save, reduced by the caster level, to prevent the paralysis.

CONJURE FIRE FROM THE AIR

Discipline: Conjuring
Preparation Time: 10 minutes
Spell Form: A charcoal rune etched onto the palm
Spell Cost: 3
Use Time: 1 action
Effect: When you rub your hands together, you create a small fire, which can be used to light a campfire, or thrown at an enemy within 30ft, causing 1d8 damage.

CREATE AN ILLUSION TO VEX THE EYES

Discipline: Conjuring
Preparation Time: 10 minutes
Spell Form: A small bag of salt
Spell Cost: 3
Use Time: 1 action
Effect: You blow the salt into the wind, creating a silent illusion up to 7ft in height and 2ft in width. The illusion can be manipulated to move around as long as you can still see it. The illusion lasts for 10 minutes or until the caster cancels the spell. Any creature looking at the spell can attempt to succeed a Mind saving throw, reduced by the caster level, to realise that it is an illusion.

REVEAL THAT WHICH IS HIDDEN

Discipline: Scrying
Preparation Time: 10 minutes
Spell Form: A scrying mirror
Spell Cost: 3
Use Time: 1 action
Effect: By peering into the scrying mirror, you are able to see the glowing yellow outline of any secret doors or hidden compartments within an 100ft area. The vision lasts for one minute before vanishing.

LEVEL 4 SPELLS

CAUSE ONE TO ACT WITH SPEED

Discipline: Charms
Preparation Time: 10 minutes
Spell Form: Stone etched with a rune
Spell Cost: 5
Use Time: 1 action
Effect: You hold the stone aloft and speak words of speed. One creature within 40ft increases its movement speed by 20ft for three rounds.

CAUSE THE FEELING OF DOOM IN ANOTHER

Discipline: Curses
Preparation Time: 10 minutes
Spell Form: A poultice of hair and bone
Spell Cost: 5
Use Time: 2 actions
Effect: You unleash the power of a potent poultice curse on one creature within 40ft. The victim feels a great sorrow wash over them as all the despair they have felt in their life up to now fills their hearts and sends them into a spiral. The victim has a setback on saves for three rounds.

CLOAK ONESELF IN DARKNESS

Discipline: Conjuring
Preparation Time: 10 minutes
Spell Form: Symbols written on the palm
Spell Cost: 5
Use Time: 2 actions
Effect: You or a creature within 30ft are shrouded in a dark fog, blocking line of sight. Anyone shrouded in darkness is attacked as if in darkness, but the shrouded creature attacks as if in daylight. The shroud follows the creature if they move. The spell lasts for three rounds.

RECALL EVENTS FROM THE PAST

Discipline: Scrying
Preparation Time: 15 minutes
Spell Form: Scrying mirror
Spell Cost: 5
Use Time: 2 actions
Effect: You can see the actions of an event up to 24 hours ago play out in a single location. Only you are able to witness these actions, which manifest as ghosts in the scrying mirror. You are able to smell and hear the events as they play out.

RID THE PITIFUL OF DISEASE

Discipline: Healing
Preparation Time: 10 minutes
Spell Form: A herbal balm
Spell Cost: 5
Use Time: 2 actions
Effect: You smear a herbal balm on a creature within 5ft to remove a single disease effect.

LEVEL 5 SPELLS

BREATHE BENEATH THE WAVES

Discipline: Charms
Preparation Time: 10 minutes
Spell Form: Wood etched with a rune
Spell Cost: 6
Use Time: 2 actions
Effect: Your charms creates a bubble around the head, allowing creatures to breathe safely underwater. Up to four creatures within 20ft gain the ability to breathe underwater for a number of hours equal to caster level.

CREATE A WILD GUST OF WIND

Discipline: Conjuring
Preparation Time: 10 minutes
Spell Form: Runes drawn on the forehead
Spell Cost: 6
Use Time: 2 actions
Effect: A strong wind builds up around you, blowing away projectiles that are shot towards you. Ranged attacks against you gain a setback for three rounds.

RESTRAIN AS IF WITH INVISIBLE ROPE

Discipline: Conjuring
Preparation Time: 10 minutes
Spell Form: Symbols written on the palm
Spell Cost: 6
Use Time: 2 actions
Effect: Up to three creatures within 20ft are bound with invisible rope and are unable to move. A successful Might save negates the effect of the spell. Affected creatures make a Might save at the end of each of their turns to end the effect.

SPEAK WITH WILD BEASTS

Discipline: Scrying
Preparation Time: 10 minutes
Spell Form: Scrying mirror
Spell Cost: 6
Use Time: 1 action
Effect: The barks, growls, squawks, and chitters of wild beasts and birds resonate in your scrying mirror, allowing you to understand their language, and they in turn can understand you. You are able to communicate with and understand the language of animals for minutes equal to your caster level. Animals do not speak in full sentences, instead using simple nouns and verbs to communicate.

SUBDUE THE WICKED

Discipline: Curses
Preparation Time: 10 minutes
Spell Form: Poultice full of hair and bone
Spell Cost: 6
Use Time: 2 actions
Effect: You throw the poultice up to 20ft. Black tendrils emerge from the poultice, slithering into the minds of your foes. The spell affects up to three creatures within 30ft of the poultice, preventing them from attacking a named creature for two rounds. A successful Mind save negates the effect of the spell.

LEVEL 6 SPELLS

BLESS THE MORTALLY WOUNDED

Discipline: Healing
Preparation Time: 20 minutes
Spell Form: Tincture
Spell Cost: 7
Use Time: 2 actions
Effect: You create a potent tincture that can revitalise those who have been severely wounded. You heal a creature within 5ft by 2d8+4 HP. The tincture can be used on a creature that is unconscious.

CONTROL THE MIND OF A BEAST

Discipline: Scrying
Preparation Time: 10 minutes
Spell Form: Scrying mirror
Spell Cost: 7
Use Time: 2 actions
Effect: You find a wild beast, such as a deer, wolf, falcon, or snake and take control of its mind for a limited amount of time. When in the mind of a beast you are still aware of what is happening around your human body and should it come to any harm your mind will snap back into its body immediately. While in the mind of a beast, you can control its body as you would your human body, but you are able to comprehend language, spoken and written. The spell lasts for one minute per class level. If the beast is killed, your mind returns to your body.

CREATE A MAGNIFICENT ILLUSION

Discipline: Conjuring
Preparation Time: 10 minutes
Spell Form: Runes written onto the fingers
Spell Cost: 7
Use Time: 2 actions
Effect: The small runes covering your fingertips glow briefly before a fantastic illusion emerges in the air before you. The illusion can be up to 15ft tall and 15ft in length and creates sound. Anyone looking at the illusion may succeed a Mind check to realise that it's an illusion. The illusion last for one minute per class level or until stopped by the caster.

IMBUE A WEAPON WITH A MIRACULOUS ENCHANTMENT

Discipline: Charms
Preparation Time: 20 minutes
Spell Form: Runes etched onto the handle of a weapon
Spell Cost: 7
Use Time: 2 actions
Effect: You draw a series of power runes onto a weapon, speaking a magical phrase to activate them. You place an enchantment on one weapon. For hours equal to the caster level that weapon deals an extra 1d4 damage. A weapon can have no more than one enchantment on it at a time.

READ THE THOUGHTS OF ANOTHER

Discipline: Scrying
Preparation Time: 10 minutes
Spell Form: A scrying mirror
Spell Cost: 7
Use Time: 2 actions
Effect: You are able to read the surface-level thoughts of an intelligent creature within 60ft. You can interpret their current emotion and what they are thinking at that moment for one minute per class level.

LEVEL 7 SPELLS

APPEAR IN A NEW LOCATION INSTANTLY

Discipline: Conjuring
Preparation Time: 10 minutes
Spell Form: Runes drawn onto the feet
Spell Cost: 8
Use Time: 1 action
Effect: The runes on your feet flash, and in an instant, you are elsewhere in the world. You are able to teleport yourself to a location within 10 miles of your current location provided that you have already been there, or it is within your line of vision.

BURN FROM WITHIN

Discipline: Curses
Preparation Time: 20 minutes
Spell Form: A straw doll that is set alight
Spell Cost: 8
Use Time: 2 actions
Effect: You craft a straw doll that, when set alight, causes searing pain in an enemy. A creature within 40ft ignites from the inside, taking 3d6 damage. If the target succeeds a Constitution saving throw, they take half damage.

GRANT THE SKIN OF STONE

Discipline: Charms
Preparation Time: 10 minutes
Spell Form: Runes etched onto a stone
Spell Cost: 8
Use Time: 2 actions
Effect: You place a charm on a creature within 5ft of you. The creature's skin becomes flexible stone that does not impede their performance. The creature gains an armour points bonus of 1 per caster level for the next three rounds. These armour points cannot be regenerated with the regroup manoeuvre.

REMOVE THE AILMENT OF AN ALLY

Discipline: Heal
Preparation Time: 20 minutes
Spell Form: A herbal balm
Spell Cost: 8
Use Time: 2 actions
Effect: You create a soothing herbal balm that is spread on the temples of a creature within 5ft. Once applied, the balm removes all adverse conditions from the creature.

SEE THAT WHICH IS INVISIBLE

Discipline: Scrying
Preparation Time: 10 minutes
Spell Form: A scrying mirror
Spell Cost: 8
Use Time: 1 action
Effect: You gaze into your scrying mirror to see any invisible creatures within your line of sight. The spell lasts for rounds equal to class level.

LEVEL 8 SPELLS

BRING PESTILENCE UPON YOUR FOES

Discipline: Curses
Preparation Time: 10 minutes
Spell Form: A poultice of bones and hair
Spell Cost: 10
Use Time: 2 actions
Effect: You throw a poultice up to 30ft away. A swarm of locusts bursts forth from the poultice, covering your enemies. All creatures within 20ft of the poultice are bitten by the locust swarm, taking 3d6 damage each and taking a setback to all saving throws for one round. A Reflex saving throw halves the damage taken.

GRANT INVISIBILITY

Discipline: Charms
Preparation Time: 10 minutes
Spell Form: A rune etched onto wood
Spell Cost: 9
Use Time: 2 actions
Effect: A creature within 20ft is subject to the magical power of your charm, turning them invisible for three rounds. As an action, you can cancel the invisibility before the effect wears off.

PROTECTION FROM THE ELEMENTS

Discipline: Charms
Preparation Time: 10 minutes
Spell Form: A rune etched onto stone
Spell Cost: 9
Use Time: 2 actions
Effect: The magic emanating from your charm covers yourself and any creature within 40ft of you for one hour per class level. While the charm is in effect, weather-based hazards cannot harm creatures under the charm.

SPEAK WITH THE DEAD

Discipline: Scrying
Preparation Time: 10 minutes
Spell Form: A scrying mirror
Spell Cost: 9
Use Time: 1 minute
Effect: You remain in a still sitting position and gaze into the scrying mirror. After a minute the ghost of an intelligent creature who died within 200ft of the vicinity is summoned and will answer questions equal to the class level of the caster. These answers do not have to be truthful and questions must illicit a 'yes' or 'no' response.

SUMMON FAIRY HORSES

Discipline: Conjuring
Preparation Time: 15 minutes
Spell Form: Runes drawn onto the hands
Spell Cost: 8
Use Time: 2 actions
Effect: You conjure up to six fairy horses from the Otherworld. The fairy horses are obedient obeying the commands of yourself and your allies. They are able to travel 50 miles in a day without the need for rest. After 24 hours the horses retreat to the Otherworld, even if they are mounted.

LEVEL 9 SPELLS

A BLESSING FROM THE GODS

Discipline: Healing
Preparation Time: 10 minutes
Spell Form: A chanted prayer
Spell Cost: 10
Use Time: 2 actions
Effect: You call out to your patron god for help. All target creatures within 30ft are healed 3d6 HP and lose any adverse conditions.

CREATE A MAGICAL WEAPON

Discipline: Conjuring
Preparation Time: 20 minutes
Spell Form: A rune drawn onto the palm
Spell Cost: 10
Use Time: 2 actions
Effect: You conjure a glimmering weapon of your choice into the hands of a creature within 40ft. The weapon has the same attributes of the type of weapon chosen, but also contains the following effects:
- +1d10 damage.
- If a creature is damaged by the magical weapon, they fall prone.
- Causes a critical hit on a 1–4.

The magical weapon lasts for three rounds. Proficiency works the same way for a magical weapon as it does with a non-magical weapon.

MOVE THROUGH SOLID MATTER

Discipline: Charms
Preparation Time: 15 minutes
Spell Form: A rune etched onto stone
Spell Cost: 10
Use Time: 2 actions
Effect: The charm allows creatures to become insubstantial for a limited amount of time. You and any target creatures within 10ft are able to pass through solid objects such as walls for rounds equal to class level.

PREDICT THE OUTCOME OF THE FUTURE

Discipline: Scrying
Preparation Time: 20 minutes
Spell Form: A scrying mirror
Spell Cost: 10
Use Time: 2 actions
Effect: The mists of time clear as you gaze into your scrying mirror. You may ask the GM three 'yes' or 'no' questions about the future and they must answer truthfully.

SUMMON A DIRE WIND

Discipline: Conjuring
Preparation Time: 10 minutes
Spell Form: A rune written onto the arms
Spell Cost: 10
Use Time: 2 actions
Effect: You create a great wind, blowing your foes across the battlefield. Target creatures within 30ft are moved 20ft in any direction, take 2d4 damage and fall prone. A successful Reflex saving throw negates the damage taken and the affected creature does not fall prone.

LEVEL 10 SPELLS

CALL UPON A GOLDEN DRAGON

Discipline: Conjuring
Preparation Time: 30 minutes
Spell Form: A rune drawn on the neck
Spell Cost: 12
Use Time: 2 actions
Effect: You summon a golden dragon to your aid. It obeys your commands, acting after you in combat. The dragon will leave after three rounds. The golden dragon may only be called once per day.

RESURRECT THE RECENTLY DECEASED

Discipline: Healing
Preparation Time: 1 hour
Spell Form: A prayer and a tincture
Spell Cost: 11
Use Time: 2 actions
Effect: You pray over the body of the recently deceased, pouring a crystal-clear tincture into their mouth. You may bring a dead creature back to life with 1 HP. The creature must have been dead for no longer than a week. For every day longer than a week the creature has been dead, add 1 to the spell casting roll.

ROT FLESH

Discipline: Curses
Preparation Time: 20 minutes
Spell Form: Bones scattered around the enemy
Spell Cost: 11
Use Time: 2 actions
Effect: You scatter animal bones around the feet of a creature within 20ft. The creature's flesh begins to blacken and rot away, falling away from the bone. Creatures of HD/level 7 or lower affected by the curse are killed. Creatures of HD/level 8 and above take 4d8 damage.

THE WORLD
OF THE
PERILOUS LAND

ITEMS OF WONDER

Whereas many fantasy roleplaying games feature fantastical and powerful magic items, in *Romance of the Perilous Land* enchanted and magical items are few and far between, many of them being legendary in their own right. It's likely that characters will have only one or two of the more powerful magical items each, becoming intrinsic parts of who they are in the world. Rarity breeds wonder, so great importance is placed on these wondrous items. In this chapter you will find a list of magical items that the characters may find on their adventures, some of which will be the objective for quests or entire campaigns.

MAGICAL CHARMS

Charms are the most common form of magical item. They are home-made and often fairly rudimentary, used by lay-folk around the country for all sorts of purposes. Charms usually have very specific uses, such as to aid with the year's harvest or to locate a witch.

Characters may only gain the benefit from one charm if they have multiple charms of the same type.

ASH STAFF

Staves crafted from the wood of ash trees are popular with overland travellers who fear they may be set upon by an adder. Adders are vulnerable to this holy wood, which is why it does an extra d6 damage when the staff successfully strikes them.

BOG VIOLET

This small flower can be placed in a coffin to prevent the dead from rising. If this is done, the chance of a corpse returning as a revenant is halved.

CONCEALED SHOE

The act of concealing a shoe within a building, usually up a chimney, is for protection against evil spirits. Concealing a shoe for a month in a hearth, up a chimney or in a bedroom protects a home from a witch entering. If the shoe is destroyed, the charm is broken, and the witch may enter. The charm lasts for two days before another shoe is required.

CORN DOLLY

Made from plaited corn sheaves and hung in the home during the harvest festival of Samhain, these little figures will summon a corn spirit to increase the likelihood of a good harvest the next year. The corn spirit is an amiable creature, but does not communicate with humans. When a corn spirit is in a village or town there is a 4 in 6 chance the next harvest will be a good one.

HAG STONE

A small stone with a perfect hole in it. The hagstone can be used to cure ailments. Once per day the user may gain an extra saving throw per hour when attempting to save against a disease.

KINGFISHER

Nailing a kingfisher to the mast of a ship increases the chance of a good fishing haul that day. There's a 4 in 6 chance of catching a large haul of fish when this charm is in place.

MISTLETOE

A sprig of mistletoe bound in cloth and kept on one's person is a charm for warding off certain magic. Once per day for one round, witches, hags, and fairies have a setback on attacks against a target with a sprig of mistletoe on their person. Mistletoe kept in this way lasts for a week before the magic dries up.

MOLE'S FOOT

The foot of a mole is hung around the neck in order to more effectively heal the wearer. While wearing a mole's foot, the wearer gains an extra 1d4 HP from resting. The magic wears off after one week.

SALT POUCH

A small pouch of salt is used to bring luck. Once per day the bearer of the salt may ignore 1 point of armour damage. The magic wears off after one week.

ENCHANTED ITEMS

The following items are enchanted and much rarer than magical charms. Some are one of a kind while others are just not commonly found in the world of mortals.

COHULEEN DRUITH (UNIQUE)

This blue cap allows the wearer to easily breathe underwater.

HAND OF GLORY

This is the enchanted hand of a recently executed individual. It will automatically pick any lock. After using it five times, the hand of glory no longer works.

POTION OF VITALITY

A clear tincture that smells faintly of rose and cinnamon. When drunk, the potion replenishes 1d8 HP. The more potent form, the major potion of vitality, replenishes 2d8 HP.

RING OF DISPEL (UNIQUE)

A ring that once belonged to Sir Lancelot, it can prevent the effects of one spell of the wearer's level or lower after it has been cast. Can be used once per combat.

SEVEN-LEAGUE BOOTS

These greenish blue boots allow the wearer to walk on the water's surface just as they would walk on land.

UNSPOKEN WATER

This vial of water from the river of the dead can cure any affliction, magic or mundane. It has 10 uses.

LEGENDARY WEAPONS AND ARMOUR

Legendary weapons and armour are the rarest kind of enchanted items, with each of them unique. Because of this, characters may only see one or two of these in their lifetimes.

ARONDIGHT

Type: Short sword
Damage: 1d8+2
Special: The sword that currently belongs to Sir Lancelot. The blade glows a subtle blue when storms are close and increases the wielder's armour points by 3.
A gleaming short sword sporting a golden hilt etched with a lion on the pommel. The blade itself glistens gold in the sunlight.

CARNWENNAN

Type: Dagger
Damage: 1d6+1
Special: This legendary dagger belonged to the King Arthur himself, but it was lost in battle and never found. It has an ornate golden hilt and its plate emits a pale glow in the moonlight. When wielding the dagger the bearer may choose to cloak themselves in shadow for three rounds. While in shadow, attacks against the wielder have a setback.

A silver dagger with an ivory and golden hilt marked with the king's seal.

COREISEUSE

Type: Short sword
Damage: 1d8+1
Special: The sword belonging to King Ban, Coreiseuse means 'wrathful' in the old tongue. After a successful attack, the target must make a Reflex saving throw. If the save is failed the target is knocked prone.

Coreiseuse is a fierce sword with a wide blade and black hilt. The word 'wrath' is carved across the blade in the runes of a long dead language.

EXCALIBUR

Type: Longsword
Damage: 1d10+1
Special: Excalibur was gifted to King Arthur by the Lady of the Lake, but eventually it was returned to the murky depths of the waters from whence it came. It is arguably the most famous legendary weapon of all. The wielder gains 10 additional armour points and gains an edge on attacks. For the magic to work, Excalibur must always be kept in its scabbard while not in use.

Excalibur is the most majestic and perfectly crafted of blades to exist in the Perilous Land. Its rounded pommel is carved into the shape of the Round Table and ripples of water for the hilt's decor.

FAIL-NOT

Type: Short bow
Damage: 1d8+1
Special: Fail-not is an ornate mahogany bow crafted for Tristan by his father. The user does not reduce their Reflex attribute by the enemy's HD in combat.
King Rivalen's enchanted bow is exquisitely carved, the tip of each limb is decorated with hawk beaks.

GREEN ARMOUR

Type: Plate armour
Armour Points: 16
Special: The origin of Green Armour is unknown, but some say it was forged by Gofannon himself. It is the toughest armour ever crafted and can withstand blows from the hardiest of weapons.
Despite resembling iron plate, the Green Armour is constructed of something far tougher – divine metal wrought by Gofannon in his almighty forge. Its colour is mossy green, decorated with arboreal symbols and a ram's head.

MERLIN'S STAFF

Type: Staff
Damage: 1d6+1
Special: This polished staff was crafted from the Great Oak of Camelot and enchanted with powers by Merlin. The staff contains 10 spell points which may be deducted instead of your own spell points when preparing spells. The spell points fully replenish at sunrise the next day.
Merlin's staff is six feet in length and covered with runic whorls that flash blue when a spell is cast through the staff.

PRIDWEN

Type: Small shield
Armour Points: 6
Special: King Uther once kept this round enchanted shield in his chamber, but it was later stolen by a servant of Mordred. Legend has it that the shield was crafted from the same wood that was used to build the boat that sails to Avalon.
This green and white target shield has a golden centre and straps created from the hide of a dun cow.

THE THIRTEEN TREASURES OF THE PERILOUS LAND

The Thirteen Treasures of the Perilous Land are powerful magical artefacts, some known and other hidden, found throughout the 11 kingdoms. These objects were first crafted by various figures throughout the ages, such as the primordial worldspeakers, the Keepers of the Secret Words and even the gods themselves. These objects have value beyond the ken of mortals and because of this some people become obsessed with discovering where they are hidden.

CAULDRON OF GOGMAGOG

Special: Eating a stew cooked in the cauldron will offer an edge on all saving throws for three hours. The cauldron can be used in this way once per day, cooking a meal for up to 10 people.
Current location: Unknown
This large black iron cauldron is embossed with the hideous face of the giant Gogmagog himself, his tongue lolling out of his mouth.

COAT OF TRUTH

Special: This glittering coat only fits those who tell them truth. If attempted to be worn by someone who is deceitful, the coat will tighten around them, inflicting 1d4 damage for every 10 seconds the coat is worn.
Current location: Unknown
A sparkling blue coat covered in foliage patterns. The Coat of Truth was created by the fairies of the Otherworld for King Ascalon.

THE GREAT CHESSBOARD

Special: The pieces on the chessboard play themselves. The current owner of the chessboard cannot lose a game.
Current location: Norhaut
This large ivory chessboard has pieces of crystal and gold. The pieces glow brightly as they move across the board. It is said the chessboard once belonged to Queen Norhaut.

HAMPER OF PLENTY

Special: This wicker hamper produces an unlimited amount of food, to the taste of the one picking from the hamper.
Current location: Unknown
This large wicker hamper was created by the goddess Aine as a gift to mortalkind when humans first arrived. Its handles resemble two swans.

HANDY HALTER

Special: As an action, the halter summons a riding horse. The horse remains until the halter is removed.
Current location: Unknown
This finely crafted leather halter was created by Epona so that she could summon a horse wherever she may be. The riding horse does not suffer from exhaustion.

HORN OF BRAN GALED

Special: This large ivory drinking horn is able to magically conjure any drink that the owner wishes. After drinking, the owner gains an edge on all saving throws for an hour. This ability may only be used once per day as an action.

Current location: Hutton

Bran Galed was one of the greatest heroes of the Perilous Land during the great expansion in the Age of Humanity. The ox horn was enchanted and offered to Bran as a gift. The carvings around the rim tell tales of the warrior's many brave feats.

MANTLE OF TEGAU

Armour Points: 2

Special: This stunning gleaming golden cloak may only be worn by a woman. The wearer has an edge on all checks for an hour. This ability can be used once per day as an action.

Current location: Unknown

The Mantle of Tegau is a brilliant golden cloak of the finest silk, flanked by two white swans and an eight-pointed star in the centre.

MANTLE OF THE OTHERWORLD

Armour Points: 2
Special: Anyone who wears the mantle is able to become invisible for 1d4 rounds. This ability may only be used once per combat as an action.
Current location: Camelot

This mantle was woven by a fairy enchantress and imbued with the maker's own magic, giving it an Otherworldly sparkle, which is particularly prominent in moonlight. A single white eye covers much of the fabric, which briefly glows yellow when its power is activated. Arthur is the mantle's current owner.

MORGAN'S CHARIOT

Special: Anyone who sits in it the chariot is instantly transported wherever they wish in the world, but never indoors. This ability can be used four times per day. The chariot seats four people.
Current location: Unknown

Also known as the Lightning Chariot, this golden chariot once belinged to Morgan the Swift, a proud warrior of Norhaut. Two great lightning bolts are engraved onto each side and the massive spoked wheels crackle with electricity.

RING OF ELUNED THE FORTUNATE

Special: Once per day, as an action, the wearer is able to become invisible for 1d6 rounds.
Current location: Unknown

This brilliant silver ring has the design of a rose twisting around a dagger. An emerald is inset in the middle. Little is known of the ring, but legend tells that it belonged to Eluned, the greatest thief the world has ever known.

SWIFTBLADE

Type: Dagger
Damage: 1d6+1
Special: The wielder may take an extra action on their turn.
Current location: Unknown

Swiftblade's silver handle is etched with magical runes that allows those who wield it to move faster than usual.

WHETSTONE OF TUDWAL

Special: When this whetstone is used to sharpen a blade, the sword does an extra d4 damage for 1d10 hours. Usable once per day per sword as an action.
Current location: Escose

A gleaming ebony stone crafted by the Keepers of the Secret Words and capable of creating the sharpest of edges.

WHITE HILT

Type: Longsword
Damage: 1d10+2
Special: When drawn from its hilt this sword's blade ignites into orange flame. If it hits in melee, the enemy must make a successful Constitution saving throw or receive a further 1d8 damage from the fire.
Current location: Camelot

Forged by the worldspeakers, the blade of white hilt glows a bright orange as flames lick up its edge. The brilliant ivory hilt resembles the body of a giant.

LOCATIONS IN THE PERILOUS LAND

The following section details some of the notable kingdoms and locations in the Perilous Land. These should give you inspiration about where to set your adventures, along with personalities and plot hooks to help you create fantastic quests for your players.

KINGDOMS

- Ascalon
- Benwick
- Camelot
- Corbenic
- Eastland
- Escose
- Listenoise
- Lyonesse
- Gore
- Hutton
- Norhaut

LANGUAGES OF THE 11 KINGDOMS AND BEYOND

While all kingdoms speak a common tongue, known as the plain tongue, each region of the Perilous Land has its own deviation of this mother language, while certain creatures also have their own languages. Players can make language checks to attempt to speak and understand these languages. For every point in Mind a character has over 13, they may choose a new language to learn at character creation.

Language	Language spoken by
Ascalonian	People of Ascalon
Bant	People of Benwick
Corlish	People of Corbenic
Draconic	Dragons, knuckers
Druid	Druids
Eastern	People of Eastland
Escose	People of Escose
Fey	Fairies, boggarts, bugbears, brownies, elves, gnomes, bogies, pixies
Giant	Giants, ogres, ettins
Linnish	People of Listenoise
Lowspeech	People of Hutton
Lyon	People of Lyonesse
Gorean	People of Gore
Gravetongue	Revenants, vampires, ghosts
Nort	People of Norhaut
Valetongue	People of Camelot

ASCALON

Ascalon is a kingdom located on the south west of the Perilous Land on the coast of the Great Sea. Ascalon is often called 'The Summerland' due to its warmer climes and near constant sunshine all year round. King Vortimer is the young monarch who rules over the kingdom, a man whose wisdom defies his years.

HYKARIA

Hykaria is the capital city of Ascalon, a grand port where cultures from overseas and the Perilous Land mingle, resulting in a lively and colourful place to live. Turbaned spice traders from the Bronze Lands arrive on red longboats, offloading sacks of saffron, nutmeg, and cumin to the delight of the Hykarian nobility, who have developed a taste for the far east. King Vortimer's Golden Guard are ever present on the white streets, emblazoned with the Horn of Hykaria and donned in polished brass. The criminal element is low in the city due to Vortimer's stringent sentencing and use of 'battle pits', where thieves and murderers are thrown to fight each other to the death, with the victor gaining a reduced sentence. Battle pits are popular with the nobility, who flock to bet on the violence with morbid glee.

Aside from Vortimer, Hykaria's most notable resident is Sir George, a former Knight of the Round Table who spend 10 years fighting abroad in battles. George is most renowned for saving a small village from a vicious dragon, earning him the nickname George Dragonslayer. Because of this fame, he is held in the highest regard and feared greatly by the dark powers for his prowess in battle.

DEWERSTONE ROCK

This mass of mossy rocks has been sitting outside of Hykaria since time immemorial and is the site of strange magic. On stormy nights unwary travellers are often set upon by prowling whish hounds, a type of black dog led by a shadowy master who some say is Death himself. This tall figure lures curious wanderers off the trail into the middle of the stone circle where he calls his hounds to do his bidding. Lately, there have been a series of kidnappings involving newborns that are said to be cursed by the houndmaster, so local villagers have put up protections against evil in an attempt to ward him off.

DUNDALE

A small farming village that sits on a wide hill overlooking the River Thy. Dundale is the site of a strange phenomenon – once a month at midnight a pig and several piglets can be seen wandering the fields near the village before fading into the distance. There are rumours of an old lady called Hegren who lives inside a hollow tree on the outskirts of the village who is responsible for conjuring the pigs. She is indeed a witch, but the pigs aren't her doing. Instead, the mound where the village stands is at a point where the window between the dead and living is thin. While the pigs are an innocuous side effect of this, there have also been sightings of figures appearing in homes during the night.

THE FORGOTTEN FOREST

Tales of the Forgotten Forest have been told for generations and because of this, few dare to venture more than a few hundred yards into its maze of gnarled trees. Those brave souls who have done so either didn't emerge from the forest or came out with blood on their garments and death in their eyes. The Forgotten Forest is the home of

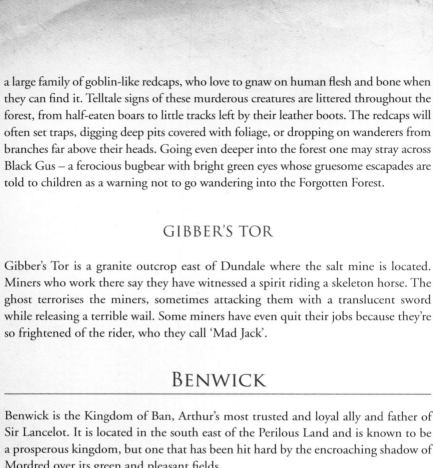

a large family of goblin-like redcaps, who love to gnaw on human flesh and bone when they can find it. Telltale signs of these murderous creatures are littered throughout the forest, from half-eaten boars to little tracks left by their leather boots. The redcaps will often set traps, digging deep pits covered with foliage, or dropping on wanderers from branches far above their heads. Going even deeper into the forest one may stray across Black Gus – a ferocious bugbear with bright green eyes whose gruesome escapades are told to children as a warning not to go wandering into the Forgotten Forest.

GIBBER'S TOR

Gibber's Tor is a granite outcrop east of Dundale where the salt mine is located. Miners who work there say they have witnessed a spirit riding a skeleton horse. The ghost terrorises the miners, sometimes attacking them with a translucent sword while releasing a terrible wail. Some miners have even quit their jobs because they're so frightened of the rider, who they call 'Mad Jack'.

BENWICK

Benwick is the Kingdom of Ban, Arthur's most trusted and loyal ally and father of Sir Lancelot. It is located in the south east of the Perilous Land and is known to be a prosperous kingdom, but one that has been hit hard by the encroaching shadow of Mordred over its green and pleasant fields.

BEYONNE

Benwick's major city, Beyonne, is ancient and splendid, with a vast history of proud kings and glorious war victories. King Ban resides in the castle Trebes with his wife Elaine, who raised the now-great knight Lancelot who serves at Arthur's side. But today Beyonne harbours within its walls cloaked rebels who serve the will of The Black Lance, knowing that to cause Benwick to crumble would be to strike a powerful blow against Arthur. A group of enchanters known as the Red Magisters have caused chaos in recent times through the weaving of dark powers, raising corpses back to life and ordering these monstrosities to attack the populace. In response, Ban has formed the Wytchguard, a group of warriors tasked with defending against undead attacks. While this has held back the tide of death, the Red Magisters are now taking their necromantic experimentations to new extremes, seeking out even more hideous beasts to do their bidding.

GOGMAGOG HILLS

This series of low chalk hills spans for three miles south of Beyonne and are home to the legendary giant Gogmagog and his 33 wicked giantess daughters. It is said that Gogmagog was the first giant of the Perilous Land, though his age is unknown. It is thought that he created the hills themselves with powerful strikes of his club and the stomping of his feet. While Gogmagog rarely ventures from his hill home, his daughters often cause problems for outlying villages, who have since erected defences such as huge wooden spikes to stop the creatures from entering and devouring villagers while they sleep. The Red Magisters have lately been consorting with the daughters in an effort to entice them to join Mordred's army. The eldest daughter Brelenda is cautious, but has accepted the offer in exchange for fresh living bodies on the eve of every full moon.

GREYCHESTER

Run by an old and noble family, Greychester is a wealthy town in Benwick whose main feature is a huge manor house which serves as home to Lord and Lady Greychester. There are wild tales tied to the manor, the most intriguing of which involves a lost fiddler and an underground maze. Beneath Greychester Manor lies a labyrinth of ancient tunnels which have never been fully explored. One day a local fiddler decided that he would be the one to map the tunnel complex. When he set off, he played his fiddle, with those watching him hearing the tune fade into the darkness. The fiddler was never seen again, although some say that he must have fallen into the realm of the fairies, where he now lives forever more.

LOWHEATH

Lowheath is a small farming village to the west of Beyonne whose people live simple lives, but who are haunted by the local crone known as Daddy Witch. This boney hag lives in a gnarled hut by a lake where no person dare venture. She is served by a group of redcaps who make life a misery for the people of Lowheath – slaughtering their livestock and in some cases kidnapping their children. In the dead of night, the eerie sound of pipes can be heard coming from the lake and the flickering of fires can be seen near the hut. Even the hardiest of Wytchguards who sought to hunt down Daddy Witch have never been seen again.

COYNE

The hamlet of Coyne is the location of a small stone church which has become known as a place not to tarry. Those who have been to the churchyard have witnessed dancing fairies with a 'fairy-cart', which in some instances has spirited church-goers away into the fairy realm. Sometimes people have returned decades later, not having aged a day and with a different personality. These 'fairy-touched' people come back with innate magical abilities, although it's not known whether they use their abilities for good or evil.

WANDLETON

Wandleton village is the site of a stone circle known as Crone's Fingers, a place of dark magical energy. Witches have been seen dancing here, singing songs to their dark mistress and cackling madly. A ghostly green knight has also been seen riding at midnight holding a tattered banner. Those who have managed to get a close look have seen his eyes burning like coals and his mare breathing fire from its nostrils.

CAMELOT

The former realm of King Uther Pendragon is now reigned over by his son Arthur, the greatest king in the land. While Arthur is well-loved by most of his subjects for his fair rule and moralistic views, there are those who wish to see him suffer. Camelot is also the home of the largest population of druids in the Perilous Land, a people who are too often shunned by those who deem themselves more 'civilised'.

THE CITY OF CAMELOT

There are few things more breathtaking than the sight of the great impregnable walls of Camelot. Within those walls are streets of pristine white, columns of marble and golden spires that reach into the azure skies. Standing proud in the centre of the city, overlooking all and sundry, is Castle Camelot, home to Arthur, Merlin and the Knights of the Round Table. Carved above the grand portcullis entranceway is Arthur's coat of arms – a shield embossed with three crowns. Behind the castle is the royal tiltyard where the knights practise and where tournaments are fought. Tournament days are the most exciting events in Camelot's calendar, where knights from around the Perilous Land come together to compete in jousting and the melee. Arthur himself has even been known to enter the fray, winning his fair share of tournaments.

But Camelot has fallen under threat from the dark powers of Mordred and Morgan Le Fay, a reluctant alliance promising to rid the kingdom of Arthur. Their fingers reach into the very city streets, with spies, assassins, and wielders of black magic working under the cover of darkness in a plot to murder the king. What was once the greatest city in all of the land is now a place where any ally of the crown must watch their backs lest they be struck down in the shadows of an alley, or come to their end at the hands of a mad mage.

The Dragon Guard patrol the city streets looking for signs of unrest and bringing justice upon those who would break the peace. In these tumultuous times Arthur has come to rely greatly of the Dragon Guard to weed out spies of The Black Lance and see that the good citizens of Camelot come to no harm. When the situation calls for it, Arthur will command his knights to aid the guard in their work.

WYTCHWOOD FOREST

The Wytchwood forest is a vast expanse of woodland to the west of Camelot city. During the Age of Doom, the Wytchwood became the haunting ground for a great number of dark denizens, from foul witches and boggarts, to shug monkeys and even the Questing Beast. Morgan Le Fay is this arboreal domain's de facto ruler, for no creature would be unwise enough to put themselves against her. For most, to venture into the Wytchwood would be certain death, but when the Age of Valour dawned Arthur led a campaign against the evils of the forest, sending questing knights to slay the monsters within – a campaign that still goes on to this day.

As one moves further into the gnarled, blackened wood they see a great many disturbing things. Twisted twig dollies hang from branches by the hundreds, swaying eerily in the stale air and animal flesh can be found strewn on the ground – a sure sign that the crones and witches who call Le Fay their mistress lurk close by.

MOUNTAINS OF ALGAARD

This sweeping mountain range runs between Camelot and Corbenic, a series of dramatic peaks that are home to the wild people of Algaard. This mountainous barbarian tribe are often mistaken as giants due to their towering stature and muscular frame, and so are greatly feared by those who choose to make the perilous journey across the range. Despite this, the wild people tend to keep to themselves and will only attack if provoked. They have mastered the art of animal husbandry, taming wolves and bears to be their ever-present companions on hunting trips in the snow. Their complexion is almost pale blue, and the men plait their beards while the women cut their hair short.

While wanderers should be wary of the wild people, there are things that lurk on the mountain that are far more terrifying. Rumours tell of a demonic cockatrice living within a cave network within the mountain, guarding a great many treasures – although nobody who is alive now has ever seen such a beast. Giants roam the foothills, preying on nearby villages while some whisper of a dragon as old as the land itself living within the foreboding caves.

TAVINOCK

This small Camelotian town stands close to the foothills of the Mountains of Algaard. A group of brigands calling themselves the Cutpurses have been causing trouble on the roads into Tavinock for a number of years. While it doesn't seem like they have an affiliation with any of the dark powers, they are not above working as mercenaries for the highest bidder. The leader, Liddia the Devious, is notorious even beyond Tavinock for her ruthlessness, even among her own ranks.

Just a stone's throw away is the ancient Tower of Elken, which has recently become the home of a hideous three-headed red etin. In the landscape surrounding the tower are remnants of the etin's victims – stone statues of warped, frightened people who have been struck by its magical stone hammer.

THE FOREST OF LIANDE

Though a far smaller forest that the Wytchwood, Liande holds no fewer secrets among its emerald trees. In the centre of the forest is a mossy stone well whose placid waters reflect like a perfect mirror. Breaking the surface of the well is said to cause a great eruption in the sky, which is when the undead knight Escalos appears to defend his well.

Close to the well is a fairy grove that serves as an entrance to Tír na nÓg – the realm of the fairies. Trooping fairies and brownies can often be found here, plotting their next move against the world of mortals.

Finally, the most numerous denizens of Liande are the druids – a peaceful and highly religious people who leave offerings to Escalos at the foot of the well in order to drink from it without suffering his wrath. The druids are a neutral party in the Age of Valour, serving only whom their gods prefer them to serve. Thus far, The Black Lance has yet to win them over and the Sisters of Le Fay know better than to meddle with the machinations of druids.

THE LOE

The Loe is a great lake close to the Forest of Liande and is home to a water nymph called Nimue, who serves as Arthur's occasional guide when Merlin isn't present. Nimue is a beautiful, dark-skinned woman who rises from the lake when summoned using the Flute of Loe, which is in Arthur's possession. She is compassionate and clever, able to outwit even the most cunning of people, including Merlin himself (for this, Merlin has a great amount of respect for Nimue). Mordred's spies have witnessed Arthur and his knights using the flute and plot to steal it from them to prevent access to the wise nymph.

Nimue has the ability to forge magic weapons in the depths of the lake. To aid Arthur in his quest against the darkness she gave him the enchanted sword Excalibur.

CORBENIC

The decaying kingdom of Corbenic is a shadow of its former self, its grey environment intrinsically tied to the ailing Fisher King. The sky bleeds red and vegetation wilts as the deadly enchantment caused by a spear wound to the king's leg slowly creeps towards his heart. While the dying monarch suffers on his throne, his gallant knights, the Order of the Fisher King, have set out on a quest to find a cure that will save him and their kingdom.

CASTLE CORBENIC

This once mighty castle is now a shell, with tattered banners waving solemnly in the breeze. The castle is empty, save for the Fisher King, who sits in his throne room awaiting the return of his knights with a cure. To prevent anyone but themselves from getting to the king in his incapacitated state, his knights have rigged the castle with deadly traps and puzzles.

THE WAILING VALLEY

The land has become barren and inhospitable, aside from the hardiest of creatures. The Wailing Valley was once home to a pleasant population of villagers, but when the environment began to fail so did their crops and livestock, leading to many having to leave the kingdom altogether. Those who remain are trained hunters who stalk the landscape in search of their next meal. Travellers from other kingdoms can easily fall into their traps and perish.

THE PLAINS OF PERRIN

These plains span hundreds of miles, with Castle Corbenic standing in the centre. These lands have since become overrun with wolves, giants, bonelesses and other ferocious creatures. The plains are dotted with tiny villages whose inhabitants have vanished, creating eerie ghost towns where the wind whispers sinister words in the dark. As in the valleys, some still remain – an order of rangers called the Bows of Perrin have effectively taken over most of the villages on the plains, led by the self-proclaimed King of Corbenic called Agravaine.

Journeying across the Plains of Perrin is a fool's errand for those unable to handle themselves in combat, as evidenced by the skeletons of villagers that litter the haunted landscape. Violent hailstorms are a frequent threat on the plains, raining ice like musket balls that can easily crack a skull open.

SUNDERED HENGE

An ancient monument created by the druids of Corbenic a millennium ago, Sundered Henge stands on a high mound in the Plains of Perrin. Each night shadows dance on the stones of the henge as the Withered Druids dance by the firelight, singing songs to dead gods and uttering magical spells to ward off the beasts that would devour them. These warped druids were once wise prophets who would act as the Fisher King's counsel, but as Corbenic decayed, so did their minds. Now they present a danger to anyone who would come across them – believing all outlanders to be demons from the underworld.

EASTLAND

Eastland lies to the south east of the Perilous Land, bordering on Benwick. Ruled by the spiteful Queen Eleanor, Eastland is sympathetic to the plight of the Sisters of Le Fay, counting the dark enchantress Morgan as an ally. Eleanor is known as a trickster, many believing she was born of fairy lineage (this happens to be true – her mother is an aristocratic fairy who wields much power in the fey realm).

HOLDHAM

The main city in Eastland is Holdham, a place of ill repute in the kingdom and the seat of Queen Eleanor's power. Castle Cart stands gaunt on a great hill overlooking the city, guarded by the queen's Black Knights – each of which is enchanted to follow her command no matter what. These Black Knights are said to be the mightiest of all warriors, even able to best Arthur's Knights of the Round in single combat.

The streets of Holdham run with the blood of sinners. Only the unwise would venture into the shadows of the night, where thieves, brigands and worse wait to rob and murder. Eleanor permits such savagery in her kingdom, believing that only the mightiest people should succeed in life, and that treachery is just a tool to build power. Despite Holdham being a city of much poverty, most who live there respect Eleanor.

LYM

The town of Lym is a stone's throw away from a knucker hole, a pool in which dwells a dragon-like knucker. The town's residents are unable to bake bread, as the smell attracts the watery beast, who devours those who get in its way. As a result of this, they must get their bread from Holdham, where merchants have inflated the price of all baked goods, knowing they can make a lot more money from the poor people of Lym. Lym has chosen many champions to lure the creature out in an attempt to slay it once and for all, but each time the knucker has swallowed these warriors whole. Queen Eleanor refuses to send her Black Knights to kill the monster, as she has a kinship with many ferocious beasts.

DRAGON'S FOREST

The knucker isn't the only dragon-like creature in Eastland, for within the darkness of the forest lives the dragon Telerax. Telerax has dark scales and a red belly, but its most notable features are its malformed wings that are too small for it to fly. While the creature does not breathe fire, it is able to spit venom, an attack that causes the body to swell and eyes to blacken. Those who are affected in such an atrocious way can only be cured by water from the pool that resides in the forest. The pool is guarded by the ghosts of those who were killed by Telerax, their undead minds poisoned to commit evil acts against the living. Lately, three witches allied with Morgan Le Fay have visited Telerax, promising to give him the greatest of wings in return for his loyalty.

WESTERFROST

A small seaside village, Westerfrost is an unusual and eerie place for outsiders to come upon. Rumours tell of seal-like creatures crawling out of the sea and shapeshifting into handsome men or beautiful women, who would then go on to marry unsuspecting Westerfrostians. These selkies will live long and happy lives with mortal-kind, but when the time comes they will return to the water, their lover in tow, to live amongst the fishes for the rest of time. Outsiders will notice how some of the villagers act abnormally, slurring their speech and using inappropriate facial expressions, offering a clue to their true nature. Should they be revealed, they will become violent, lashing out at the one who outed them.

SHERWOOD

Sherwood is the most infamous forest in the Perilous Land because of one particularly famous resident – Robin Hood. Hood is the leader of a group of rangers known locally as the Merry Men of Sherwood, although it should be noted that several women are part of their numbers including the Lady Marian, a strong-willed assassin and second in command. The Merry Men make their homes in the trees, camouflaging their bodies and faces as not to be spotted while they hunt their quarry. Despite being branded as outlaws by Queen Eleanor, they are not mere petty criminals, but it is true that they live outside of the law of the land. Hood only targets the corrupt influential members of society – hypocrites, killers, con artists and tyrants – all of whom walk the halls of the Queen's court on a daily basis.

ESCOSE

Also known as the Northlands, Escose is the northernmost kingdom of the Perilous Land. This bleak but beautiful land is known for its miles of hill-land, enchanting lakes and fierce barbarian warriors. Escose is ruled by King Nuit, a benevolent monarch with a fierce temperament. He does not like to meddle in the machinations of other kingdoms and has no interest in war with anyone, but will not hesitate to defend his borders.

The poison of The Black Lance is beginning to filter into Escose, particularly among the barbarian tribes.

LILARNATH

The mighty ancient city of Lilarnath is hewn from the very rock of the Orin Mountains. The Castle Larn is the largest in all the Perilous Land, with the ceiling of the throne room coated in glittering diamonds. The people of Lilarnath are taller than most, with many sporting red hair and intricate patterned tattoos that denote their family name. Each night a giant bell rings out over the city to ward off the 'grey folk' – vicious giants who live in the mountains and hills around the city. King Nuit occasionally sends a retinue of knights into the mountains to slay these foul beasts. Due to the dangerous nature of this quest, the king throws a feast in honour of the knights who will be venturing into the mountains. The people of Lilarnath offer gifts of flowers and kisses to the brave few who ride out at dawn after the festivities.

THE LITTLE ISLES

Off the west coast of Escose lie the Little Isles, a group of mostly uninhabited islands save for the Red Stag tribe. These barbarians rarely venture onto the mainland, preferring to be surrounded by the sea. The waters are home to kelpies, who drag mortals to their doom in the frigid inky blackness. While the Red Stag are used to the kelpies, travellers from the mainland are often enchanted by these creatures, meeting an untimely end.

The Grey Folk have made their home on one of the islands, having sailed over on their black boats from the frozen lands to the north. While they generally keep to themselves, they have been known to attack barbarians.

THE CAVE OF MHORR

This subterranean dwelling is the home of several fairies and a Cat Sìth called One-eyed Meg, on the count of its singular yellow eye. Meg guards treasure, both mundane and magical, appearing to treasure hunters as a cat, but transforms into her true witch form and steals their souls. As a result, human bones litter the cave floor and the ghostly cries of her victims echo in the darkness.

THE LONELY FOREST

On the misty highlands, the Lonely Forest sits, a maze of pines that dwells in silence. This is the domain of Ghillie Dhu, a fairy who uses moss to camouflage himself from mortals who would seek him out. Under the cover of darkness, he is known to punish trespassers by biting and clawing at them, remaining unseen. The large lake beside the forest is haunted by the Stoor Worm, a water dragon with a head like a mountain and two huge round eyes. Its length is not known, other than it could stretch hundreds of miles beneath the lake. Seeing the Stoor Worm emerge from the lake will put fear into the heart of even the bravest warrior. While it cannot remain for long outside of water, the giant creature has been known to slither through the forest and along the nearby hills searching for a meal.

LISTENOISE

Listenoise is located in the north west of the Perilous Land and is notable for its many lakes, earning it the moniker 'Lakeland'. The kingdom is ruled over by King Pellinore, a bearded old man who was a great friend of Uther Pendragon and is a dear ally of Arthur's. His son, Percival, is a member of the Knights of the Round Table and his daughter Dindrane is a gifted enchanter who serves in his court as his most trusted advisor.

OROFAISE

The white tower of Thane can be seen for miles beyond the city of Orofaise – a comparatively small city compared to places such as Camelot or Beyonne. While the much-loved King Pellinore is in charge, it is actually his daughter Dindrane that makes courtly decisions. She is a kind-hearted, courageous woman who forged a great friendship with Lady Guinevere of Camelot. She has inherited her father's quest to hunt down the strange creature known as the Questing Beast, a monster that Pellinore's father and great grandfather had tried to vanquish all of their lives. Now Pellinore is too old to hunt, Dindrane has taken it upon herself to do her father proud and slay the beast.

Like many places in the Perilous Land, Orofaise has become a breeding ground for the dark powers and, because of the royal family's obsession with the Questing Beast, they have been too distracted to notice the evil element growing under their very noses.

CASTLE ROCK

This old gothic structure takes on the visage of a grand castle from afar, but as one grows closer the castle appears to age and crumble. Castle Rock is the dwelling place of the half-fairy cunning woman Guendolen, who has the power to entice people to stay with her for years on end, forgetting their previous life and swearing loyalty to only her. This enchantment has led to part-fairies being born and becoming integrated into Listenoise society, possessing innate magical abilities.

DREADWOOD FOREST

This ancient forest to the south of Orofaise is a haven for outlaws who like to ambush travellers. Knights who have walked through the Dreadwood have reportedly seen a huge black dog whenever there is a storm. After the storm has passed, thunderstones are left scattered around the area, serving as charms to ward off evil. It isn't known what the dog wants, whether it is friend or foe, but some risk a trip into the wood after a storm to collect the thunderstones.

Wolves are also native to the forest, and some have also seen a mysterious woman walking with the wolves, as if she was part of their pack. The wolf woman is known as Wild Brangaine.

CAMLANN

This peaceful plain is the location of several small settlements built along a winding river that runs all the way through Camelot. Dindrane has heard that people living here have seen the Questing Beast, but no tracks have been found. Locals say that the sun always shines on Camlann.

THURROW'S PEAK

The foggy hills of Thurrow's Peak border on Norhaut, but to travel during the night would be to invite misfortune. A spirit known as the Lantern Man, a type of will-o-wisp, leads travellers over the edge of embankments, sending them tumbling to their doom. Several ogres live in caves near the peak and can smell the sweat of a traveller as they pass. It's not unknown for ogres to set traps to catch their prey before eating them alive.

LYONESSE

A large kingdom to the east, bordering on Listenoise and Norhaut, Lyonesse is ruled by King Meliodas and his wife Isabelle. Meliodas is warm to King Arthur, but believes that the threat of Mordred is not something he should be worrying about – after all, his army is the envy of all in the Perilous Land. Despite this belief, Isabelle is more cautious, eager to have him forge an alliance with Camelot for the good of the kingdom.

CITY OF LIONS

The seat of power in Lyonesse, the City of Lions is a sprawling coastal city forged by the burgeoning fishing trade. King Meliodas is a divisive figure in the city, with staunch supporters of his rule pleased with his inward-looking protectionist politics, while his detractors criticise him for acting like a bully, passing harsh laws for even the most minor of offences. His wife Isabelle believes that an alliance with Camelot will give him a much-needed image boost while being able to do some real good for the wider continent.

Meliodas is fearful of magic and will put those who practise it, whether for good or evil, in prison or burn them at the stake. This hardline stance against cunning folk has led to a rebellion sympathetic to the Sisters of Le Fay who call themselves the Burning Chapter. This organisation consists of a network of magic users who aim to end the king's reign with violence.

THE GOLDEN PLAINS

Rolling hills, crystal streams and emerald fields cover a vast stretch of land west of the City of Lions. The Golden Plains are beauty incarnate and many who live there have long and happy lives in their quaint villages, disturbed by few incidents. But as the rebellion of the Burning Chapter grows, so do disturbances in this idyllic land.

The wise woman Ester Crow has seen visions of homes burning, a great winged shadow blotting out the sun, and the rise of evil fairies summoned by robed enchanters from their realm. This portent has shaken the nerves of many a villager on the plains and some tell tales of giant wolves, chattering little creatures, and even of catching glimpses of dragons in the sky.

SCARLET FOREST

The Scarlet Forest swallows hundreds of acres of Lyonesse, being by far the largest forest in the Perilous Land and the one that holds the most secrets. It is said that nobody has managed to explore the entirety of the forest, those who try end up becoming lost and die. This is the domain of the Green Man – an old man with a mossy beard, green skin and leaves covering his body. He is taller than even the hill giants, but can make himself smaller if the task requires it. The Green Man is the embodiment of the forest and is its guardian, seeing that no harm comes to the flora and fauna within. He strides through the undergrowth singing with the birds, covering vast distances in a short amount of time.

The last remaining unicorns are known to graze deep in the forest, particularly close to fairy rings where they are protected. Lyonesse once had herds of unicorns until they were hunted to near extinction for the healing properties in their horns. A unicorn head even hangs above King Meliodas' throne, killed by his own hands.

Other mighty beasts roam the forest, such as the golden griffins who perch in the branches of strong oaks, packs of grey wolves who howl at the full moon, and the little gnomes who make their homes from toadstools and hollow sycamores.

DENDRIDGE

The village of Dendridge is located close to the Scarlet Forest and is notable for the old fortification on its outskirts where the red ettin Gornus resides. This three-headed giant does not bother the villagers much if they offer him a human sacrifice at the beginning of each year. In this harrowing ceremony a black mark is placed upon the door of the one who is to be sacrificed – the eldest in the household.

GORE

The kingdom of Gore is known as 'The kingdom from where no stranger returns'. It has historically been an enemy of Camelot and has been scarred by war for centuries. In an attempt to fortify Gore from invaders, the old king Uriens called upon giants to sunder the land, drawing it away from the rest of the Perilous Land. He connected the land by two bridges – the Sword Bridge and the Water Bridge.

GAIHOM

Gaihom in the capital of Gore, ruled by Meliagrant, an evil knight who is consumed with jealousy of Sir Lancelot and believes him to be an inferior knight despite Lancelot being known the land over as a great warrior. As a result, Meliagrant will pay a great bounty to anyone who can bring Lancelot to his court, alive, to do battle with him. The king is currently in possession of The Great Chessboard, one of the 13 treasures of the Perilous Land.

The city itself is heavily fortified with thick walls and hundreds of guards patrolling the high walkways. The water itself is filled with serpents and morgens – water spirits that lure people into the depths.

Gaihom is not a happy city. Meliagrant rules with an iron fist and has no love of diplomacy. Even his own advisors worry on a daily basis whether they will end up on the wrong end of the chopping block, such is Meliagrant's foul temper and stubbornness. The knight is also paranoid of losing an inch of grip on his kingdom, constantly watching over his back for spies from other realms.

DUERGAR HILL

This small mountain is named after the duergar that reside within it, a race of dwarves who have no love for humanity, often leading travellers to their doom with their mysterious glowing lanterns. Meliagrant has tried time and again to rid the hills of these creatures, but his soldiers always return in fright and of shorter numbers. Some say that a golden dragon also lives within the hill, using the duergar to lure wealthy merchants into its cave. This is true – the dragon Fealtor resides deep within the hill where he has a symbiotic relationship with the dwarves. Occasionally if Fealtor hasn't eaten in awhile, he will fly into a mighty rage, causing all the earth in the kingdom to quake.

THE HUNTING GROUNDS

This plain of 300 acres is known as The Hunting Grounds because of The Wild Hunt, an event that occurs when the moon goes dark and the spirits of the

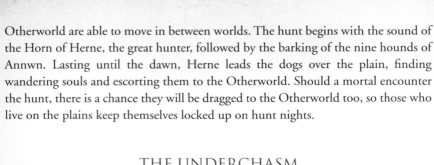

Otherworld are able to move in between worlds. The hunt begins with the sound of the Horn of Herne, the great hunter, followed by the barking of the nine hounds of Annwn. Lasting until the dawn, Herne leads the dogs over the plain, finding wandering souls and escorting them to the Otherworld. Should a mortal encounter the hunt, there is a chance they will be dragged to the Otherworld too, so those who live on the plains keep themselves locked up on hunt nights.

THE UNDERCHASM

Centuries ago King Urien of Gore ordered a great fortress to be built as a way of defending against the marauding armies to the west who would attack Gore on a frequent basis. The fortress was the most magnificent ever built and was said to be impenetrable. Indeed, no army ever made it through the walls of the fortress. Urien was so impressed with the structure that he decided to move his wealth into the fortress where he knew no enemy could ever reach it. His most valuable treasure was the enchanted shield called Pridwen, which could deflect any blow. For decades the fortress stood strong and none could break through its walls to access Urien's treasure. But one day the dragon Fealtor, who lives in Duergar Hill grew hungry and angry, throwing himself into a fit of rage. The rage was so powerful that it shook the ground, causing an earthquake that razed towns. As a result, a yawning pit opened beneath the fortress, sending the structure tumbling into the earth, treasure and all.

Now only a great trench exists where the fortress once stood, but adventurers risk their lives rappelling down the walls to find an entrance to the building, which in common lore is called the Underchasm. None have yet found a way in, but they know that if they were to get inside they would find treasure beyond their wildest dreams.

HUTTON

Hutton lies to the north west of the Perilous Land, bordering Escose, Listenoise and Norhaut. Queen Izolda rules this kingdom, a strong leader whose pure heart and tactical mind have won her the love of her subjects. Izolda has a good relationship with Pellinore of Listenoise and is one of the most ardent supporters of King Arthur's quest to unite the kingdoms against the forces of darkness, not least because of the threat Mordred poses in the neighbouring realm of Norhaut.

THE CITY OF HUTTON

The city of Hutton was founded on the western shores for ease of trading on the water. The scent of sea salt and haddock linger around its ports and the deafening sound of gulls can be heard echoing over the waves dashing against the rocks. As a result of overseas trading, Hutton has become a beacon of commerce in the north, turning it into a prosperous and affluent place. However, this has made it attractive to overseas raiders and land invaders who seek to rob the city of its wealth. Hutton's heraldry is emblazoned with a unicorn flanked by two swords, representing its majesty and splendour, but also its fierce history in battle. Izolda herself is a trained warrior who has joined her armies on the field on multiple occasions.

WHITTEN MOOR

This emerald moorland has become the stomping ground of a gigantic dun cow, a beast known to trample people to death should the spring that it drinks from dries up. Lately a malicious witch from the nearby wood has enchanted the spring so that it no longer produces water, just a steady stream of dust. The dun cow is now on a rampage through the moor, smashing homesteads, breaking bones, and running people into the dirt. People are afraid to walk the trade paths between towns in case they come face to face with the dun cow.

PEG'S WELL

Crossing over the River Riddle, a traveller would come upon a well with a stone figure sitting atop it resembling a crooked old woman. Walkers have been known to be dragged into the well by a malevolent spirit known locally as Peg of the Well. Some who drink from the well find that later they fall ill, with some dying of their malady.

THE RADIANT WOLD

North of the Whitten Moor lies the Radiant Wold, an elevated wooded area of great significance to the ancient druids who have since departed this place. The wold is hallowed ground where the druids were said to have first communed with the earth goddess Anu, whose realm is the moon, air and the ways of magic. There the trees grow taller than any in the Perilous Land, their pure white bark reflecting the brilliant sunlight like a beacon. The rarest flowers and mushrooms grow in the wold, planted by Anu as a gift to the druids. Now the druids have departed, the trees have become home to creatures such as shug monkeys, who have be heard howling into the night, and several bugganes who have nested in the area. Other beasts also make their home here, like the grey wolves and black bears, who are attracted to the lingering magic of Anu.

NORHAUT

Norhaut is a realm in the north east of the Perilous Land. Since the Age of Doom, Norhaut has become plagued with the forces of darkness, with Mordred now residing there in his Dread Tower where he commands his evil domain. Norhaut was lost in the War of Shadow, when Mordred led an army of humans and beasts against King Mark, who fell to Mordred's spear. Now, Norhaut is cast under a cloud of evil, its people enslaved by The Black Lance if they don't show willing to take up arms against Camelot. Here, Mordred's army grows by the week, but he knows that he needs more than just numbers to overcome Arthur – he needs magic.

BRIODA

Under the reign of King Mark, Brioda was a flourishing city that rivalled even Camelot. Now, with Mordred installed as its ruler, there is nothing but pain and anguish in its streets. His Draconian Guard keep the populace in check, dealing out severe penalties for speaking out against Mordred. As a result, pockets of rebels have created an underground network who plan to reclaim Norhaut. This group, known as the Shining Spear, put their lives at risk to plant spies throughout the city and even installing moles in the Dread Tower. Mordred has become aware of the group's existence after finding that his handmaid was planning to assassinate him. To make an example of her, he had the handmaid flung out of the top window of the tower onto the iron railings below and proclaimed that anyone who would attempt to usurp him would receive an even worse fate.

THE FOREST OF FALDOR

The blackened branches of the trees of Faldor curl in the ever-present mist that blankets the forest floor. Here lurk mist hags, bugbears, evil fairies, and other malevolent spirits – this was a place avoided by people even before Mordred invaded with his dark forces. There are rumours that one of the 13 treasures of the Perilous

Land is hidden somewhere in the forest, but these tales are as old as the forest itself and nobody remains who knows whether it's true. When Mordred caught wind of this rumour he send his dark knights to investigate, but they never returned.

THE VILLAGE OF GNOMES

Deep within the Derrigan Wood a true marvel can be witnessed. Hundreds of large toadstool mushrooms of all colours fill an area of the wood, each mushroom being the home to one of the Derrigan gnomes. The gnomes never venture out of the wood, having heard ill tidings of Mordred's evil. However, those of pure heart who visit the gnomes are greeted with kindness and merriment. Lud, the Lord of Gnomes, sits on his flower throne smoking a great pipe and whiling his days away pondering. It is said that he is one of the wisest creatures to ever exist and he will answer any question posed to him. Some adventurers have gone to him seeking aid in answering great questions of diplomacy, strategy and love.

THE WHISPERING CAVERNS

This cave system, located 50 miles east of Brioda, goes deep into the Twilight Mountains and has historically been a location for adventurers to explore after rumours surfaced of an ancient royal burial site hidden somewhere within. Families of pottons can be found in the first few chambers, the bane of hunters who live in the surrounding areas. Those brave souls who have ventured further have seen ogres, spriggans and some even say a dragon sleeps somewhere in one of the large chambers. Indeed, the whispering that can be heard through the tunnels and chambers is supposedly the sound of the dragon speaking to the ghosts of the queen who was buried here.

BLACKBONE PORT

A haven for pirates and scallywags, Blackbone Port has so far been unaffected by Mordred's forces. To say that the port is lawless would be an understatement. Murder is rife on the streets and poverty is the highest in all of the Perilous Land. Despite this, Blackbone Port attracts those looking for adventure, with pirates willing to pay a pretty penny for deeds (some fair and others terrible). It's tradition to toss a coin in the green waters to appease the storm hag that haunts the coast.

GODS OF THE PERILOUS LAND

The various deities of the Perilous Land hold sway over their domains, from hunting and nature, to luck and the arts. The pantheon of this roleplaying setting is based on the Celtic gods of old whose various forms are commonly found across the continent through art, heraldry and architecture. While in the Perilous Land there is no doubt that these gods and demigods exist, meaning atheists are few and far between, most people and communities pray to a patron deity – one that has a special significance to their way of life or personality. It is recommended that players select a patron god or goddess for their character to help enrich the roleplaying experience.

AINE

Domain: Love, fertility, summer
Symbol: Swan
Common Class Patrons: All

Aine is the goddess of love, fertility, and the summer and an important deity for farmers who pray to her for a good crop yield. During a wedding ceremony Aine is evoked through the symbol of the swan, which represents a blessing to the newly married couple. When walking the mortal soil, Aine transforms into a swan or a red mare, spreading a message of love and acceptance wherever she goes.

CERNUNNOS

Domain: Forest, wild animals, wealth
Symbol: Antlers
Common Class Patrons: Rangers, barbarians, thieves
Cernunnos is a popular patron god amongst rangers, having the wild as his domain. He wears shining beads around his neck and has an impressive set of mighty antlers sprouting from his head, which has led him to be referred to as 'The Horned One'. Many members of the Iron Hawks revere Cernunnos in order to keep themselves safe during their months in the wilderness, while thieves call upon the blessings of Cernunnos for wealth and prosperity.

EPONA

Domain: Horses, fertility
Symbol: Horse and foal
Common Class Patrons: Knights, barbarians
Epona is the goddess of horses and riding, who herself takes the form of a white mare much of the time, occasionally transforming into a woman when the situation requires. Soldiers' barracks often have her symbol carved into the masonry. She is also deemed the goddess of fertility, which is the reason her symbol appears at the bedside of women who are due to give birth.

FACHEA

Domain: Poetry, creativity
Symbol: Harp
Common Class Patrons: Bards
Appearing as a beautiful young woman carrying a golden harp, Fachea is the personification of creativity and a patron of many bards, particularly in the southern regions of the Perilous Land. She is present in the shanties sung in port taverns, the tales of daring adventure by firelight and the murals on the ceilings of grand palaces.

GOFANNON

Domain: The forge
Symbol: Hammer and anvil
Common Class Patrons: Knights, thieves

Known as 'The Divine Smith', Gofannon is the god of the forge, crafting tools, weapons and armour with his sacred hammer and anvil. Gofannon is worshipped by blacksmiths, knights, and even thieves, who bless their thieves tools with his grace. He is particularly revered in northern lands such as Norhaut and Escose, and is depicted as a man striking an anvil with a large hammer.

LUGH

Domain: The Sun, crafts, the arts
Symbol: Sun
Common Class Patrons: Bards, cunning folk

Lugh is the lightbringer, the one who bathes the world in glorious sunshine. He carries with him his blazing hot, invincible spear which must be stored in a vat when not in use lest it accidentally sets the world on fire. Lugh is skilled in many crafts and has become a patron god for artisans and artists alike, along with the druids who revere him for his warming sunlight.

MORRIGAN

Domain: Death in battle, nature's guardian
Symbol: Raven
Common Class Patrons: Cunning folk, knights

Morrigan, also known as the Queen of Phantoms, is the goddess of death and war, appearing alongside warriors in battle to fight alongside the side she favours. To witness Morrigan join one's side in battle is to be reinvigorated, as certain victory is close at hand. Morrigan has a dual role as the guardian of nature, keeping unwanted beings from desecrating the earth that she deems sacred. As a result, some nature-revering witches have come to worship her as their patron goddess. Similarly, some knights pray to Morrigan for her aid in war.

NODENS

Domain: Healing, hunting
Symbol: Dog
Common Class Patrons: Rangers, cunning folk

Nodens is the god of healing, whose mending hands can cure all disease and sickness that ails a mortal. He is joined by his hounds, whose licking tongues also have celestial healing properties. Nodens carries a silver trident and rides a chariot through the depths of the sea, pulled by aquatic horses. Village healers will pray to Nodens while making restorative balms, ointments, and tinctures in order to bestow magical potency on their ingredients.

MATH

Domain: Magic
Symbol: Staff
Common Class Patrons: Cunning folk

Math is the god of magic and enchantments, the greatest sorcerer god there ever was. He is able to transform his enemies into animals, though he has mercy on those whose misfortune is not of their own making. He is depicted as carrying a staff and is worshipped by those who would use magic to help others, such as Merlin.

TARANIS

Domain: Thunder
Symbol: Wheel
Common Class Patrons: Barbarians

Taranis is the god of thunder and storms and a patron of seafarers across the Perilous Land who pray to him for calm seas. He has a great white beard and conjures crackling thunderbolts in his mighty hands to hurl at the earth. Of all the deities, Taranis is the largest and most brutal in his ways.

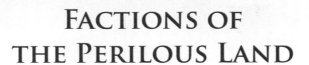

FACTIONS OF THE PERILOUS LAND

To fight a war, one must have allies. The Great Search brought together factions of allies, from the chivalrous Knights of the Round Table to the legendary huntsman The Merry Men of Sherwood. Likewise, the powers of evil brought together their own groups bent on dominating Camelot and the Perilous Land itself.

Factions add another element to gameplay through flavour that sparks great opportunities for roleplay. Players are encouraged to choose one of the Allies of Camelot to join and note on their character sheet. Each faction write-up contains information on joining the group and rules when operating within them. Again, these rules are designed to enhance roleplay and give players a good idea of their characters' personal quests.

ALLIES OF CAMELOT

THE KNIGHTS OF THE ROUND TABLE

Standing for chivalry, honour, and good, the Knights of the Round Table were founded by King Arthur in Camelot to help fight the forces of evil in the Perilous Land and keep Camelot from falling. Each knight has trained in the elite art of battle since they were young. While the original members were only allowed to be males of noble blood, Arthur eventually abolished this requirement after The Great Search, knowing that he would need as many trained allies as possible to combat the rising tide of darkness brought about by Mordred and Morgan Le Fay. Sir Lancelot is Arthur's closest companion and one of the greatest warriors in the land, entrusted to lead The Great Search in the north. Sir Percival is as intelligent as he is capable with a blade. He has been tasked with aiding the Order of the Fisher King in finding magical artefacts, weapons, and an elixir to cure the Fisher King. Others, such as Sir Gawain and Lady Guinevere, form the core knights who undertake dangerous quests to hunt magical beasts terrorising the land.

BECOMING A KNIGHT OF THE ROUND TABLE

The knights are made up of the bravest and most able warriors in the Perilous Land, but Arthur does permit people who are not of noble blood, or male, to join their ranks so long as they can prove their worth. Prospective knights start their career as squires as they train themselves in both body and mind. A Knight of the Round Table has the authority to form a band of warriors known as Blades of Arthur, who can be of any character class. The Blades of Arthur will be presented with quests by their knight leader, which they must undertake without the aid of the knight. Once a Blade of Arthur reaches level 8 and have proved themselves sufficiently, they can be knighted by Arthur in Camelot.

FACTION RULES

- Blades of Arthur each receive a silver medallion depicting the Arthurian crown as proof they serve the king's court.
- Once knighted, members have access to the royal armouries located around the Perilous Land. These contain an assortment of weapons, armour, and elixirs to aid in battle. Only one of any type of equipment may be taken by any one person at a time, i.e. one weapon and one set of armour.
- Once knighted, members have the opportunity to have a seat at the Round Table and help determine the fate of Camelot and the Perilous Land.
- 10% of any treasure obtained in a quest must be given to the court of Camelot via a knight based in the local region.
- The penalty for treason against the crown is often death by hanging. A jury will decide whether the perpetrator is guilty or not. A knight may be stripped of their knighthood and exiled instead of facing death, depending on the severity of the crime.

THE MERRY MEN OF SHERWOOD

Robin Hood is the charismatic leader of the Merry Men, a band of outlaws who live off the land and carry out good deeds while punishing the wicked. Robin has been tasked by King Arthur to defend the wild places of the world from the encroaching evil. The Merry Men are Robin's loyal followers and believers in his crusade against the corrupt. Most of them are rangers, able to expertly track their quarry and survive in the wilderness. Despite their name, not all members are male, with Lady Marian being one of the most experienced rangers in their ranks. While Robin is based in the vast Sherwood Forest, he has expanded his Merry Men into woodlands across the Perilous Land, with many of the original members, such as Little John and Will Scarlet, leaving Sherwood to form their own bands. The mission statement of the Merry Men is: "Do no harm to those less fortunate, or the goodly knight." Their main purpose is to punish corruption that lurks in the higher orders of society, such as the nobility and the clergy.

BECOMING A MERRY MAN OF SHERWOOD

The Merry Men specifically look for those who are able to handle themselves in the wild and have a disdain for corruption. Merry Men are expected to shirk material things and live in the wilderness – they do not crave gold or fame, but instead they are happy in the knowledge that they are doing justice. Prospective Merry Men are often given a series of challenges, such as surviving naked for a week in the forest or stealing a purse from a corrupt aristocrat unnoticed. Rangers and thieves usually make the best Merry Men, but they are open to all classes.

FACTION RULES

- 50% of treasure gained from a quest must be redistributed to the poorest in society.
- Merry Men are part of a wider network of forest dwellers who aid each other when needed. When in a forest, there is a 1 in 6 chance you will find another Merry Man.
- If Robin calls on you to undertake a job, you must do it or be forced to leave the Merry Men.

THE ORDER OF THE FISHER KING

Corbenic, the kingdom of the Fisher King, is a crumbling grey wasteland where plants seldom grow aside from weeds. The Fisher King is dying, having suffered from a leg wound from an enchanted spear; as the life force drains from him so too does life wither from his kingdom. The ailing monarch gathered his remaining knights to create the Order of the Fisher King, a group that seeks to find magical artefacts that could cure their King's leg and ensure his kingdom flourishes once more. These gallant few have joined forces with Camelot to find enchanted equipment to use against Mordred, with the promise that if the Knights of the Round Table discover a revitalising elixir, they will offer it to the Fisher King.

BECOMING A KNIGHT OF THE ORDER OF THE FISHER KING

The Order of the Fisher King consists solely of warriors from Corbenic who have sworn fealty to their monarch. Being treasure hunters, knights of this group are expected to understand the values and magical properties imbued in certain artefacts and to resist the temptation to keep them for their own gain. Loyalty to the Fisher

King is their first priority and any member must swear an oath on the standard to retrieve a cure for him at all costs. Members of the Order can only be knights.

FACTION RULES

- You will not stand in the way of retrieving a cure for the Fisher King. Doing so is an act of treason and is punishable by death.
- You may keep and use magical treasure as long as it is to aid the pursuit of the cure.
- You will act with honour and dignity at all times, as treachery and deceit is the way of Mordred.

FELLOWSHIP OF ENCHANTERS

During The Great Search, master magician Merlin and his retinue of wizarding disciples scoured the land far and wide to find cunning folk who could use their abilities to help defeat the darkness. From grand cities to lowly hamlets, Merlin discovered those rare people gifted with the ways of magic, although many lived alone in the wilderness and didn't care much for news outside of their small lives. Still, others rose to the occasion and formed the Fellowship of Enchanters, for without magic Camelot would not stand a chance against the ways of Morgan Le Fay.

BECOMING A MEMBER OF THE FELLOWSHIP OF ENCHANTERS

Quite simply, the Fellowship of Enchanters only counts cunning folk amongst its ranks. But many of these magical types live solitary existences and tend to look out only for themselves, so Merlin has required an oath from his enchanters to only use magic to further the cause of Camelot and to safeguard the Perilous Land. Those discovered dabbling in the more sinister arts, or using magic to harm the innocent, will be considered enemies of Camelot.

FACTION RULES

- Magic must only be used to enable good to prevail.
- Natural things are friends: do no harm to nature unless your life is put in danger.
- You must frequently report your activities to Merlin via letter.

IRON HAWKS

Hardened monster slayers, the Iron Hawks are the last bastion of righteousness in the northernmost reaches of the Perilous Land. Bors the Younger leads this band of warriors, wandering from town to town with the sole purpose of finding and destroying the dark allies of Mordred. Bors is a gruff veteran of battle and despite his dislike for authority, he recognises that the threat the land is facing is beyond him alone and so agreed to join Arthur in his crusade. The Iron Hawks are formed by a mixture of fighters, with no consistent skill set aside from being able to kill evil creatures. The life of an Iron Hawk isn't as glamorous as that of a Knight of the Round Table, as they are often seen as mercenaries looking to make a quick coin.

BECOMING A MEMBER OF THE IRON HAWKS

Bors isn't trusting of outsiders, but after proving themselves against the hordes of darkness he will allow someone into the Iron Hawks. He does not want his members swearing oaths of bravery to him – he would rather see this sentiment manifest as action rather than mere words.

FACTION RULES

- If an Iron Hawk is wounded in battle, they are not to be left behind.
- Magical items are treacherous and are to be handled with caution. Stay away from them unless you have no choice.
- If you are interrogated by the forces of darkness, you should sooner take your own life than give away information.

THE DARK POWERS

There are two main powers of darkness in the Perilous Land who oppose the ruling of King Arthur: The Black Lance and Sisters of Le Fay. These two factions will prove to be challenging antagonists for the allies of Camelot, providing a wealth of conflict for your adventures. It isn't recommended that players create characters aligned to either of these evil factions; *Romance of the Perilous Land* is a game of heroism and good deeds rather than treacherous and wrong-doing.

THE BLACK LANCE

Mordred was once one of the greatest Knights of the Round Table. His commitment to training in arms bordered on obsession, spending many lonely nights cloistered away in his quarters practising with a variety of weapons. While others thought he was just trying to be an exemplary warrior, he was in fact plotting the downfall of his uncle, Arthur Pendragon. Mordred was of the belief that the throne of Camelot belonged to him and that, with the help of Merlin, Arthur was merely an imposter who had usurped Uther. To Mordred, the sword in the stone was a trick, so he committed himself to becoming a greater warrior than even his king in order to one day best him in battle. However, to do this he would need to raise a great and powerful army – something he was unable to do under Arthur's watchful eye – so he hatched a plan. One day Mordred led a handful of knights on a quest to hunt down the Witch of Gravenstone, but instead led them straight into a trap. With the aid of the witch and her dark familiars he slayed the knights and left his battered armour at the scene to make it appear that he had been captured. After that, he fled to the kingdom of Norhaut to amass his forces under the banner of The Black Lance.

Mordred began to form an alliance with the dark enchanters of Norhaut, promising them that when Camelot was his, he would give them freedom to practise their evil works unimpeded by lawmakers. He even made pacts with spirits and monsters, having them pledge their service to him in exchange for mortal flesh, treasure, and other desires of malignant creatures. Word spread across the Perilous Land of Mordred and his goals, and more people sympathised with him. Soon The Black Lance had spies and warriors in all corners of the land, coming together with one goal in mind – overthrow the rulers of Perilous Land and take their rightful place as leaders in a new, chaotic world of beasts and dark magic.

Now, Mordred operates from the Dread Tower in Norhaut, commanding his magicians and monsters to do his bidding. He knows that it isn't long until Camelot is ready to fall, but first he must weaken the other kingdoms, turning them against Arthur if he can, and destroy the allies of Camelot.

SISTERS OF LE FAY

In the darkness of the dense Wytchwood Forest the enchantress Morgan Le Fay reigns supreme. Aside from Merlin, she is perhaps the most powerful magician in the land but would instead use her powers to see Camelot crumble into dust. Le Fay believes that all creatures, good and evil, should have the right to live and thrive in the world. These beliefs go against the rule of Arthur and many leaders in the Perilous Lands, who wish to banish evil beings from the world in order to prevent darkness taking over. Because of this Le Fay formed the Sisters of Le Fay, a faction that rallies against civilisation, wanting the world to be reclaimed by nature and her beasts.

While Le Fay is aware of Mordred's efforts to overthrow Arthur, she isn't necessarily a loyal ally of The Black Lance, but sees them as a means to an end. She is happy to use Mordred's forces for her own gain, and in the end plans to destroy both him and Camelot. The Sisters of Le Fay have grown further afield than just the Wytchwood Forest, for many people also wish for nature to reclaim the Perilous Land and become the true ruler of men.

Non-Allied Factions

In all of the Perilous Land there are groups who have their own agenda, allied neither with Camelot nor the dark powers of Mordred and Morgan Le Fay. These factions can range from a guild of assassins to a clandestine organisation of witches. It is up to the GM whether they will allow for player characters to be a part of any of these factions, and for the player to come up with a good reason as to why they are a member of such a faction.

THE KEEPERS OF THE SECRET WORDS

The most mysterious of groups in all the realms, the Keepers of the Secret Words is a band of wise sages who live deep in the Algaard Mountains in their humble tower. It is said that five hundred years ago the gods themselves gave to humans the ten secret words that would both create and destroy. While most used these words for good, creating better lives for their people, a minority, known as the Red Magisters, grew mad with the desire for fortune and conflict, using the words to level towns and depose kings. They brought fire and brimstone onto their fellow man, scorching the earth and murdering thousands. Those who had done only good with the words created a sweeping army led by wizard generals, and marched on the Red Magisters. After the bloody battle most of the Red Magisters were dead, along with a large number of the Keepers. Those who remained decided that the words should never again be let loose into the world unless there was dire need. Ten of these wizards made their home in the mountains where they remain to this day, each harbouring one of the secret words.

Because of their location, the Keepers are rarely if ever encountered, leading monastic lives of silence. Knowing they could hold the key to stopping the powers of darkness, Arthur once sent several knights on a quest to gain the secret words. However, the Keepers would not speak, and the quest was a failure.

Despite being destroyed centuries ago, some Red Magisters still survive in Benwick where they are allying themselves with the Sisters of Le Fay.

THE WARD

Little instills fear in people's hearts like the mention of The Ward, a notorious network of assassins found throughout the Perilous Land, with a headquarters in Lyonesse where the shadowy figure who leads the faction resides. The Ward are known by their insignia, the triple wolf head – a symbol of their ferocity, cunning and organisation. Many a noble and high-ranking official has become the target of The Ward, who are masters of stealth and knife-play, using the cover of darkness to their advantage. To call upon The Ward, one must have two things: connections and wealth. Those who have been slain by the assassins are branded on the forehead with a W, a scare tactic used to send a message to others on behalf of the client.

GUARDIANS OF AVALON

Avalon is a mystical island said to lie off the coast of Camelot, a place where the spirit goes once the corporeal body has passed on. The body would be traditionally placed in a boat and taken away to Avalon by water spirits. The Guardians of Avalon are two fairy knights who guard the boat to the Isle of Avalon, only allowing the dead to cross the waters. The guardians wear bright white plate armour that glows with starlight, and wield the two Celestial Swords, the most powerful blades aside from Excalibur. The guardians do not speak with their mouths, but their voices are conjured in the heads of those they wish to communicate with. They are able to do this over long distances, anywhere in the world. It is said that they know the names of all who exist and will exist in the future.

Mordred seeks to conquer Avalon and take both of the Celestial Swords for himself as part of his plan to become king of Camelot, though every effort thus far has been thwarted by the power of the guardians.

THE DEAD DOGS

The Dead Dogs are also referred to the Terror of Eastland – a large group of brigands who are known for murdering, torturing, and pillaging. Their leader, Thane Gyrak, is the most wanted man in all of Eastland after he ordered one of Queen Eleanor's most trusted advisors to be left naked in the middle of a forest with nothing but the blood of an elk covering him. His body was later found after being torn to shreds by wolves.

The Dead Dogs operate from a moving encampment, usually located in dense woods, protected by magic to ward off beasts and spirits who would do them harm. These brigands most often target wealthy merchants with road ambushes, but they have been known to raid small villages for food and money. While Gyrak is bloodthirsty, he does not permit the killing of children or those who are unable to defend themselves.

THE CHILDREN OF MÓRRÍGAN

In the forests of Norhaut the Children of Mórrígan live – a coven of witches who act as guardians of the land. Also known as the Wild Witches, the coven worships the goddess Mórrígan, who oversees the earth and the beasts that live off the land. While they will not harm the innocent, they are wrathful towards those who seek to harm the things they protect, using spells of fear and illusion to confuse and terrify their quarry.

PERSONALITIES OF THE PERILOUS LAND

This section details the different personalities who inhabit the realms of the Perilous Land; from kings and queens to warriors and magicians, these are some of the most important people that player characters could come across. Each personality has been statted up just like a player character, rather than using the system from the bestiary. GMs are encouraged to include some of these personalities in their adventures or campaigns.

KING ARTHUR OF CAMELOT

As a boy Arthur had no idea who he really was – he was a rambunctious child with a rebellious attitude, but after pulling the sword Clarent from the stone it was clear that he was bound for greatness. Arthur is the king of Camelot and head of the Knights of the Round Table – a fair and just man who wishes to unite the kingdoms of the Perilous Land to stave off the evil of Mordred and Morgan Le Fay. He is a strong and capable fighter, master tactician and wise leader who can do diplomacy as well as he performs in battle.

KING ARTHUR OF CAMELOT			
Level/HD	**HP**		**Age**
10	80		27

Class	**Background**	**Faction**	**Deity**
Knight	Outlaw	Knights of the Round Table	Gofannon

Might	**Reflex**	**Charisma**	**Constitution**	**Mind**
25	19	18	20	16

Armour Points	**Weapon Damage**
12 (plate armour)	d10 + 6 (Excalibur [longsword])

Save Proficiencies
Might, Reflex

Skills
Athletics (Might), Riding (Might), Perception (Mind), Stealth (Reflex), Thievery (Reflex)

Class Features
Aid the Defenceless, Weapon Expert, Never Surrender, Valiant Effort, Double Strike

Talents
Shield Expert, Mighty, Leadership, Improved Leadership, Armour Recovery, Hardy

Languages
Common, Valetongue

Equipment
Excalibur, plate armour, shortbow, 20 arrows, quiver, 5 torches, flint and steel

LADY GUINEVERE, KNIGHT OF CAMELOT

Raised by a blacksmith, Guinevere learned to fight from an early age. These skills came in useful when she was attacked by wolves when she was out collecting firewood, managing to fend them off with a battered short sword her father gave her when she was seven years of age. When she grew up she wanted nothing more than to join the Knights of the Round Table, but they wouldn't let a woman of common blood become part of their ranks. However, when Arthur began The Great Search, he lifted this restriction to enable him to build a great army of knights to battle Mordred, and so Guinevere trained with the knights and eventually was bestowed the title 'Lady'.

LADY GUINEVERE, KNIGHT OF CAMELOT		
Level/HD	**HP**	**Age**
7	49	25

Class	Background	Faction	Deity
Knight	Artisan	Knights of the Round Table	Lugh

Might	Reflex	Charisma	Constitution	Mind
20	17	15	18	16

Armour Points	Weapon Damage
15 (plate armour and wooden shield)	d6 + 3 (flail)

Save Proficiencies
Might, Reflex

Skills
Athletics (Might), Riding (Might), Survival (Mind), Perception (Mind), Nature (Mind)

Class Features
Aid the Defenceless, Weapon Expert, Never Surrender, Valiant Effort

Talents
Dodge, Quick Step, Sprinter, Armour Recovery

Languages
Common, Valetongue

Equipment
Flail, plate armour, wooden shield, 3 torches, dagger

SIR LANCELOT

Sir Lancelot is King Arthur's closest friend and confidant, in addition to being one of the greatest warriors in all of the Perilous Land. He is an expert jouster and current champion of the melee tournament in Camelot. Not even Arthur himself comes close to Lancelot's valour and strength, making him seem perfect in the eyes of other knights. It was Lancelot who led The Great Search for new knights to join Camelot and who entered the courts of kings and queens to extend a hand of diplomacy.

SIR LANCELOT		
Level/HD	HP	Age
10	83	28

Class	Background	Faction	Deity
Knight	Guard	Knights of the Round Table	Gofannon

Might	Reflex	Charisma	Constitution	Mind
26	20	16	17	15

Armour Points	Weapon Damage
15 (plate armour and wooden shield)	D8 + 5 (spear)

Save Proficiencies
Might, Reflex

Skills
Athletics (Might), Riding (Might), Survival (Mind), Perception (Mind), Intimidate (Charisma)

Class Features
Aid the Defenceless, Weapon Expert, Never Surrender, Valiant Effort, Double Strike

Talents
Armour Recovery, Swift Recovery, Mighty, Quick Step, Critical Blow, Monster Hunter

Equipment
Spear, plate armour, lance, lantern, oil, chalk

Languages
Common, Valetongue

ROBIN HOOD

Outlaw, thief, and vigilante. Robin Hood is the most renowned and feared ranger in the land, stalking Sherwood Forest with his band of Merry Men and targeting the corrupt. An expert tracker and the greatest bowman of his generation, Hood and his cohorts live off the land, preferring to take money and valuables from those in power to distribute amongst the poorest in society.

ROBIN HOOD		

Level/HD	HP	Age
10	83	32

Class	Background	Faction	Deity
Ranger	Outlaw	Merry Men of Sherwood	Cernunnos

Might	Reflex	Charisma	Constitution	Mind
17	24	21	16	19

Armour Points	Weapon Damage
8 (leather armour)	d10 + 5 (longbow), d6 + 2 (dagger)

Save Proficiencies
Reflex, Constitution

Skills
Nature (Mind), Acrobatics (Reflex), Survival (Mind), Stealth (Reflex), Thievery (Reflex)

Class Features
Herbalism, Mortal Enemy, Deadly Shot, Split Shot, Snap Reflexes

Talents
Connected, Critical Blow, Fleetfoot, Jack-of-all-Trades, Razor Bow, Wilderness Expert

Equipment
Longbow, leather armour, dagger

Languages
Common, Eastern

MORDRED OF THE BLACK LANCE

Stewing in seething hatred for King Arthur, his uncle who took the throne through sorcery, Mordred began a campaign to take Camelot by force under the banner of The Black Lance. Once a great knight of the Round Table, Mordred led a retinue of knights to their doom before fleeing Camelot to begin amassing his army. He is a proficient warrior who prefers to meet his foes in single combat, rather than sneaking around their backs.

MORDRED OF THE BLACK LANCE		
Level/HD	**HP**	**Age**
10	82	25

Class	Background	Faction	Deity
Knight	Aristocrat	The Black Lance	Taranis

Might	Reflex	Charisma	Constitution	Mind
25	21	15	20	19

Armour Points	Weapon Damage
12 (plate armour)	d12 + 5 (claymore)

Save Proficiencies
Might, Reflex

Skills
Athletics (Might), Riding (Might), Survival (Mind), Languages (Mind), Intimidate (Charisma)

Class Features
Aid the Defenceless, Weapon Expert, Never Surrender, Valiant Effort, Double Strike

Talents
Armour Recovery, Swift Recovery, Mighty, Leadership, Critical Blow, Darksight

Equipment
Claymore, plate armour

Languages
Common, Valetongue

MERLIN

Merlin, the wise enchanter who has been at Arthur's side since his birth, is one of the most powerful cunning folk in the Perilous Land. He is Arthur's closest friend and confidant, acting as a sounding board for the king and counsel in trying times. The Great Search saw the wizard gather together rare cunning folk to join his Fellowship of Enchanters, whose goal is to use magic as a force for good against a common enemy.

MERLIN		
Level/HD	**HP**	**Age**
10	44	74

Class	Background	Faction	Deity
Cunning Folk	Scholar	Fellowship of Enchanters	Math

Might	Reflex	Charisma	Constitution	Mind
17	19	20	17	26

Armour Points	Weapon Damage
6 (cloth armour)	d6 + 3 (Merlin's staff)

Save Proficiencies
Mind, Charisma

Skills
History (Mind), Magic Knowledge (Mind), Religion (Mind), Bluff (Charisma), Languages (Mind)

Class Features
Spellcasting, Magic Discipline

Talents
Magic Sensitivity, Mystical Intuition, Trained Caster, Master Healer, Leadership, Witchfinder

Spell Prepared
Imbue a Weapon with a Miraculous Enchantment, Bless the Mortally Wounded, Grant the Skin of Stone

Equipment
Staff, cloth armour, scrying mirror

Languages
Common, Valetongue, Fey, Gravetongue, Druid, Giant, Gorean

MORGAN LE FAY

Known as the Dark Enchantress, the Shadow of Wytchwood and the Bane of Arthur, Morgan Le Fay is a mysterious cunning woman who has vowed to destroy Arthur for his crusade against the creatures of darkness who she has allied with. While she is relatively young for an enchantress, she almost rivals Merlin with her magical expertise. She leads her network of witches and cunning folk, the Sisters of Le Fay, who have risen up around the Perilous Land to support her in her cause against Camelot.

MORGAN LE FAY		
Level/HD	**HP**	**Age**
9	40	36

Class	**Background**	**Faction**	**Deity**
Cunning Folk	Artisan	Sisters of Le Fay	Morrigan

Might	**Reflex**	**Charisma**	**Constitution**	**Mind**
17	18	18	16	21

Armour Points	**Weapon Damage**
6 (cloth armour)	d6 + 2 (staff)

Save Proficiencies
Mind, Charisma

Skills
Magic Knowledge (Mind), Bluff (Charisma), Religion (Mind), Perception (Mind), Nature (Mind)

Class Features
Spellcasting, Magic Discipline

Talents
Magic Sensitivity, Mystical Intuition, Trained Caster, Wilderness Expert, Darksight

Spell Prepared
Bring Pestilence Upon your Foes, Restrain as if with Invisible Rope, Cause Limbs to Stop Moving

Equipment
Staff, cloth armour, poultices, scrying mirror

Languages
Common, Valetongue, Fey, Giant

THE PERILOUS
LAND BESTIARY

fter the Age of Doom, the land has come under threat by a great many monsters. In this chapter you will find a list of creatures and peoples that inhabit the Perilous Land, from mundane animals such as bears to fantastical creatures such as knuckers. While this book should provide a wide array of enemies for players to encounter on their heroic journeys across the Perilous Land, monsters have been designed in a way that make them easy to create on the fly, using a universal number to determine the majority of their stats.

HOW TO READ CREATURE STATS

Creatures in *Romance of the Perilous Land* are designed to be simple to reference and use in the game. They have two attributes that you should be aware of: hit dice (HD) and the target number (TN). The HD is the number of d6s that are rolled to determine the creature's hit points (HP), and the bonus it adds to its HP. Each creature includes their average HP in parenthesis. The higher the HD, the more challenging the enemy. Just like player characters, enemies have armour. The total HD will reveal the creature's armour points. These attributes are written out on the creature's stat block.

The TN is always equal to the creature's HD+10. The TN also determines the number of spell points a magic-wielding enemy has.

For example, an HD3 creature rolls 3d6+3 to determine its HP. Its TN is 13. It also has three armour points. If it were able to cast spells, it would have 13 spell points.

Creature stats also contain the names of the attacks it can use. Sometimes it will have more than one attack name, which means that it can attack multiple times on its turn. If this is the case, the creature can choose to attack more than one target with each. Each attack has a damage die and damage bonus assigned to it, which is written beneath the attack on the creature's stat block. Each attack is labelled as melee or ranged, with the distance it can attack targets at included with the latter. Damage dice and damage bonuses are assigned to creature HDs as follows:

HD	Damage Die
1	d4+1
2	d6+2
3	d6+3
4	d6+4
5	d8+5
6	d8+6
7	d8+7
8	d10+8
9	d10+9
10	d10+10

Creature stats list the number that are likely to appear in an encounter against the players. This is expressed as a range of number, with a minimum and maximum (i.e. 1–3) to offer the GM a guideline as to how many should be included in a given situation. Some creatures such as wolves hunt in packs while others, such as black dogs, are strictly solitary.

Creatures also have special features, which is a specific rule just for that creature. This could be a different kind of attack, or an effect that changes combat in some way.

USING TARGET NUMBERS FOR ATTRIBUTE CHECKS, SAVING THROWS AND CASTING SPELLS

If a creature needs to make an attribute check or a saving throw, they must roll equal to or under their TN, reducing the level of the opponent if the check is contested.

For example, an HD3 brigand with a TN of 13 needs to roll a saving throw. Their opponent is level 2 so the brigand must roll their new TN of 11.

Some creatures will already have spells prepared, which will be listed in their stats. To cast spells, creatures need to roll equal to or under their TN, reducing the TN by the level of the spell they are casting, as a player character would.

For example, a gnome with TN 12 is casting a level 3 spell. For the spell to work, it must roll a 9 or lower.

THE BESTIARY

ADDER

HD: 1   **TN:** 11
HP: 1d6+1 (4)
Armour Points: 1
Attack: Venomous bite (melee)
Damage: 1d4+1
Number Appearing: 1–6
Special: Adders can poison with their bite. If the adder causes damage, the target must make a successful Constitution saving throw. If they fail, they are poisoned and must take 1 HP damage at the beginning of each turn for 1d4 rounds. If the target is already poisoned, they cannot be poisoned a second time until the poison has worn off. Attacks with a weapon made of ash wood do an extra 1d6 damage against adders.

Adders are small snakes that generally grow up to between 60 and 75 cm in length. Their body carries distinctive zig-zag patterns, making it easily identifiable up close. These snakes inhabit the undergrowth on the edge of woodland and can often be found in the open countryside, preying on small rodents such as field mice and voles. They are not aggressive creatures, shying away from humans if they are disturbed, but if provoked they can deliver a nasty venomous bite.

In common lore, adders are portents of ill fortune, and therefore are greatly feared throughout the land, particularly in villages near forests and fields where they dwell. While they are seen as servants of evil, the shedded skin of an adder can be used for remedies to cure diseases. The dried skin of a fully-grown adder can be treated for one week and crushed into powder to be dissolved in a hot soup, giving a 3 in 6 chance that someone inflicted with a disease will be healed in 1d4 days.

Assassin

HD: 5 **TN:** 15
HP: 5d6+5 (22)
Armour Points: 5
Attack: Short sword (melee) or short bow (ranged, 80ft)
Damage: 1d8+5
Number Appearing: 1–6
Special: If the assassin has an edge against an opponent, a bonus 1d4 sneak attack damage is gained.

Assassins can be found in every major city in the Perilous Land, organised into guilds that offer their services to those wealthy enough to afford them. They dress in black, carrying lighter blades and bows, striking like lightning in the dark, or taking a more subtle approach to assassination such as a drop of poison in the target's drink. Assassins of The Ward are the most skilled and feared in the land, leaving the brand of a 'W' on those they have slain.

Banshee

HD: 5 **TN:** 15
HP: 5d6+5 (22)
Armour Points: 5
Attack: Claw (melee) or wail (ranged, 80ft radius)
Damage: 1d8+5 (claw)
Number Appearing: 1–4
Special: A banshee can make a wail attack, affecting 1d6 creatures in a 50ft radius. Those affected by the wail must succeed a Mind saving throw or make a full movement away from the banshee for the next 1d4 rounds. The banshee may only use a wail attack three times per combat.

Banshees are spectral beings of the restless dead who inhabit cairns and other grave sites. Their body is an eerie translucent blue, with long spindly fingers and near-skeletal features. Its face has two sunken eyes pierced with glowing green pupils while its mouth extends to inhuman proportions when it howls. During the hours of sunlight, banshees retreat into their graves until the sun sets and the stars begin to twinkle, which is when they emerge at full power.

Banshees often appear after a particularly traumatic death – with a larger number of the beings materialising when the deceased is a more notable member of the community, such as an aristocrat or monarch. They gather around the vicinity of the corpse for 2d6 days, attacking those who try to come near with their almighty wailing, sending people fleeing in terror.

BARBARIAN

HD: 3 **TN:** 13
HP: 3d6+3 (13)
Armour Points: 3
Attack: Axe (melee)
Damage: 1d6+3
Number Appearing: 1–10
Special: Once per combat a barbarian may go into a rage. For the next three rounds it gains a bonus 1d4 to damage inflicted.

When the land was old, barbarians were the rulers of the Perilous Land. Warrior tribes are feared by city-dwellers, who have conjured stories of cannibalistic giants wearing face paint. Despite this, barbarians form close-knit communities that look out for each other and know the importance of family and friendship. Barbarians are strong folk who often eschew armour, preferring to trust their natural strength and constitution than chainmail or plate. In battle they can be ferocious, flying into a frenzied blood rage as they hew through the enemy ranks.

BEAR

HD: 3 **TN:** 13
HP: 3d6+3 (13)
Armour Points: 3
Attack: Claw and bite (melee)
Damage: 1d6+3
Number Appearing: 1
Special: A bear is able to pin its target to the ground. After a successful claw attack, the target must make a Reflex saving throw. If they are unsuccessful, they are pinned to the ground and restrained. While pinning, the bear does not have to roll when making a bite attack – it just rolls damage.

Bears are large, powerful creatures that roam the woodlands and mountains. While bears tend to stay out of the way of people, running across one could end in a savage death. Corbenic has the highest population of bears in the Perilous Land, particularly around the foothills of the Mountains of Algaard where they tend to breed. Some barbarian tribes venerate bears, co-existing with them without too much trouble.

BLACK DOG

HD: 4 **TN:** 14
HP: 4d6+4 (18)
Armour Points: 4
Attack: Bite (melee)
Damage: 1d6+4
Number Appearing: 1
Special: Black dogs strike fear into the hearts of their enemies. Anyone attacking a black dog in melee must make a Mind saving throw. If they fail, they take a setback to the attack.

Black dog legends are rife around particularly rural parts of the Perilous Land. They are described as huge hounds, up to 6ft in length, with saucer-like eyes that glow like burning coals. They can be found in moorlands and on forgotten fields where few members of humanity dwell, but sometimes they venture into church graveyards to frighten the locals. Black dogs have many names depending on where they are found. These names include Black Shuck, Barghest, and Gytrash. It is a terrible omen to hear the baying of a black dog when out walking on the moors, for it is often linked with certain doom. The very sight of one of these terrible ghostly beasts is enough to drive one to madness through fear.

Some black dogs serve as familiars to evil cunning folk – a trend that is becoming more popular with those who follow The Black Lance. However, a rare few of these creatures are benevolent, helping guide travellers through dangerous terrain. It was reported that during The Great Search, Merlin was aided by a black dog, that led him and his men through a particularly dangerous swamp where all manner of fearsome beasts dwelt.

BLUECAP

HD: 1 **TN:** 10
HP: 1d6+1 (4)
Armour Points: 1
Attack: Bite (melee)
Damage: 1d4+1
Number Appearing: 1–2
Special: The bluecap's blue flame glows brightly when there is danger nearby.

Bluecaps are squat relatives of fairies who inhabit underground chambers and mines, leading miners to mineral deposits and warning them of cave-ins with their bright blue flame. It is rare for anyone to get close to a bluecap without it vanishing into the darkness, but if one was able they would find the creature to be entirely coloured blue, with tiny black polished eyes and mottled skin. Its fingers end in black claws and its legs are short with booted feet. Because of their helpfulness, miners leave offerings of milk and honey deep within the mines to appease their fairy guardians and ensure safe passage. Bluecaps are unlikely to attack people, being benevolent creatures of the Seelie Court, however if they feel threatened or are attacked they will use their sharp fangs to puncture and rend flesh.

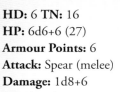

BODACH

HD: 6 **TN:** 16
HP: 6d6+6 (27)
Armour Points: 6
Attack: Spear (melee)
Damage: 1d8+6
Number Appearing: 1–6
Special: Once per combat a bodach can take on its shadow form for 1d6 rounds. While in shadow form, attacks against the bodach have a 2 in 6 chance of missing.

Bodachs are grotesque humanoid creatures that resemble terrible naked old men with wrinkled faces and bulbous yellow eyes. Their thorn-like teeth part to reveal a blackened lolling tongue that ends in a point, an appendage used for tasting its victim's hair before devouring them.

Bodachs are also known as 'shadow beings', creatures conjured from the magical darkness that surrounds the graves of dead cunning folk. Over decades the shadow becomes sentient and takes on the wretched form of the bodach, which is imbued with the dreadful traits of its dead master. Once awakened from shadow, bodachs softly creep into houses in the dead of night when all are slumbering, crawling down the chimney, and swiftly stealing away children from their beds before their parents know what has happened. They often leave behind the smell of rotten egg, which lingers for weeks in a child's bedroom.

Bodachs are known to be natural tricksters who love to make a bargain they never have any intention of keeping. Sir Gawain of the Round Table was once deceived by a bodach, who had stolen away a young prince. The bodach said that if Gawain left 100 gold pieces and a saucer of milk on the king's hearth and waited three days then the prince would be returned safely. After the knight did this he waited for the bodach to arrive, but he never came. Instead, the creature had told some local dark fairies that there was milk and gold to be found by the king's hearth, so the castle was overrun by the creatures. Gawain hunted the double-crossing bodach to its lair to find a pot of stew cooking and the creature licking its dry lips, the prince nowhere to be found.

Many consider bodachs to be omens of death – if one is seen in the vicinity of a town or village, people are known to stay indoors for upwards of a month for fear they will be struck down by a deadly ailment.

BOGIE

HD: 5 **TN:** 15
HP: 5d6+5 (22)
Armour Points: 5
Attack: Claws (melee)
Damage: 1d8+5
Number Appearing: 1–2
Special: Once per day for 2d6 hours, a bogie can disguise itself as an elderly human. If it is damaged by an attack while it's disguised it will revert to its true form. Anyone making a Mind check to see through the disguise rolls with a setback.

Bogies are a type of shapeshifting fairy whose true form resembles a humanoid with bright white glowing eyes, pointed ears and clothing made of oak leaves. They are agents of the Unseelie Court who like nothing more than tricking people before luring them into the dark Otherworld.

Bogies usually turn into elderly humans and ingratiate themselves into a community with their charming words and seemingly good-hearted actions. Over a series of months or even years they gain the trust of others before putting their murderous plans into motion, bringing humans into the Unseelie Court where they are trapped forever or devoured by its denizens. There are few ways to determine whether a kind older person is a bogie or not. The air around a disguised bogie grows noticeably colder, which is why they often operate during the winter months. There is also a smell of cinnamon when a bogie is close by, which is why many pretend to be bakers to explain the smell.

Bogies are weak against fire. If attacked with fire, magical or mundane, a bogie takes an extra 1d6 damage. Holding a flame close to a bogie will cause it to recoil in terror.

BOGGART

HD: 1 **TN:** 11
HP: 1d6+1 (4)
Armour Points: 1
Attack: Claws (melee)
Damage: 1d4+1
Number Appearing: 1–6
Special: Once per day as an action a boggart can make a check against its TN to turn near invisible for 1d3 rounds. Attacks against it have a setback while near invisible.

A boggart is a malevolent, mischievous creature that enjoys causing chaos among humankind by smashing crockery, souring milk, and stealing small farm stock such as chickens and piglets. They are small, ugly creatures that resemble small, dirty grey-skinned humans with pointed ears and green teeth. They are covered in matted grey hair and reek of rotten fish, which can be smelled from around 100ft away. Some boggarts are known for living in marshes, creeping out to kidnap babies and children before dragging them into their lairs where they hang them from the ceiling by ropes. Because of their ability to turn almost invisible, it can be hard to spot a boggart, but its tracks are distinctive claw prints.

If a boggart remains close to milk for more than an hour, the milk sours.

BONELESS

HD: 3 **TN:** 13
HP: 3d6+3 (13)
Armour Points: 3
Attack: Engulf (melee)
Damage: 1d6+3
Number Appearing: 1
Special: After a successful engulf attack, the target must make a Reflex saving throw or become engulfed in its fleshy body for 1d4 rounds. At the beginning of each round the target takes 1d4 damage from being crushed. While a target is engulfed they are restrained. The engulfed target may make a Might test and if successful they are no longer engulfed. While the boneless has a creature engulfed, it moves at half speed. The boneless can move 50ft.

The boneless is a disgusting fleshy jelly creature, about 3ft in height and about 7ft in length, that waits on pathways to chase down and engulf its victims. It is large and white with frog-like features and although it has no discernable limbs it can move at great speeds. Bonelesses are particularly prevalent when the weather is foggy and damp, as travellers often mistake their shape for a body on the road before rushing to investigate. Legend has it that a boneless used to be a greedy person, who, through their constant jealousy and avarice slowly turned into a large blob creature that seeks only to devour. This is a common story told to children throughout the Perilous Land to teach them a lesson about greed and possessiveness.

Witches sometimes use the smelly ichor the boneless sweats after feeding as an ingredient in their magical concoctions. Three drops of this potent liquid is enough to paralyse an adult human for 1d6 days.

BRIGAND

HD: 2 **TN:** 12
HP: 2d6+2 (9)
Armour Points: 2
Attack: Short sword (melee) or shortbow (ranged, 80ft)
Damage: 1d6+2
Number Appearing: 3–6
Special: Brigands gain an edge on Stealth checks when concealing themselves in natural terrain such as trees and bushes.

Brigands are outlaws who live by their own code. They often ambush parties on the road, extorting them and holding the more wealthy people hostage in hope of a ransom. Many brigands used to be soldiers who found that they could make profit from their skills through petty crime. While brigands rarely resort to murder, some are happy to kill if the situation becomes desperate. Wanderers in places where brigands operate should be aware of traps, such as leaf-covered pits, created to ensnare their victims before tying them up. They will always have a leader, usually the one who has shown the most strength out of the group.

The most infamous band of brigands in the Perilous Land operate in Eastland, calling themselves the Dead Dogs. This ruthless group of bandits are known for stringing their victims from trees to let the wolves find them – or worse.

BROWNIE

HD: 2 **TN:** 12
HP: 2d6+2 (9)
Armour Points: 2
Attack: Bite (melee)
Damage: 1d6+2
Number Appearing: 1–3
Special: If a brownie is gifted a treasure with a value of more than 50gp there is a 4 in 6 chance it will leave a location in peace and never return.

Brownies are small spirits, about 3ft in height, who attach themselves to families and reside in their household, usually against the family's wishes. They have dirty brown hair, often covered with a hood, and have a hole where their nose should be, giving them a rather frightening look. Their clothes are haphazardly stitched together using stolen material from different families, with their heads often adorned by a floppy red cap (though these should not be confused with redcaps, whose hats are stained in human blood). Brownies become more active around the harvest time, popping up in stables, kitchens, and pantries. Sometimes they will lend a helping hand by doing household chores such as sweeping the floor and darning socks, but they will expect a gift in return for their hardship.

They can be easily insulted and are prone to rage if they are criticised or pitied. Brownies can usually be kept from mischief with daily offerings of milk and porridge.

BUGGANE

HD: 6 **TN:** 16
HP: 6d6+6 (27)
Armour Points: 6
Attack: Claw/gore (melee)
Damage: 1d8+6
Number Appearing: 1–4
Special: Bugganes may take on human form for six hours per day. A successful Mind check will reveal the creature is a buggane.

The buggane is an ogre-like creature that stands 7ft tall, with a mane of filthy black hair, long yellowed claws and large tusks jutting from its lips. It is a ferocious but curious beast that likes to blend with human civilisation using its shapeshifting powers, although its human disguise still retains its shaggy black hair and long nails. If its true nature is discovered the buggane will launch into a murderous frenzy, using its immense strength to tear apart its victims. They are most often found in crumbling ruins, forests, or caves. Bugganes are unable to cross running water.

BUGBEAR

HD: 3 **TN:** 13
HP: 3d6+3 (13)
Armour Points: 3
Attack: Bite (melee)
Damage: 1d6+3
Number Appearing: 1–3
Special: A target that is damaged by a bugbear must make a successful Reflex saving throw or reduce their armour by an additional 2 points (if the target has any armour points remaining). This extra damage only affects armour.

Bugbears are large evil creatures who dwell in the depths of dark woods, usually in caves or makeshift tree shelters. They resemble black bears with the faces of pale wrinkled goblins. They are often served by smaller creatures like boggarts and redcaps, who help them track down their next meal. Despite looking like bears, bugbears have some intelligence and have been known to speak to humans in a rumbling voice. While the majority of bugbears tend towards the powers of darkness, a rare few are neither evil nor good. Some even say they have been saved by bugbears when they have been in need.

Their tales are told to keep children from wandering too deep into the forest, where these hideous hairy creatures will feast on their flesh. Their powerful metal-like claws are strong enough to rend armour.

CAT SIDHE

HD: 4 TN: 14
HP: 4d6+4 (18)
Armour Points: 4
Attack: Claw (melee)
Damage: 1d6+4
Number Appearing: 1
Special: A cat sidhe can transform into a witch as an action. They can only change eight times, turning into a cat forever on the ninth time.

A magical fairy cat often found in the highlands of Escose, a cat sidhe spends much of its time as a black cat the size of a dog, but occasionally transforms into a witch. They often dwell within caves on their own, enjoying the still silence. If their meditative state is broken by an intruder, they will pounce, using their claws to rip their victim apart, or if they are outmatched they will transform into a witch and use magic.

During the festival of Samhain a cat sidhe will bless a household that leaves a saucer of milk for it, but curse those that don't make an offering with cows whose udders can no longer provide milk.

COCKATRICE

HD: 7 TN: 17
HP: 7d6+7 (32)
Armour Points: 7
Attack: Peck (melee) or stone gaze (ranged, 60ft)
Damage: 1d10+7 (peck)
Number Appearing: 1
Special: The Cockatrice's gaze can turn its victims to stone. After the cockatrice

makes a successful stone gaze attackthe target of the attack must make a successful Mind saving throw or become paralysed. Once the cockatrice is dead, those who had become stone turn back to flesh.

The cockatrice has the head of a cockerel, the scaly body of a lizard and a dragon's tail. The beast stands 6ft tall and can turn a person to stone with just a look. Cockatrices are rare beings who live deep in the forest or occasionally in dark caves. They are able to see perfectly in the dark, which is how they prefer to hunt. There used to be many more cockatrices before the Age of Valour, but Arthur decreed them to be too dangerous to exist and had them hunted by his knights. The Sisters of Le Fay have been known to domesticate and use cockatrices as mounts. These witches, known as stonegaze riders, are blind, either by nature or having blindfolded themselves, so they won't accidentally be turned to stone. To make up for their lack of sight, they have spent years honing their other senses, so they gain no setbacks from combat.

CORPSE CANDLE

HD: 2 **TN:** 12
HP: 2d6+2 (9)
Armour Points: 2
Attack: Lure (ranged, 100ft)
Damage: None
Number Appearing: 1–4
Special: The corpse candle can make a lure attack against a target it can see. The target must succeed a Mind saving throw or fall under its spell for 1d6 rounds. While under a corpse candle's spell, the only action a target can make is to move towards the corpse candle. They must do this, even if moving towards the creature puts them in danger (i.e. falling over a ravine). The corpse candle may only make a lure attack three times per combat.

Corpse candles are portents of doom. They say that if you see one of these ethereal beings you are soon to take your last breath. These floating orbs of eerie light are often seen on dark roads, or in forgotten fields and dangerous marshlands, hovering in the air and dancing softly in the breeze. Corpse candles are able to lure their victims over the edge of cliffs, into lakes or straight into the jaws of a bigger beast. Because of this, evil monsters such as bugbears, redcaps, and eachies gather where corpse candles frequent, in the hope of using the corpse candles as bait.

CRONE

HD: 3 **TN:** 13
HP: 3d6+3 (13)
Armour Points: 3
Attack: Iron claws (melee) or terrifying visage (ranged, 40ft)
Damage: 1d6+3 (iron claws)
Number Appearing: 1–3
Spells Prepared: Witch Doll (x3), Have Vision in Dark Places
Special: A crone can create a terrifying visage. 1d4 targets within 40ft that she can see must make a successful Mind saving throw or become restrained for 1d4 rounds. A crone may do this up to three times per combat.

Crones are evil entities that live close to water, creeping out on dark nights to steal away victims from their beds. Their faces resemble impossibly old women with straggly grey hair and long, crooked noses. They walk with a hunch, shuffling quickly along at an alarming speed. Anyone who wanders too close to their lake dwellings are dragged in by their boney fingers where they meet their

watery fate. Those who try to escape have only to look on the crone's terrible countenance to be frozen on the spot, unable to move a muscle as the creature approaches.

CU SIDHE

HD: 4 **TN:** 14
HP: 4d6+4 (18)
Armour Points: 4
Attack: Bite (melee) or baying (ranged, 50ft)
Damage: 1d6+4 (bite)
Number Appearing: 1
Special: As an attack, the cu sidhe may let out a loud baying. If it is successful, 1d4 targets within 50ft must succeed a Mind saving throw or recieve a setback to attacks for 1d4 rounds. The cu sidhe can only make a baying attack three times per day.

The cu sidhe is a large fairy dog, roughly the size of a young bull, that leaves massive paw prints in the hills near fairy mounds. It has a mossy green coat and large, dark, solemn eyes. Being the guardian of the gateway between the Perilous Land and the Otherworld, it will attack anyone attempting to trespass into the fairy realm with its huge jaws. It is said that the creature lets out three mighty bays and on the third anyone who can hear them must get to safety or be hunted down and viciously attacked by the fairy dog.

The cu sidhe will allow entry to the Otherworld if the one who wishes to pass between worlds has an invitation from the Fairy Queen, or they can prove that they wish no harm on the fairy race. Offerings of enchanted items usually help with this.

DRAGONS

Dragons are among the most enigmatic and feared beings in all of the Perilous Land. There are several types of dragon that haunt the countryside of kingdoms, from the biting north to the warm climes of the southern realms. Dragons are huge lizards with massive wingspans and yellow serpent-like eyes. They make their lairs in mountains, swamps, and even underground, emerging to feed on livestock and humans. In their lairs they hoard vast amounts of riches, taking gifts of gold and jewels from local settlements in exchange for their safety.

DRAGON, GOLDEN

HD: 7 **TN:** 17
HP: 7d6+7 (32)
Armour Points: 7
Attack: Bite/bite (melee) or poison breath (ranged, 40ft)
Damage: 1d8+7
Number Appearing: 1
Special: A golden dragon breathes poison in a 40ft line, ignoring obscuring cover. Those damaged by the poison breath must succeed a Constitution saving throw or become poisoned, suffering 1d6 damage at the start of every turn for 1d6+1 rounds. The golden dragon is only able to use poison breath three times per combat. The golden dragon is able to fly as its movement.

Golden dragons are the most regal of the dragon family, with shimmering golden scales and bronze spines running down their massive bodies. Golden dragons are not as ferocious as other dragons, usually keeping to themselves unless their lair is being trespassed. They are able to breath a noxious poisonous cloud that can kill in an instant – deadly when confined to underground chambers where they most often reside.

DRAGON, RED

HD: 9 **TN:** 19
HP: 9d6+9 (40)
Armour Points: 9
Attack: Bite/bite/claw (melee) or fire breath (ranged, 50ft)
Damage: 1d10+9 (bite and claw)
Number Appearing: 1
Special: A red dragon breathes fire in a 50ft line. Anyone caught in the fire breath must succeed a Reflex saving throw or take 6d6+9 damage. If the save is successful, the damage is halved. The red dragon may only use fire breath three times per combat. The red dragon is able to fly as its movement.

The red dragon is the most common type of dragon, with glands in its mouth that allow it to breath jets of fire hot enough to melt steel. They are most often found deep in mountain caves and grow the largest out of all the dragon species in the Perilous Land — measuring 30ft in length.

DRAGON, WHITE

HD: 8 **TN:** 18
HP: 8d6+8 (36)
Armour Points: 8
Attack: Bite/bite (melee) or ice breath (ranged, 40ft)
Damage: 1d10+8
Number Appearing: 1
Special: A white dragon breathes ice in a 40ft line. Creatures damaged by the ice breath must succeed a Reflex saving throw or become frozen in place for 1d6 rounds. The white dragon may only use ice breath three times per combat. The white dragon is able to fly as its movement.

The white dragon is a cousin of the larger red dragon. Rather than breathe fire, the white dragon breathes a freezing cold mist that freezes those it comes into contact with, making it every bit as deadly as the red dragon. White dragons prefer to make their lairs on the top of snowy mountains or by the side of cool lakes.

A white dragon was discovered beneath the foundations of Camelot's castle after it was first built. Realising that the castle walls would continue to crumble as long as the dragon remained beneath it, Merlin conjured the illusion of a red dragon, which the white dragon chased for days until it was weak and fell back into its pit and fell into an eternal sleep. The pit was filled in and the castle walls were rebuilt. After that, the white dragon became the enduring symbol of Camelot.

DRAKE

HD: 6 **TN:** 16
HP: 6d6+6 (27)
Armour Points: 6
Attack: Bite (melee)
Damage: 1d8+6
Number Appearing: 1–3
Special: At the beginning of the drake's turn, it regenerates 1d4 HP.

Drakes are the smallest members of the dragon family, measuring up to 10ft in length, and are unable to fly or use a breath weapon. However, they do have the ability to heal their wounds while in combat, making them a tough opponent even for the hardiest of warriors. Drakes are known to attack merchants as they travel between towns, and many are blamed for sheep and cattle being devoured.

DRUID

HD: 4 **TN:** 14
HP: 4d6+4 (18)
Armour Points: 4
Attack: Staff (melee)
Damage: 1d6+4
Number Appearing: 1–20
Spells Prepared: Rid the Pitiful of Disease, Cloak Oneself in Darkness, Find Safe Sustenance in the Wild
Special: Druids can bless a creature within 10ft with the grace of their patron god as an action. The creature gains an edge on saving throws for the next round. They may only do this three times per combat.

The word druid means 'knowing the oak tree'. Druids are people who worship at the altar of nature, praying in forest groves and forbidding themselves for writing any of their beliefs. They are wielders of magic, drawing energy from the roots, bark, and leaves around them. Druids act as counsel to many of the leaders of the Perilous Land, giving sage advice in times of great need.

Druids wear robes of natural greens and browns and cover their faces in tattoos that tell the story of the gods. Their homes are small hovels built from mud, clay, wood, and leaves, adorned with charms dedicated to the gods. The high priest –'the anointed one' – is said to have direct access to the gods and is able to converse with them after hours of meditation by the great fire. The high priest is revered by his or her people, taking many husbands and brides through their impossibly long lives. Servants of kingdoms far and wide will travel great distances to receive counsel from a high priest, whose word on any matter is final.

DUERGAR

HD: 3 **TN:** 13
HP: 3d6+3 (13)
Armour Points: 3
Attack: Axe (melee)
Damage: 1d6+3
Number Appearing: 1–10
Special: Duergar automatically render themselves near invisible when in shadows. Anyone attempting to attack the creature when in this state must make a Mind saving throw to harm it. If it is unsuccessful, there is a 3 in 6 chance the attack will miss. If a Duergar is exposed to natural sunlight it may be killed if it takes at least 1 HP of damage.

Duergar are grey and ugly wild dwarves found across the Perilous Land. They wear lambskin and smell of ammonia. They carry copper lanterns with them in order to lead travellers astray in the dark, causing them to mis-step and often drown in a bog or stumble into a ravine.

Duergar are malevolent beings that disappear before the dawn. They secret themselves away in dirt warrens and lay still until the night comes. Should one be unearthed during the daylight they are entirely vulnerable and can be killed with a swift blow.

DUN COW

HD: 3 **TN:** 13
HP: 3d6+3 (13)
Armour Points: 3
Attack: Trample (melee)
Damage: 1d6+3
Number Appearing: 1
Special: A target damaged by a trample attack must succeed a Reflex saving throw or become prone.

Dun cows are massive cows the size of houses who graze in rolling fields, often found in more southerly kingdoms. Their hides and ribs are prized by hunters, but battling against one of these monsters can prove tough as their mighty hooves are used to trample assailants into the ground.

EACHY

HD: 7 **TN:** 17
HP: 7d6+7 (32)
Armour Points: 7
Attack: Choke (melee) or bite (melee)
Damage: 1d10+7
Number Appearing: 1–4
Special: When an eachy does damage with a choke attack, the target must make a Might saving throw or become restrained for one round.

An eachy is a slimy, mossy humanoid creature that lurks in the depths of lakes. They have large powerful arms that are used to strangle their victims to death. Its head resembles that of a python, with yellow eyes and two sharp fangs. Eachies can lay in wait for their prey for days, not needing to breathe underwater. Local people sometimes refer to them as snake people and ward their villages with all manner of charms to prevent them from entering. However, there are others who venerate the eachy, believing them to be the spawn of gods. The Cult of the Snake formed around this belief, with its practitioners dressing in moss and dancing by the waters where the creatures dwell. At the beginning of each harvest someone from the cult is chosen as a sacrifice and is thrown into the waters where the eachy inevitably drags them under.

ELF

HD: 2 **TN:** 12
HP: 2d6+2 (9)
Armour Points: 2
Attack: Staff (melee) or longbow (ranged, 150ft)
Damage: 1d6+2
Spells Prepared: Replenish the Battered and Bruised (x2), Dazzle with Glittering Lights (x2), Good Luck Charm (x2)
Number Appearing: 2–10
Special: Elves are not affected by difficult terrain in a forested area.

Elves are short creatures, standing around 4ft tall, who are close relatives of the fairy. While male elves resemble small old men, the females are beautiful, angelic beings. They live in meadows and forests and can be found near magical places such as standing stones and fairy circles. While elves are generally friendly, if they are crossed they will seek ruthless vengeance, from stealing babies to outright murder. Because of their innate magical abilities, elves have been targeted for recruitment by the Sisters of Le Fay, who now rank many elves among their numbers. These have become known as night elves, for they have turned away from the light towards the powers of darkness.

ETTIN

HD: 5 **TN:** 15
HP: 5d6+5 (22)
Armour Points: 5
Attack: Stone hammer (melee)
Damage: 1d8+5
Number Appearing: 1–3
Special: When an ettin hits with a stone hammer attack, the target must make a successful Reflex saving throw or become paralysed for the next five rounds.

The ettin is a hulking giant with three ferocious heads – each with its own

personality (which can often lead to internal conflicts). It carries a hammer that, when it strikes its victim, turns them to stone. They often build forts close to civilisation and demand a tax from local landowners or, in some circumstances, a sacrifice. This has led to some villages local to an ettin fort to perform an annual selection to offer as a tribute to the creature. Should they not do so, the ettin will wreak havoc on the village.

FACHAN

HD: 5 **TN:** 15
HP: 5d6+5 (22)
Armour Points: 5
Attack: Kick (melee) or eye blast (ranged, 60ft)
Damage: 1d8+5
Number Appearing: 3–5
Special: When a target is damaged by an eye blast attack, they must succeed a Reflex saving throw or become blinded for one round.

Fachans are bizarre beings with a single leg, a single arm, and a solitary eye. These creatures are thought to be cast-off experiments of evil enchanters and have the ability to blind their victims with a bright light emanating from their eye. Fachans can be found in lonely and desolate places, such as crumbling towers and old ruins, particularly where cunning folk reside. While they cannot speak, they can emit a horrible screeching sound that pierces the soul, a sound usually heard before the fachan attacks.

FAIRIES

Fairies number among the most magical beings in the Perilous Land and are found throughout the continent. These small humanoid creatures have butterfly-like wings that grow back if removed and their skin glows white, making them easy to spot in the dark. Fairies are denizens of the Otherworld, a parallel dimension of fairy kingdoms. While there are multiple types of fairy, they can be split into two groups: the fairies of the Seelie Court and the fairies of the Unseelie Court.

The Seelie Court, also known as The Summer Court, is a race of light fairies who use their powers to bring good into the world, although they are not above playing mischievous pranks on humans. The Seelie Court is governed by the fair Queen Una, most powerful of fairies. The Unseelie Court, or The Winter Court, is a place of darkness, where dark fairies, boggarts, and bogles dwell. Unlike the fairies of the

Seelie Court, these creatures are malevolent and often violent, taking great joy in assaulting travellers at night, slaying cattle, and causing chaos in homesteads. The Unseelie Court is overseen by the dark Queen Mab – sister of Una.

There are various ways to access the Otherworld, the most common being through a fairy mound, a natural circular structure that becomes a portal to the Otherworld at certain times of the month – most often at night. Some fairies also use the magic of standing stones to transport themselves home.

FAIRY, SOLITARY

HD: 4 **TN:** 14
HP: 4d6+4 (18)
Armour Points: 4
Attack: Fairy sword (melee)
Damage: 1d6+4
Spells Prepared: Cause the Alert to Slumber (x2)
Number Appearing: 1
Special: Solitary fairies are able to fly.

Solitary fairies are the most malicious and feral of the fairy race. They often invade households to smash crockery and even set fire to the home. These nasty creatures can be a particular problem to homesteads located near forests or standing stones, where gateways to the Otherworld are more likely to exist. If the solitary fairy is outmatched, it will attempt to talk its way out of a fight, using lies and tricks as a means of self-preservation.

FAIRY, TROOPING

HD: 2 **TN:** 12
HP: 2d6+2 (9)
Armour Points: 2
Attack: Fairy mace (melee) or fairy bow (ranged, 60ft)
Damage: 1d6+2
Spells Prepared: Dazzle with Glittering Lights (x3)
Number Appearing: 3–6
Special: Trooping fairies are able to fly. Ranged attacks against a trooping fairy take a setback.

Trooping fairies are the aristocrats of fairy realm, holding high-ranking positions in both Seelie and Unseelie Courts. They usually travel in processions, using their numbers to overwhelm opponents. Their clothing is made of silk and gold, woven together from the silk of rare worms found in the Otherworld. Trooping fairies are often courteous and well-mannered, no matter which court they come from. Their words can be convincing, but when words fail they are not afraid to start a fight.

FAIRY, QUEEN MAB

HD: 7 **TN:** 17
HP: 7d6+7 (32)
Armour Points: 7
Attack: Fairy spear (melee)
Damage: 1d8+7
Spells Prepared: Create an Illusion to Vex the Eyes, Cause the Feeling of Doom in Another, Create a Wild Gust of Wind
Number Appearing: 1 (unique creature)
Special: Queen Mab is able to become human-sized at will. While in fairy form she is able to fly.

Queen Mab is ruler of the Unseelie Court, a powerful magic-user with pale skin and twisted black horns protruding from her forehead. She can grow to the size of a human to walk among humankind, her horns retracting back into her head to complete the disguise. Morgan Le Fay herself has been meeting Queen Mab on moonless nights to persuade her to join her fight against King Arthur, though Mab has not been given an offer good enough to take her up on this yet.

FAIRY, QUEEN UNA

HD: 8 **TN:** 18
HP: 8d6+8 (36)
Armour Points: 8
Attack: Fairy sword (melee)
Damage: 1d10+8
Spells Prepared: Control the Mind of a Beast, Bless the Mortally Wounded, Create an Illusion to Vex the Eyes
Number Appearing: 1 (unique creature)
Special: Queen Una is able to become human-sized at will. While in fairy form she is able to fly.

Queen Una reigns over the Seelie Court and is well-loved by her fairy subjects. She is known as the most beautiful creature to set foot in the mortal world. Many who see her fall in love in an instant, following her to the Otherworld where they spend their lifetime in servitude to their new queen. Una is able to grow into a full-size human, although even when disguised her skin emits a fairy glow. Una is a kind soul, but has a great wrath if she is crossed. During The Great Search, Merlin visited the Otherworld to gain Una as an ally to Camelot, but the queen has refused until Arthur deems himself worthy of her help.

FINFOLK

HD: 5 **TN:** 15
HP: 5d6+5 (22)
Armour Points: 5
Attack: Fishing spear (melee)
Damage: 1d8+5
Number Appearing: 1–10
Special: Finfolk can shapeshift to look like fishermen and fisherwomen at will. A successful Mind check will reveal the true nature of the creature.

Finfolk are humanoid fish people with large bulbous eyes and dour faces who live in cold waters to the north and north east of the Perilous Land where they hunt fishermen with their long, serrated spears. As shapeshifters, they can alter their appearance to resemble a fisherman who has fallen overboard. When the unassuming sailors rescue the creature it proceeds to kill them or drag them into the depths to its family waiting below. Finfolk are territorial creatures and will attack if a vessel strays into their waters.

GARGOYLE

HD: 3 **TN:** 13
HP: 3d6+3 (13)
Armour Points: 3
Attack: Claw (melee)
Damage: 1d6+3
Number Appearing: 1–6
Special: Gargoyles are able to fly. As an action, once per combat a gargoyle may regenerate 1d10 HP.

Gargoyles were originally created as ornamental aspects of masonry, carved on the sides of castles and forts. However, during the Age of Doom a group of enchanters brought many of these gargoyles to life as grotesque winged servants. They are

slightly smaller than the average human, with large bat-like wings and sharp protruding incisors. Their stone skin is able to magically regenerate over time.

GHOST

HD: 5 **TN:** 15
HP: 5d6+5 (22)
Armour Points: 5
Attack: Cold touch (melee)
Damage: 1d8+5
Number Appearing: 1–10
Special: Mortal weapons do half damage to ghosts (rounded down), while attacks from spells or magic weapons do an extra 1d6 damage.

Ghosts are the incorporeal remnants of the dead – a restless spirit whose work on earth is not yet done. Particularly violent ghosts are known as poltergeists. Ghosts can appear anywhere, but most often appear in graveyards, ruins, and old forests.

GIANT

HD: 6 **TN:** 16
HP: 6d6+6 (27)
Armour Points: 6
Attack: Club/slam (melee)
Damage: 1d8+6
Number Appearing: 3–8
Special: Giants are able to smell magic from up to 200ft away, including magic items or spell casters.

Giants are well known for terrorising villages and stealing livestock to eat. While many used to exist, wars were waged against these great creatures and they are now fewer in number, though they are still a force to be reckoned with.

GNOME

HD: 2 **TN:** 12
HP: 2d6+2 (9)
Armour Points: 2
Attack: Claws (melee) or sling (ranged)
Damage: 1d6+2
Spells Prepared: Change the Mundane into Treasure (x3), The Voice of a Hound (x2)
Number Appearing: 5–20
Special: Gnomes may reroll a failed attack once per combat.

Gnomes are defenders of gold, often kept deep within the ground where they live. They have huge underground networks of gnome villages that have never been seen by mortal eyes. As intrinsically magical beings, gnomes are able to travel to the Otherworld to attend the Seelie (and Unseelie) Court. As a result, gnomes will often be found wherever fairies dwell.

GOGMAGOG

HD: 9 **TN:** 19
HP: 9d6+9 (40)
Armour Points: 9
Attack: Club/slam/slam (melee)
Damage: 1d12+9
Number Appearing: 1 (unique creature)
Special: If Gogmagog deals damage with all attacks, the target falls prone and is restrained for 1d4 rounds. Gogmagog is able to smell magic from up to 400ft away, including magic items or spell casters.

Gogmagog is the oldest and largest of the giants, a 20ft tall lumbering behemoth who wields a tree trunk as a club. He lives inside the earth with his daughters, who venture out to bring him his food in the form of cattle and humans. While Gogmagog usually keeps himself holed up in the ground, nearby magical events such as spellcasting or someone using a magical weapon is enough to stir him to rise to the surface. There are some who believe that Gogmagog was the first being in the Perilous Land and he will also be the last after finally destroying all of civilisation. There are even small sects who worship the giant in the hopes that he will once again reclaim the land as his own.

GREEN KNIGHT

HD: 8 **TN:** 18
HP: 8d6+8 (36)
Armour Points: 8
Attack: Axe/axe (melee)
Damage: 1d10+8
Spells Prepared: Restrain as if with Invisible Rope (x3)
Number Appearing: 1 (unique creature)
Special: For every round the Green Knight survives, his damage is increased by +1 up to a maximum of +8.

The Green Knight is a headless enigmatic magical being who is covered in the colour green, including his skin. He rides a phantom steed and carries a great battleaxe with him. The more he fights, the stronger he becomes and few live to tell the tale. Some say that he has come from the underworld to haunt the living, killing mortals and taking their souls. Others say that he has been cursed by a witch to roam the plains, unable to pass on into the next life. Either way, stories of the Green Knight are prevalent all around the Perilous Land.

GREEN MAN

HD: 7 **TN:** 17
HP: 7d6+7 (32)
Armour Points: 7
Attack: Claw/claw (melee) or strangle vines (special)
Damage: 1d8+7
Spells Prepared: Control the Mind of a Beast (x2), Replenish the Fractured and Wounded
Number Appearing: 1 (unique creature)
Special: The Green Man can cause vines to erupt from the earth and strangle its enemies. This affects one target within 60ft. If the attack is successful, the target must succeed Reflex saving throw or take an additional 1d6 damage and become strangled. The target cannot take any actions on its turn, but may roll a Reflex saving throw at the end of each turn to attempt to break free of the vines. While the target is being strangled, the Green Man does an automatic 1d6 damage to the target. The Green Man may only use strange vines three times per combat.

The Green Man is the custodian of nature and the embodiment of the Scarlet Forest in Lyonesse. It is a large humanoid creature made of vines, bark, and leaves, standing 11ft tall. It likes to stroll through the forest, helping the plants grow and healing sick flora and fauna. It acts as guardian of its realm, wrapping vines around trespassers with ill intent and strangling them to death. Throughout the world the Green Man has become a widespread symbol of nature and many worship him as a god, though he is not officially a deity.

GRIFFIN

HD: 3 TN: 13
HP: 3d6+3 (13)
Armour Points: 3
Attack: Peck (melee)
Damage: 1d6+3
Number Appearing: 1–4
Special: Griffins are able to fly.

Griffins are hybrid beings with the body of a lion and the head and wings of an eagle. They are larger than an adult stallion with massive talons used to rend flesh. They most often nest in deep forests (golden griffins) and high in the mountains (grey griffins) away from human civilisations. Some humans have attempted to tame the beasts in order to turn them into methods of transportation, but very few have been able to do so. Griffins often appear on heraldic coats of arms as representations of courage and heroism.

GUARD, CITY

HD: 2 TN: 12
HP: 2d6+2 (9)
Armour Points: 2
Attack: Short sword (melee) or shortbow (ranged, 80ft)
Damage: 1d6+2
Number Appearing: 2–20
Special: None

The typical city guard wears leather armour and carries a sword or bow. They are often found patrolling the streets in search of those who dare to break the law, or are posted on city gates or walls. They are generally trained to a low standard.

GUARD, ROYAL

HD: 4 TN: 14
HP: 4d6+4 (18)
Armour Points: 4
Attack: Spear (melee) or longbow (ranged, 150ft)
Damage: 1d6+4
Number Appearing: 2–10
Special: Once per combat a royal guard may spend an action to replenish all their armour points.

Royal guards are in charge of security around the royal palace, joining the monarch as part of their royal detail when they travel. They wear sturdier armour than regular city guards and gain more respect from the public.

HAGS

Hags are found in lonely places throughout the Perilous Land. They are spirits in the guise of wretched old women with long, crooked noses, and yellowed fingernails, often found draped in tattered cloaks. They are creatures of evil intent who delight in the misery of others, whether it's causing their ships to capsize using their elemental powers or materialising in the dark corner of a child's room before snatching them away into the mist. What's more, hags are powerful opponents and care not for morality – they know only evil. Even the Sisters of Le Fay stay away from locations where hags are found, knowing the power they wield. There are several types of hags, but all of them live for centuries, growing more gnarled as the years go by.

HAG, MIST

HD: 7 TN: 17
HP: 7d6 (24)
Armour Points: 7
Attack: Claw/claw (melee) or fog (ranged, 60ft)
Damage: 1d8+7 (claw)
Spells Prepared: Cloak Oneself in Darkness (x2), Create a Wild Gust of Wind (x2)
Number Appearing: 1
Special: The mist hag can create a 30ft x 30ftft area of fog within 60ft of her. The fog blocks line of sight and acts as darkness for anyone inside the area of fog or attacking

into the area of fog from outside. The mis hag may only use fog twice per combat.

Mist hags walk lonely moors groaning monstrously – a sound that sends shivers down the spines of those who hear it. They have the dark appearance of a spectral wraith, floating over the ground and obscured by mist. When a fog rolls into a village near the hag's hunting grounds, villagers ensure their doors and windows are bolted as they wait silently for the creature to pass through.

HAG, RIVER

HD: 8 **TN:** 18
HP: 8d6+8 (32)
Armour Points: 8
Attack: Claw/strangle (melee)
Damage: 1d10+8 (claw/strangle)
Spells Prepared: Protection from Elements, Subdue the Wicked, Witch Doll
Number Appearing: 1
Special: River hags are able to shapeshift into a desirable woman once per day for 1d4 hours.

River hags are the most numerous type of hag, found close to bodies of waters like lakes and rivers. Their skin is green and their hair is seaweed, perfect for camouflaging against a river bank. They have the power to change their visage into a younger, more beautiful woman in order to charm people into coming with her to the water's edge, where they reveal their true guise before dragging them in.

HAG, STORM

HD: 8 **TN:** 18
HP: 8d6+8 (32)
Armour Points: 8
Attack: Claw/claw (melee) or lightning strike (ranged, 50ft)
Damage: 1d10+8
Spells Prepared: Witch Doll (x2), Protection from Elements, Cause Limbs to Stop Moving
Number Appearing: 1
Special: Storm hags can call upon lightning from the tips of their fingers, shooting a 50ft line of electricity at a target. If the attack is successful, the target must succeed a Constitution save or become paralysed for 1d4 rounds. The storm hag may only use lighting strike three times per combat.

Along the battered cliffs of Escose fishermen live in fear of the storm hag, a witch who can control the weather to create violent storms with booming thunder and destructive lightning. Many a time boats have capsized as a result of an angry storm hag's magic. They live in caves near the sea, often in cold, hard to reach places where they decorate their lairs with the bones of dead sailors.

HAWK

HD: 1 **TN:** 11
HP: 1d6+1 (4)
Armour Points: 1
Attack: Claw (melee)
Damage: 1d4+1
Number Appearing: 1–3
Special: Hawks can fly.

Hawks are common birds of prey found across the realms. They have hooked beaks used to tear the flesh of their prey and sharp talons to grip them in flight. Hawks are often trained to be used as hunting birds.

HERNE THE HUNTER

HD: 9 **TN:** 19
HP: 9d6+9 (40)
Armour Points: 9
Attack: Chain/chain/chain (melee) or longbow/longbow (ranged, 150ft)
Damage: 1d10+9
Number Appearing: 1 (unique creature)
Special: Herne can blow his horn as an action. Anyone within 100ft must make a Mind saving throw or become restrained. They may make a Mind save at the end of their turn to see if the effect wears off. Herne may only use his horn twice per combat.

Herne the Hunter is a malevolent spirit who wears stag antlers on his head and rides a ghostly mare. The rattle of chains can be heard as he approaches, his eyes burn like hot coals. When he blows his horn a nightmarish wail echoes through the air, terrifying all who hear it.

Incubus

HD: 5 **TN:** 15
HP: 5d6+5 (22)
Armour Points: 5
Attack: Claw (melee) or charm
Damage: 1d8+5 (claw)
Spells Prepared: Cause the Alert to Slumber (x3)
Number Appearing: 1–4
Special: An Incubus may use a charm attack on a target within 40ft. If successful, the target must succeed a Charisma saving throw or fall under the Incubus' control. While under their control, the Incubus may use the target's actions as if they were its own. The target may make a Charisma saving throw at the end of each of her turns to break the charm. The Incubus cannot attempt to charm a target that it has previously charmed that day.

An incubus is an evil spirit that magically charms both men and women to fall in love with it. While under its spell, the incubus controls their minds. If an incubus impregnates a woman, she will die after giving birth, the baby of which will be a young incubus. An incubus cannot stand the light of day, so will only be seen during the night. During daylight hours they retreat into the dark caverns of the world where they slumber.

Kelpie

HD: 4 **TN:** 14
HP: 4d6+4 (18)
Armour Points: 4
Attack: Trample (melee) or drown (special)
Damage: 1d6+4
Number Appearing: 1–2
Special: One target within the kelpie's line of sight must make a successful Charisma saving throw or be forced to mount it. Upon mounting, the kelpie will move to the nearest body of water. Every round a mounted target fails a save, they take 1d6 drowning damage. The kelpie may only use drown twice per combat.

Kelpies are horse spirits that appear close to rivers or large bodies of water, often hiding themselves amongst other horses. Using magical charms, they make themselves seem irresistible for riders, who are lured into mounting them. But once their victim is in place, the kelpie then rides into the water in order to drown the rider, re-emerging to trick another poor soul.

KING OF CATS

HD: 3 **TN:** 13
HP: 3d6+3 (13)
Armour Points: 3
Attack: Claw (melee)
Damage: 1d6+3
Number Appearing: 1 (unique creature)
Special: The King of Cats can speak all languages.

    The King of Cats is an enchanted black cat who leads a great procession of cats through the country, often speaking of ill omens to befall human settlements. He is not a malicious being, but nor does he wish to serve humankind. He occasionally visits witches to speak of portents of the future. Mordred wishes to use the knowledge the King of Cats possesses for his own gain.

KNIGHT

HD: 4 **TN:** 14
HP: 4d6+4 (18)
Armour Points: 4
Attack: Longsword (melee) or short bow (ranged)
Damage: 1d8+4
Number Appearing: 2–6
Special: A knight can choose to take any non-magical damage inflicted on another creature within 5ft creature.

    Knights are skilled warriors who can be found in nearly every kingdom of the Perilous Land. Most knights obey a code of chivalry and honour, such as the Knights of the Round Table, but there are also knights who are devious, cunning and backstabbing, such as Mordred's knights of The Black Lance. Knights are often clad in heavy armour and are well-practised with a wide array of weapons, from daggers to claymores.

KNUCKER

HD: 7 **TN:** 17
HP: 7d6+7 (32)
Armour Points: 7
Attack: Bite/tail whip (melee)
Damage: 1d8+7
Number Appearing: 1
Special: After damaging a target with its tail whip attack, the target must succeed a Reflex saving throw or be knocked prone.

The knucker is a distant relative of the dragon family, often inhabiting lakes – or 'knucker holes' – for hundreds of years, sneaking out to devour livestock and frighten farmers. Occasionally they will drag humans down into their murky lairs where they will feed on their flesh and bones. Knuckers grow between 15ft and 30ft in length and are often mistaken for dragons, despite their lack of wings. They are ferocious monsters who use their tail to whip their victims, shattering bone and causing them to go limp before devouring them with their massive maw.

LAVELLAN

HD: 2 **TN:** 12
HP: 2d6+2 (9)
Armour Points: 2
Attack: Bite (melee)
Damage: 1d6+2
Number Appearing: 1–5
Special: The lavellan has a venomous bite. If a target is damaged by a bite attack, they must succeed a Constitution saving throw or take 1d4 extra venom damage.

A lavellan is a large ferocious rodent that makes its nest in waterways, near lakes and in city sewers. Their bite is highly venomous, but their skin is prized for being able to cure a variety of ailments. Cities often employ pest catchers to hunt levellan who are found nesting beneath the streets. These "Lavvies", as they are jokingly referred to as, are usually the poorest members of society who are seen as expendable.

LEANASHE

HD: 6 **TN:** 16
HP: 6d6+6 (34)
Armour Points: 6
Attack: Claw (melee)
Damage: 1d8+6
Number Appearing: 1–4
Special: If the leanashe damages a target with its bite attack, the target's next attack is made with a setback.

The leanshe is a vampiric spirit that haunts barrows and is mainly found in Norhaut and Camelot. They are spirit beings of the restless dead who rise from their graves to drain the life force from the living. Their face resembles a skull, with bright shining green eyes and a shock of blue hair that erupts in flame when it devours its victim.

LUBBER FIEND

HD: 4 **TN:** 14
HP: 4d6+4 (18)
Armour Points: 4
Attack: Slam (melee)
Damage: 1d8+4
Number Appearing: 1–3
Special: The lubber fiend regenerates 2d6 HP after drinking a saucer of milk.

Lubber fiends are household spirits in the same family as brownies. They resemble large hairy men, around 7ft tall, with lizard-like tails and large circular yellow eyes. While they are muscular and can do damage if they want, lubber fiends are actually helpful beings who like to help around the house in exchange for a saucer of warm milk left in front of a roaring fire every night. If this offering is not left they can be quite mischievous, pulling pranks on the owners of the house until their get their milk. Some lubber fiends have taken a darker turn, having worked within the Unseelie Court. These creatures will seek to harm people while they sleep at night.

MERFOLK

HD: 3 **TN:** 13
HP: 3d6+3 (13)
Armour Points: 3
Attack: Claw (melee) and lure (special)
Damage: 1d6+3 (claw)
Number Appearing: 1–10
Special: When a merfolk uses its lure attack, all creatures within 50ft must succeed a Mind saving throw or move 30ft towards the merfolk. The merfolk may only use its lure attack twice per combat.

Merfolk are water-dwelling creatures with the upper body of an attractive human and the lower body of a large fish with glistening scales of many colours. Merfolk can be found close to the shore where they unwittingly lure sailors onto the rocks with their beauty and dream-like voices. Most are peaceful beings who are curious about the world on the land and there have been times when mortal and merfolk have fallen in love, thought this union has always ended in disaster. They build great underwater cities on the seabed or at the bottom of deep lakes. Should one discover an injured merfolk washed up on the shore, they will be rewarded with grand treasures for healing them. There does exist a more malicious form of merfolk called a merrow, who trap people in lobster pots beneath the ocean as a warning to other fishermen not to venture into their watery realm.

NUCKELAVEE

HD: 8 **TN:** 18
HP: 8d6+8 (36)
Armour Points: 8
Attack: Spear/spear (melee)
Damage: 1d10+8
Number Appearing: 1–3
Special: A nuckelavee can make a melee attack up to 15ft away from its target.

Nuckelavee are hideous-looking creatures that resemble a skinless man fused with a demonic horse, their eyes burning like coals. The creature has abnormally long arms in which it carries a black spear covered in the flesh of its victims. Its very breath is able to rot crops and farmers blame long spells of drought on the presence of a nuckelavee. Because of the many superstitions that have arisen about of these creatures, people who live in coastal regions where nuckelavee are more prominent never say the name without uttering a prayer to their gods. Farmers have awoken to find their fields filled with the corpses of livestock, the nuckelavee standing over the grisly scene with a grin on its face.

OGRE

HD: 8 **TN:** 18
HP: 8d6+8 (36)
Armour Points: 8
Attack: Club/club (melee)
Damage: 1d10+8
Number Appearing: 1–5
Special: If an ogre successfully deals damage with two consecutive club attacks the target is pushed back 10ft and falls prone.

Ogres are large hairy bearded humanoids with large teeth and mighty appetites for human bones. Their skin is grey and their eyes like black jet and their breath stinks of rot. Ogres usually grow up to 13ft tall, but some of the more ancient beasts can be more than 18ft. They tend to live in old ruins or in damp caves close to forested areas where they can hunt deer, although humans are their favourite food to eat. While they are not particularly intelligent, they do function in tribal societies and are found throughout the Perilous Land. Some of these tribes have been seduced by The Black Lance in the promise of all the humans they can eat.

PECH

HD: 4 **TN:** 14
HP: 4d6+4 (18)
Armour Points: 4
Attack: Claw (melee) or shortbow (ranged, 80ft)
Damage: 1d8+4
Number Appearing: 3–10
Special: Pech roll with an edge when attacking in melee.

Pech are little people found most often in Escose. Despite their short stature they have strong, muscular arms and can quickly overwhelm their target. They are said to be able to brew magical ales from heather that will increase the strength of those that drink the concoction. Pech were among the first beings in the Perilous Land, existing alongside giants when the world was young, which is why many believe they had to brew potions to make them mighty. They are responsible for some of the great and ancient megaliths found around Escose.

PIXIE

HD: 1 **TN:** 11
HP: 1d6+1 (4)
Armour Points: 1
Attack: Claw (melee)
Damage: 1d4+1
Spells Prepared: Dazzle with Glittering Lights
Number Appearing: 2–10
Special: Pixies can fly.

Pixies are small creatures, no bigger than a domestic cat, who are rarely seen by humans. They have inherently magical powers and most are helpful to those that stumble across them. However, there are those who cause havoc in households, smashing objects and in some cases setting furniture alight. These events are often blamed on ghosts.

POTTON

HD: 3 **TN:** 13
HP: 3d6+3 (13)
Armour Points: 3
Attack: Short sword (melee)
Damage: 1d6+3
Number Appearing: 2–10
Special: Pottons can dig in the ground at their walking speed.

Pottons are squat creatures with large hands and broad shoulders who live in the stumps of ancient trees and underground cave networks where large numbers can be found. Human hunters blame pottons when they cannot find any game, even if there are no pottons in the area. They wear brown leather jerkins covered in moss and have a pungent odour. Pottons feed mainly on boar, deer, fish, and mushrooms and don't usually go out of their way to harm people unless their lairs are invaded.

QUESTING BEAST

HD: 10 **TN:** 20
HP: 10d6+10 (45)
Armour Points: 10
Attack: Claw/Claw/Tail/Bite (melee)
Damage: 1d10+10
Number Appearing: 1 (unique creature)
Special: The Questing Beast is immune to magical spells of level 5 and under. It takes half damage from non-magical attacks (this does not include attacks from magical weapons).

With the head of a snake, the body of a leopard, the feet of a hart, and haunches of a lion the Questing Beast is one of the most dreaded creatures in all of the Perilous Land. Its deafening cry is like the bark of a large dog. The Questing Beast is pursued by Princess Dindrane of Orofaise whose bloodline have hunted the creature for over a century to no avail. It leaves in its wake great destruction, with villages levelled by the mighty beast, all its inhabitants devoured or left for dead. Morgan Le Fay has become obsessed with capturing the creature and using it as a weapon against Arthur. The Order of the Fisher King also have need of the Questing Beast, for its blood is said to have healing properties. The Questing Beast is a unique creature, with only the one believed to have ever existed in the Perilous Land.

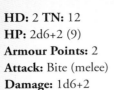

REDCAP

HD: 2 **TN:** 12
HP: 2d6+2 (9)
Armour Points: 2
Attack: Bite (melee)
Damage: 1d6+2
Number Appearing: 2–5
Special: When a redcap deals damage with a bite attack, the target must succeed a Might saving throw or take an extra 1 damage from blood drain.

Murderous little goblin creatures, redcaps inhabit abandoned castles and keeps, crumbling ruins and old forests where they ambush travellers to drain their blood. Their caps are coloured red from being dipped into the still-fresh blood of their victims. They have eyes that burn in the night, claw-like fingernails and the faces of grotesque old men. Seasoned travellers have learned to avoid so-called 'red roads' where redcaps have been spotted in the past. Their iron boots leave deep imprints in the soil and their voices can be heard chattering in the foliage on quiet, lonely nights.

RED MAGISTER

HD: 8 **TN:** 18
HP: 8d6+8 (36)
Armour Points: 8
Attack: Staff (melee)
Damage: 1d10+8
Spells Prepared: Create a Wild Gust of Wind, Grant the Skin of Stone, Dazzle with Glittering Lights, Witch Doll
Number Appearing: 1–5
Special: For two actions, the Red Magister writes a rune of protection on the ground in front of them. As long as they are within 5ft of the rune, they are immune to sneak attacks.

In the days of old the Keepers of the Secret Words were handed the first magics from the gods. While the majority used these words for good, a faction that became known as the Red Magisters used this magic for power and destruction. They dress themselves in scarlet robes and carry twisted, blackened staves etched with various runes. While most died out decades ago, a small group of Red Magisters remain in Benwick, though there have been reports of sightings further afield.

REVENANT

HD: 6 **TN:** 16
HP: 6d6+6 (27)
Armour Points: 6
Attack: Claw (melee)
Damage: 1d8+6
Number Appearing: 1–3
Special: A revenant is able to regenerate all HP after resting for six hours in their grave (or equivalent). In the daylight, halve the revenant's total HP.

A revenant is the animated corpse of an individual who has been brought back to life through a need for revenge. Their flesh is usually rotten, their eyes sunken back into their heads, and they cloak themselves in the shroud they were buried in. Problems with revenants have led to a trend in cremations in some parts of the Perilous Land, although some believe that burning a corpse prevents its soul from passing on to the afterlife. Revenants are able to rest during the day to rebuild their damaged bodies so that at night they are at full strength to carry out their evil deeds.

SCEADUGENGA

HD: 4 **TN:** 14
HP: 4d6+4 (18)
Armour Points: 4
Attack: Bite (melee)
Damage: 1d8+4
Number Appearing: 1–5
Special: A sceadugenga can transform into a human child at will as an action. A successful Mind saving throw will determine that the child is a sceadugenga because of its pitch black eyes.

The Sceadugenga ('shadow-goers') are dark creatures that haunt the forests of the Perilous Land. In their natural form they are spindly hunched shadow beings with red eyes and a large maw full of serrated teeth. They are able to transform into children, integrating into human society and becoming adopted by families. They may wait months until they make their move, taking on their true form and devouring their helpless parents with glee. Some stay trapped as children, unable to turn back, though their black eyes may give them away as a spirit creature.

SELKIE

HD: 3 **TN:** 13
HP: 3d6+3 (13)
Armour Points: 3
Attack: Claw (melee) or shortbow (ranged, 80ft) or bite (melee in seal form only)
Damage: 1d6+3
Number Appearing: 1–3
Special: A selkie is able to turn into a seal and back to human form at will as an action. When they take on human form, they shed their seal skin. If their skin is taken, the owner has a 1 in 3 chance of becoming the selkie's master. If this happens, the selkie must obey all commands given to it by its master until the master relinquishes the skin or dies.

Selkies, or 'seal folk', are seals by day, but dark-haired human by night. While they are more often female, there are some male selkies who exist. Their seal skin falls off close to their sea lair and they head into civilisation. Some start families with mortals, only to return to the sea years later. If someone is to steal the skin of a selkie, there is a high chance that they will become the creature's master.

SHELLYCOAT

HD: 3 **TN:** 13
HP: 3d6+3 (13)
Armour Points: 3
Attack: Spear (melee)
Damage: 1d6+3
Number Appearing: 3–10
Special: Attacks against a shellycoat with light ranged and light melee weapons have a setback.

Shellycoats are water-dwelling creatures whose backs are covered in large seashells. They resemble humanoid fish, standing a head shorter than the average human and bearing a set of viciously sharp teeth. They carry spears crafted from spiked shells that are designed to do maximum damage when attacking. They live in lakes, rivers, and the ocean and often go into territorial battles with merfolk who they despise.

SHUG MONKEY

HD: 6 **TN:** 16
HP: 6d6+6 (27)
Armour Points: 6
Attack: Claw (melee) or howl (special)
Damage: 1d8+6 (claw)
Number Appearing: 1–5
Special: A shug monkey may make a howl attack that affects all creatures in a 50ft radius (except other shug monkeys). If a howl attack is successful, the target must succeed a Mind saving throw or take a setback to saving throws and attack rolls for 1d4 rounds. The shug monkey may only use how twice per combat.

The shug monkey is a shaggy creature with facial features resembling a demonic monkey. The creature lives in forests located to the south of the Perilous Land, preferring warmer climes, making their homes in the branches of large trees. Locals stay away from so-called 'shugland', where these vicious beasts dwell. When threatened, they let out an echoing howl that can turn the blood of the bravest warrior cold. Some say the shug monkey is related to the werewolf, having once been a human that has magically transformed into this arboreal monster.

SLAUGH

HD: 5 **TN:** 15
HP: 5d6+5 (22)
Armour Points: 5
Attack: Longsword (melee) or longbow (ranged, 150ft)
Damage: 1d8+5
Number Appearing: 1–8
Special: Reduce damage to the slaugh by non-magical weapons by 3.

The slaugh is a rugged warrior spirit who has returned to the mortal realm as a member of the Host of the Unforgiven Dead, an army who refuse to stop fighting even when all wars are over. These ghosts are clad in a green ethereal armour, carry swords and bows and can march for months or years across the land until they meet an opposing force. Mortal weapons have little effect against them. Battles between the living and the Host have been fought in the history of the Perilous Land, the most recent in Benwick.

SPRIGGAN

HD: 7 **TN:** 17
HP: 7d6+7 (31)
Armour Points: 7
Attack: Slam/claw (melee) or whirlwind (ranged, 60ft)
Damage: 1d8+7
Number Appearing: 3–6
Special: When a spriggan deals damage with a whirlwind attack, the target must succeed a Reflex saving throw or be thrown backwards 10ft and be knocked prone.

Spriggans are tall tree-like creatures found in barrows, ruins, and caves guarding treasures. They are hideous to behold, with long limbs and the faces of wrinkled old men. When displeased, they can conjure violent whirlwinds to sweep away treasure hunters before battering them with their bark-like limbs. Spriggans often appear in groups, ambushing adventurers who seek the precious objects they guard, circling their quarry before attacking. Some believe that they are the ghosts of giants, while others think they are conjured by nature herself.

Tiddy mun

HD: 4 **TN:** 14
HP: 4d6+4 (18)
Armour Points: 4
Attack: Claw (melee)
Damage: 1d8+4
Number Appearing: 1–4
Special: If the tiddy mun is attacked at dusk, there is a 2 in 6 chance the attack will miss.

Tiddy muns or 'greencoaties' are squat humanoids, no larger than a toddler, with long white beards and large bulbous noses. They live in and around bogland, hiding in the murky waters. They wear grey cloaks that make them difficult to see at dusk, which is the time they are most active, luring people into the bogs by calling out, pretending to be a traveller who has become lost in the bog. Nearby villagers offer them buckets of water as an apology for trespassing on their land and to keep them from encroaching on their villages.

Trow

HD: 2 **TN:** 12
HP: 2d6+2 (9)
Armour Points: 2
Attack: Mace (melee) or sling (ranged)
Damage: 1d6+2
Number Appearing: 3–10
Special: Once per day for 1d3 rounds a trow may turn invisible.

The trow are a small race of magical beings with long, pointed noses and large ears, who dress themselves in material they steal from local settlements. They are most often found around ancient burial mounds where they sing songs and dance in the moonlight. While they are not malicious creatures, preferring to shy away from humanity, turning invisible when they need to, they will defend their burial mounds when required. Locals refer to them as 'truncherfaces' due to their ugly looks, but most respect their space and leave them well enough alone. They very rarely venture out in the sunlight, preferring to emerge when the sun has set.

Unicorn

HD: 3 **TN:** 13
HP: 3d6+3 (13)
Armour Points: 3
Attack: Gore (melee)
Damage: 1d6+3
Number Appearing: 1
Special: A unicorn is able to heal another creature it touches by 3d6 HP. It can do this as an action three times per day.

Unicorns were once commonly found in the Perilous Land, but over the centuries they have been hunted to near extinction due to the medicinal properties found in their horns. The chemical alicorn is made when the horn is ground to a powder and added to rainwater. This potent potion is able to heal even the most grievous of wounds. Unicorn hunting has been outlawed in the majority of kingdoms as their numbers have dwindled. Only the most valiant are able to come within metres of a unicorn, and only the most pure of heart manage to receive a healing blessing from the creature. Mordred has dispatched The Black Lance to hunt down the last of the unicorns in order to create a supply of the alicorn elixir.

Urisk

HD: 2 **TN:** 12
HP: 2d6+2 (9)
Armour Points: 2
Attack: Kick (melee) or sling (ranged, 50ft)
Damage: 1d6+2
Number Appearing: 1–5
Special: Urisks ignore difficult terrain.

Urisks are the offspring of humans and fairies, with the legs and hooves of a goat and a body resembling a green, large-eyed bald creature with large curled horns. They live in caves, often by a waterfall where they like to catch fish and sing strange songs in the moonlight. They are shunned by human society and so have become friends with the wildlife around them, having the ability to speak with animals and plants.

VAMPIRE

HD: 7 **TN:** 17
HP: 7d6+7 (32)
Armour Points: 7
Attack: Claw/claw (melee) or drain (melee)
Damage: 1d8+7
Number Appearing: 1–6
Special: If a vampire does damage with a drain attack, it gains 1d6 HP. A vampire is able to shapeshift into a wolf or bat as an action, each with the following stats:

- Wolf
  HD: 7 **TN:** 17, **HP:** as vampire, **Armour Points:** 7, **Attack:** Claw/bite (melee), **Damage:** 1d10. **Special:** If another wolf is within 5ft, the wolf gets a second bite attack
- Bat
  HD: 7 **TN:**17, **HP:** as vampire, **Armour Points:** 7, **Attack:** Swoop/bite (melee), **Damage:** 1d10, **Special:** Can fly.

Vampires are nocturnal beings who live unnaturally long lives so long as they have a frequent supply of human blood. Because of this blood thirst, vampires stalk cities at night, slipping into bedchambers and draining the blood of sleepers, leaving two puncture holes in their necks from their protruding fangs. Vampires cannot venture into the daylight; those that do immediately catch fire and are reduced to ash. It is said that the vampire is not native to the Perilous Land, having been brought over by traders from eastern lands.

WEREWOLF

HD: 8 **TN:** 18
HP: 8d6+8 (36)
Armour Points: 8
Attack: Bite/claw (melee)
Damage: 1d10+8
Number Appearing: 1–5
Special: If damaged by a bite attack, the target must succeed a Constitution saving throw. If they fail, in 1d4 days they are infected with the lycanthropy disease and they take a setback on all saving throws. 1d4 days after that they become a werewolf themselves, unable to change back to human form unless by magical means.

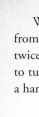

Werewolves were once humans who were infected with lycanthropy after a bite from another werewolf. Werewolves are much larger than ordinary wolves, up to twice the size, and far more ferocious. After being bitten, it can take up to eight days to turn into a werewolf and there are few non-magical cures. It is said that keeping a handful of wolfsbane on one's person can help ward off these creatures.

WITCH

HD: 6 **TN:** 16
HP: 6d6+6 (27)
Armour Points: 6
Attack: Claw (melee)
Damage: 1d8+6
Spells Prepared: Cause the Feeling of Doom in Another, Witch Doll (x3), Break Skin out into Boils
Number Appearing: 1–3
Special: The witch may use an action to create a 5ft protective circle. While in the circle, the witch has 10 extra armour points that cannot be regenerated with a regroup action.

Witches are cunning folk who practise magic for malevolent purposes. They are usually shunned from society, living solitary lives in caves or deep woods where nobody can see them work their infernal magic. On certain moonless nights, witches gather together to dance naked around the fire, stomping and chanting in a frenzied circle. Most witches have one or more familiars, small animals or spirits who are connected to them on a spiritual level. The Sisters Le Fay are mostly witches. Male witches are called warlocks.

WOLF

HD: 3 **TN:** 13
HP: 3d6+3 (13)
Armour Points: 3
Attack: Bite (melee)
Damage: 1d6+3
Number Appearing: 3–8
Special: If another wolf is within 5ft, the wolf gets a second bite attack.

Wolves are canines that live in forested areas, hunting in packs. While they usually eat deer or rabbit, if they happen upon a traveller they will happily devour them. Some barbarian tribes have tamed wolves to aid them in the hunt, but they are strictly not pets – they are free to come and go as they please. Wolves are hunted for their fur pelts to aid survival during the winter months, as well as trophies for the aristocracy.

YETH HOUND

HD: 5 **TN:** 15
HP: 5d6+5 (22)
Armour Points: 5
Attack: Pounce (melee)
Damage: 1d8+5
Number Appearing: 2–6
Special: Yeth hounds cannot be blinded or be the target of an effect that causes fear.

Yeth hounds are large black headless dogs who roam moorlands, emitting strange cries in the night. While they are able to tear a human limb from limb with their powerful steel-like claws, they do not tend to venture close to civilisation and very few people have even encountered a yeth hound. The most frequent sightings have been to the south of the Perilous Land.

GUIDE FOR GAME MASTERS

This section contains some useful advice for GMs running adventures in the Perilous Land. Game Mastering is an entirely different beast than being a player in a game. As a game master it's your job to facilitate the adventure, manage the flow of the story, present interesting personalities and situations to the players and provide a framework for the whole group to form a joint narrative.

RUNNING A CAMPAIGN

Games of *Romance of the Perilous Land* can last just one night for a quick adventure, a few months for a shorter campaign, or even a number of years for an epic-length campaign. Campaigns are simply a string of adventures using the same player characters. The beauty of running campaigns is that the players have room to progress, gain levels, and explore the world with their characters. Some people like to run a series of adventures that have no common component or story arc – they will wrap up one adventure and go straight onto the next one. This is similar to the 'adventure of the week' format that was popular in TV shows in the 1980s and early 1990s. There can sometimes be small commonalities between adventures, such as recurring characters, but on the whole the campaign isn't interlinked. The advantages to this campaign format is that the GM doesn't have to think about continuity or consequence, so this type of campaign is often easier to prepare for. The disadvantages are that you lose much of the immersion that is present in an interlinked campaign and players can't become as invested in the characters of your world if they're unlikely to ever see them again.

Other groups prefer to play campaigns where each adventure is linked through one or more common threads, creating a wider story arc over time. Player characters will meet recurring protagonists and antagonists along the way, create bonds with NPCs and immerse themselves in one story. This campaign format is often more rewarding for those who enjoy seeing the consequences of their actions, as it allows player characters to impact the world and set off chains of events that could have ramifications for them further down the line. For example, in one adventure they retrieve a gnarled black staff from the Wytchwood imbued with magical potency, but they are unsure how it works. However, in three adventures' time, they discover that it belonged to a witch who has been hunting them down for weeks in order to find the right time to defeat them and take back her staff. Of course, interlinked campaigns with a wider arc can take more preparation time for the GM, who must think about what certain personalities should be doing at certain points in the story and planning how player character actions have affected the world around them.

TYPES OF CAMPAIGN

Romance of the Perilous Land is a game of adventure at its heart. Brave heroes undertake quests, rescue those in harm's way, and ultimately attempt to rid the land of the darkness that arose in the Age of Doom. But adventure isn't the only flavour of campaign that you can play.

POLITICAL INTRIGUE

The Perilous Land contains 11 different kingdoms, each with its own kind of governance and disposition against Camelot. In a political intrigue campaign, player characters will often be diplomats who are attempting to unite the kingdoms under the banner of Camelot, using their wisdom and guile more than pure strength to win over kings, queens, dukes and barons to join their cause. Political games are less about combat against monsters, although that can be a component, and more about matching wits against the aristocracy. The hallmarks of this kind of campaign are treachery, war, and hard-fought deals, and are usually roleplay-heavy. A political intrigue campaign is well-suited for classes such as bards, thieves, and knights.

HORROR

The Age of Doom brought with it impossible creatures of shadow, evil beasts that lurk in the darkness, and twisted enchanters who bend the black forces of the universe to their will. A horror campaign is about creating an atmosphere of dread where heroes sometimes feel helpless against the tide of evil they find themselves up against. These kinds of campaigns work better when the focus is on just one or two monsters rather than hordes of brownies or redcaps. Horror adventures should build tension, with the monster only revealed towards the end in all its grotesque glory. Each adventure should be a mystery, with heroes following a series of clues that lead them further down the path of horror. Cattle are found mutilated in a field, with locals seeing strange lights at midnight in the same field. Horrific wooden dolls are found hanging from the ceiling of a child's bedroom. Something is leaving letters scrawled in pig's blood on the duchess's pillow. There are many creatures in the bestiary that suit horror well, such as hags, witches, revenants, ghosts, vampires, werewolves, incubi, finfolk, and gargoyles.

HACK AND SLASH

Sometimes it's fun just to forget about story and focus on the action. Hack and slash, otherwise known as 'dungeon crawling', is a style of game that is suited to campaigns where adventures aren't interlinked. In these campaigns heroes delve into ruined temples, forgotten dungeons, crumbling towers, and mighty castles to battle monsters and find treasure. Hack and slash adventures focus on lots of enemies, and a variety of them, often filling large underground structures such as catacombs and caves. This campaign type is great for groups who prefer combat over roleplaying. Quests are usually simple – requiring the heroes to retrieve an item or defeat a specific enemy lurking in the deeper levels of a sinister dungeon.

LOW FANTASY

Romance of the Perilous Land is inherently fantastical, with heroes often coming up against magic and monsters. Low fantasy is a genre that eschews some of the tropes of 'high' fantasy such as wide varieties of monsters and powerful magic for a more subdued version of fantasy, also known as 'sword and sorcery'. In a low fantasy campaign, magic is rare and reality is more gritty and desperate. In low fantasy, the Perilous Land has crumbled in the Age of Doom and Camelot is the last bastion of hope in a sea of evil. Cunning folk exist, but in much smaller numbers and their powers are seen as god-like

to most people. There are fewer fantastical creatures such as fairies, with the majority being large beasts such as knuckers, black dogs, and drakes. The real monsters in low fantasy are humans, who are often treacherous and cannot be trusted.

HISTORICAL FANTASY

Historical fantasy can be described as having even fewer fantastical elements than low fantasy. This type of campaign is more grounded in medieval reality, where people fear magic and monsters, but they are merely figments of their imaginations. Witches and cunning folk are either apothecaries or mad individuals who are sought for their wisdom. Magic and enchanted items are merely stories and cannot be used in the game.

NARRATIVE VERSUS TACTICAL PLAY STYLES

There is more than one way to play a roleplaying game, with the two main ways being narrative and tactical.

NARRATIVE ROLEPLAYING

Also known as 'theatre of the mind' roleplaying, the narrative method eschews battle maps, miniatures and generally any props in favour of a heavily descriptive game. In this style, the players tend to stay in character more often, putting on voices and generally acting like their tabletop counterpart. Combat is handled through description, too, with the GM explaining what is happening at that point in time and the players narrating what their characters are doing. The narrative roleplaying method is generally the most immersive way to play, as there are fewer distractions to pull you out of the game, such as moving miniatures around a battle map. However, the drawback is that both the GM and the players will carry a bigger mental burden in remembering where they are at a given point and what is going on in the encounter, especially if the GM introduces new elements part way through the battle. Here are some tips for using the narrative style:

- **Sketch out the current location:** While theatre of the mind play doesn't use tactical maps, it can be useful for everyone to have the current location drawn out on a piece of paper to avoid confusion.
- **Repeat the current circumstances:** Because of the mental burden on players, it's helpful for the GM to repeat whatever has just happened to set

the scene in a combat round. For example, it's the thief's turn, so the GM explains that two bugbears are attacking the bard, while a witch has just paralysed the barbarian. This helps set the scene so the current player is clear on what they should be doing.

- **Handwave exact distances:** Using a tactical battle map, players know exactly how far their characters can move, but in narrative combat this is more abstract. Assume that both players and opponents can reach each other in a single movement at the beginning. Use the far, near, and close movement method to move in and out of range. Also, assume that anyone firing in ranged combat can reach any opponent.

- **Try cool stunts:** GMs should encourage players to try new things in battle. Narrative play is perfect for this, whether they want to kick over a table, duck behind it and blind-shoot a crossbow at a giant, or scissor-kick a brigand off the edge of a cliff, let the players experiment with combat and give them a ruling based on what they want to do. More often than not this will be a simple attribute check.

- **Give the players the benefit of the doubt:** Things can get confusing in narrative combat and maybe a player isn't imagining the situation the same way as you, so give them the benefit of the doubt where you can.

TACTICAL ROLEPLAYING

While narrative roleplaying lives almost entirely in the collective imagination, the tactical style of play uses miniatures, maps, and dioramas to help bring the game to life. While general social roleplaying will by default be more theatre of the mind, combat becomes a much more strategic affair, with players manoeuvring their miniatures or tokens into the most optimum spots to take on their opponents. Tactical roleplaying reduces the mental burden that narrative gaming has by having terrain features and character locations visualised on a map, allowing players and GM alike to quickly see where they are in relation to others in an encounter. With a map, you can measure the distance needed to shoot an arrow, or who would be affected by a certain spell. However, this can remove from the immersion of the game, as having everything in front of you puts less emphasis on description. It can also slow the game down as players are more likely to spend longer thinking about their positioning and what they will be doing a turn ahead. Here are some tips for playing a tactical style game:

- **Describe actions:** Because it's easy for tactical combat to fall into players just declaring they are attacking creatures, encourage them to describe how they strike their opponents and how they're moving around the battlefield.

- **Plan ahead:** Tactical combat can be less fluid than narrative combat, so encourage players to plan what they will be doing on their turns while others are acting, which should speed up proceedings.
- **Use terrain features:** Using a map means it's easier to show terrain features, whether it's thick snow, slippery ice or a huge crevasse. Terrain on a battle map adds depth and tactical nuance to the game.
- **Try cool stunts:** In the same way that stunting should be encouraged in narrative play, players should be able to try tricks and feats to spice things up and empower them.

CREATING ADVENTURES

One of the best things about being a GM is being able to create your own adventures to play with your friends. Adventures provide a framework for the group to tell a collaborative story, whether it spans one night or a series of sessions. This section contains advice on how to create an adventure.

AN IMPORTANT NOTE WHEN CREATING AND RUNNING ADVENTURES

It's important to note that there is a difference between Game Mastering an adventure and telling a story. When you tell a story, you have all the narrative beats figured out and you know exactly where the tale is heading. The main characters will go to the mountain to fetch the enchanted lamp, they will fight the bugbears, then they will discover a magical boat to sail across the river and they will finally have a showdown with the main antagonist. When you're running an adventure you have to remember that it's not just you who is playing – the players need to be active participants in the story, making decisions that affect the narrative. This is what is known as 'player agency' and it's a vital part of what makes a roleplaying game different from one person just telling a story. So don't go into an adventure having a concrete ending in mind and don't be afraid to veer off the plot you had in your head. Your players will thank you for it.

Choose your setting

Start by selecting the location where you want your adventure to be set. This book provides information on each of the 11 kingdoms and areas within those kingdoms, so choose one that strikes a chord with you. This might be because it contains a particularly interesting monster, or that there's scope for political intrigue involving the court in that kingdom. The Perilous Land is riddled with dangerous foes, tyrants and hidden enchanted treasure, so there are many options when it comes to selecting a setting.

CHOOSE SEVERAL LOCATIONS WITHIN YOUR SETTING

Once you have selected your setting it's time to narrow down a handful of locations that will be important in the adventure. This could be a deep cave, a little hamlet, and a dark forest. You don't need to know what will happen there just yet, but knowing where the adventure will take place will help with the next steps.

Select a main enemy and their motive

Every good story has an enemy who's out to thwart the good guys and your adventure should be no exception. Choose an interesting enemy to provide the conflict in your adventure, whether this is trying to reach a certain goal before the player characters or putting roadblocks in the way to stop the heroes reaching their own goals. A good enemy needs a motive – why are they taking these actions? For instance, if your main enemy is Morgan Le Fay, then why is she seeking a certain treasure? Giving your enemies a motive will help you to understand how they react to the player characters. The enemy should be tied to one or more of your locations in some way. In this case, Morgan Le Fay might have travelled to the forest and have made camp in search of this treasure, which you may decide resides within the deep cave.

CREATE ONE OR MORE SECONDARY
ENEMIES AND THEIR MOTIVES

Secondary enemies are likely not as powerful as the main enemy, but they are there to provide further barriers or added complications for the heroes. These enemies may or may not serve your main enemy. In fact, it's sometimes a good idea to have multiple enemy factions working towards their own goals in order to keep the players guessing. For example, Morgan Le Fay is searching for the sacred mirror of Alara, so you decide that her second-in-command, the witch Esmeralda, is leading a group of five witches to find it because Esmeralda wants to please her mistress. But you also decide that another secondary enemy is guarding the mirror – a golden dragon, who you decide has guarded the mirror for centuries because if it was lost his power would diminish and he would eventually die. So now you have two secondary enemies at odds with one another. Again, make sure your enemies are tied to locations. Here it would make sense for Esmeralda and her witches to be exploring the forest and the dragon to be living in the cave.

CREATE A MAIN ALLY WITH MOTIVES
CONNECTED TO ONE OR MORE ENEMIES

Adventures usually begin with someone offering the heroes a quest and this is usually an ally. This ally should be connected in some way to one or more of the enemies in your adventure, whether directly or indirectly. An example of an indirect connection would be the ally has found evidence of a witch camp in the forest near his home and fears for his family. A direct connection would be that the ally is the sole friend of the golden dragon, who has told him that there are witches abroad in the hunt for magical treasures. Like your enemies, the main ally needs a motive to call upon the heroes' help. It should be noted that while sometimes an ally may turn out to be an enemy, this is generally not a good idea when running a roleplaying game. Players can often feel cheated and made to feel stupid if the friend they have made is a trickster, so unless there's a good reason for doing this it's best to steer clear of this idea. In this instance, let's have a farmer as a main ally, who has seen evidence of witch activity close to his farmstead – eerie chants in the night, strange smells, and burned-out fires. His motive is that he is terrified of what they may be planning and is concerned for his family's safety.

CREATE ONE OR MORE
SECONDARY ALLIES WITH MOTIVES

Secondary allies are there to offer further guidance or even complications for the players. They may have no connection to the main ally, but they will have a connection to the enemies or their motives. Don't create too many allies – two or three is usually a good number – so you don't get overwhelmed when preparing your adventure. In our hypothetical adventure, we may have a village baker whose child became lost in the forest where the witches have been seen and asks the heroes to help find her, adding a secondary objective for the player characters – the child. In this case, the child was in the woods collecting chestnuts when she was captured by the witches, who will use her as a human guinea pig to test the power of the mirror. We might also add a scholar who has a map of the cave warrens where the golden dragon lives, and promises to show them a secret entrance for a cut of any treasure that is to be found. With these characters we have clear motives – one who desperately wants to see their child again, one who wishes to escape her captors, and one who just desires riches.

MAP OUT AND STOCK YOUR LOCATIONS

Now that you have a good idea about what your enemies and allies want in the adventure, it's time to start building out your locations and stocking them with items and opportunities for conflict. While some groups like to play theatre of the mind games without miniatures or battle maps, it's still a good idea to sketch out your locations so you can better describe them to your players during the adventure. Write brief descriptions of your locations, even if it's just a few words like 'damp and earthy' to describe a basement. When stocking a location, you're adding individual elements that the players can collect or interact with. For example, you may decide that one of the cave chambers is home to the corpse of a long-dead adventurer wearing a pack containing some dried herbs and four gold pieces. You might then drop a child's shoe into the forest, belonging to the missing child – a clue tied to one of the allies – but to add a complication you have the shoe surrounded by a pack of hungry wolves. You may then decide that the witches have set traps around their camp, so create several hazardous pits covered with leaves in their vicinity.

NOTE DOWN YOUR PLOT HOOKS

A plot hook is how players are drawn into an adventure. It's best not to force players into the adventure – they will have a much better sense of agency if they decide how to take on the quest. Because you have multiple enemies and allies it should be easy to draw out several plot hooks to get the players involved. In the example adventure, we have the following hooks:

- The farmer wants the players to investigate the potential witch sightings.
- The scholar knows of a treasure of great power in an underground warren within the forest.
- The baker wants the players to bring her child back safely.
- The players may have heard that Morgan Le Fay is on the move and has been spotted in this locale.

With these hooks the players could approach the adventure in a multitude of different ways, making them feel more immersed in the game.

START YOUR ADVENTURE

Now you have all your ingredients in place, it's time to start the adventure. Notice how we have only focused on what NPCs are doing in the adventure and not given the player characters strict objectives? This is because as a GM you have no control over what the players do – your job is to have the NPCs react to their actions. Remember that events are going to happen regardless of what the players do. The witches will be constantly acting along with their motives in the background; the scholar may still seek the secret passage even if the player characters don't oblige to helping him; and the baker may decide to go into the woods to look for her child herself if the players miss this hook. Think of an adventure as a pressure cooker. You have lots of elements interacting and changing based on player and NPC motives – nothing is happening in a vacuum. Make sure that player actions have consequences. If they decide to go with the scholar to the cave, the consequence might be that the witches ransack the farmstead in search of the enchanted mirror. If they manage to kill the witches before they get the mirror, what happens when a rogue scholar finds it instead? This method of creating an adventure leads to a living environment, rather than a static one, ensuring that the players feel like their actions have meaning.

RUNNING COMBAT

Combat is a key part of *Romance of the Perilous Land*, where characters get to test their mettle against the plethora of villains and monsters that haunt its kingdoms. These battles should be tense and exciting, with swords clashing, arrows flying, spells weaving, and claws slashing. Here are some tips to help you run great combat encounters.

BE DESCRIPTIVE

When you boil combat down to its constituent parts, it's just a series of rolls and maths, which on its own isn't terribly exciting. This is why the GM should make encounters descriptive, throwing in little details that help paint a picture in the shared player imagination. The storm hag doesn't just walk over to the knight and hit him; she eerie floats towards him, her eyes fixed on his, grinning wickedly before suddenly striking him in the arm with her clawed hand. If she manages to successfully hit the knight, she tears a gouge in his armour as if it were tissue paper, grazing him. The GM should also encourage the players to describe how they attack. If they manage to kill an enemy, allow them to express how they land the killing blow – it's likely they will come up with something cool (and gruesome).

KEEP THINGS MOVING

Combat should be fast and furious, so any slowdown can pull the players out of the game. Make sure you are familiar with the rules for combat or have them to hand during an encounter so you can quickly reference anything that crops up. If you don't know a rule and can't find it, make an executive decision to keep things moving along and have another player look it up while you get on with the game.

VARY THE CHALLENGE

Player characters shouldn't just be fighting enemies with HDs equivalent to their levels. While this provides a relatively equal challenge, it's not a realistic scenario in a world of peril. Don't be afraid to pit the heroes against creatures a couple of HD levels above their class levels. Once in a while you may even want to throw something even more powerful at them, particularly if they have done something silly, such as walking into a dragon's lair when the local villagers have specifically warned of a gargantuan dragon residing there. Likewise, throw lower HD creatures at them to give them the satisfaction of cutting through a horde of easier enemies for a cinematic feel.

USE TERRAIN FEATURES

Whether you're playing on a battle map with miniatures or have a theatre of the mind style of play, terrain features add an extra element to combat. Have walls to duck behind, trees to climb, bogs to slow them down, or hazards that can cause problems if encountered on the battlefield. Terrain allows players to think tactically about how they position themselves, leading to more interesting encounters.

HAVE COMBAT GOALS

The default combat encounter is to kill all the opposition, which is fine, but sometimes setting other goals for players to achieve keeps combat fresh. Perhaps an enemy is trying to escape and the player characters have to stop this from happening otherwise they will alert a larger warband. In this encounter, you might want to include some difficult and blocking terrain, as well as enemies that will get in the way to prevent them from achieving their goal of stopping the runner. Another idea could be the heroes find themselves in a burning village and they must fight off a group of marauding creatures while saving people from the blaze. Not every combat needs goals other than decimating the opposition, but think about including them for key encounters.

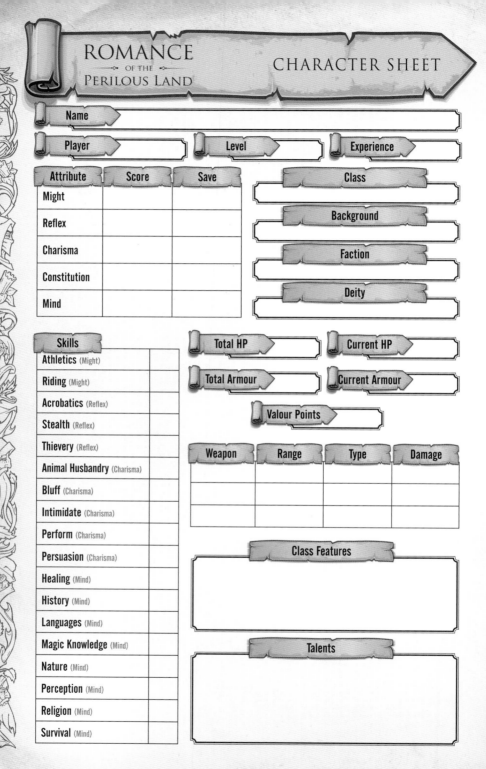

ROMANCE
OF THE
PERILOUS LAND

CHARACTER SHEET

Name

Player

Level

Experience

Attribute	Score	Save
Might		
Reflex		
Charisma		
Constitution		
Mind		

Class

Background

Faction

Deity

Skills

Skills	
Athletics (Might)	
Riding (Might)	
Acrobatics (Reflex)	
Stealth (Reflex)	
Thievery (Reflex)	
Animal Husbandry (Charisma)	
Bluff (Charisma)	
Intimidate (Charisma)	
Perform (Charisma)	
Persuasion (Charisma)	
Healing (Mind)	
History (Mind)	
Languages (Mind)	
Magic Knowledge (Mind)	
Nature (Mind)	
Perception (Mind)	
Religion (Mind)	
Survival (Mind)	

Total HP

Current HP

Total Armour

Current Armour

Valour Points

Weapon	Range	Type	Damage

Class Features

Talents

Description

Backstory

Languages

Equipment

Notes

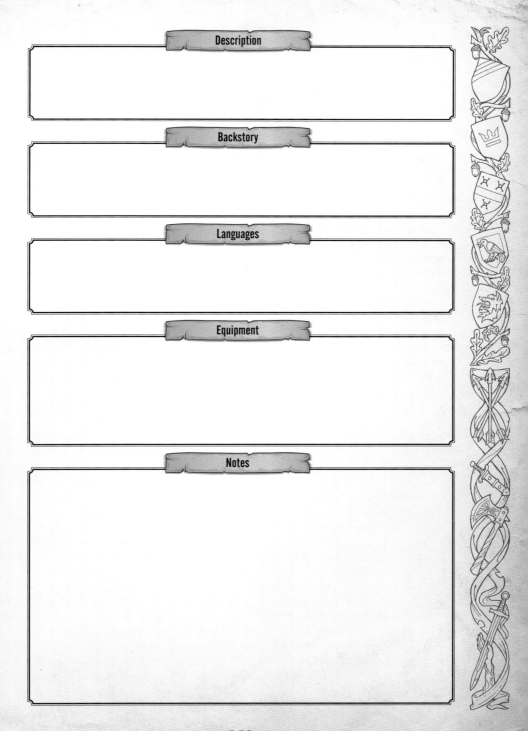

253

INDEX